Tony Bury, born in 1972 in Northampton, England, has had a passion for writing songs, poems and short stories since an early age. He has taken it more seriously since having kids, writing several children's books and screen plays as well as the Alex Keaton series of crime novels. *Inside Edmund Carson* is the first book in a new series.

INSIDE EDMUND CARSON

Also by Tony Bury

The Alex Keaton Series:

Intervention Forgiven
Intervention Needed
The Intervention

Tony Bury

INSIDE EDMUND CARSON

Vanguard Press

VANGUARD PAPERBACK

© Copyright 2017
Tony Bury

A CIP catalogue record for this title is
available from the British Library.

ISBN 978 1 78465 254 8

*Vanguard Press is an imprint of
Pegasus Elliot MacKenzie Publishers Ltd.*
www.pegasuspublishers.com

First Published in 2017

**Vanguard Press
Sheraton House Castle Park
Cambridge England**

Printed & Bound in Great Britain

Dedication

For Maria… who still loves me!

The Early Years

Chapter 1

"Edmund…"

"Edmund…"

Oh my god, I swear that woman's voice goes straight through me.

"Get up, Edmund."

I pull the covers closer and snuggle back down. I don't want to get up, and I don't want to go to school. I am going to stay here for the rest of the day.

I pull my head out of the covers just enough to see the clock. It's only 8:02. She must have been shouting for fifteen minutes, fifteen minutes, what is up with that woman? I can hear footsteps coming up the stairs, and they are heavy. They are not my mum's footsteps, but Dad's. My door springs open.

"Edmund, get up, please."

I lift my head back out of the covers.

"OK, Dad, I will be down in a minute."

I throw him a smile. The door closes.

Dick.

I pull the covers round myself again. Two minutes later I throw them off me. I get up and head for the shower. It takes me twenty minutes to shower. I relieve myself whilst thinking about Caroline and Miss Walker. As the shower finishes so do I. I dress and go down for breakfast. Entering the kitchen she is at the stove and he is reading the paper.

"Morning, darling." I don't answer her. She has been screaming at me most of the morning what does she expect from me? I give a little grunt and sit at the table. There is nothing in front of me.

You have been fucking shouting me for half an hour; at least have breakfast ready when I get here!

She brings my breakfast over: a cold bacon sandwich. What is the point in giving me cold food? I push it to one side. At least cook me warm food if you are going to shout at me all morning.

"So, Edmund, any plans for today?" I look over at him. He doesn't even bother to drop the paper to look at me when he talks.

Yes, Father, bunk off school, as it's a waste of my time being there. Then pick Caroline up from college and fuck her senseless over this kitchen table. That's my plan. Sound good?

"Not really, Dad, school and then some homework, I guess."

"That's good, that's good."

The prick didn't hear a word I said.

I pull the sandwich back and cover it in brown sauce. I eat my breakfast in silence. Breakfast is always silent; we have nothing to say to each other. They don't want me here. And let's face it, if they aren't going to buy me a motorbike, then

14

why would I want them here? What the hell good are they to me?

"So, dear, I have made you lunch and I will leave you some food in the fridge as it is our dance lesson tonight, so dinner won't be until around seven thirty." I stand up and take the lunch, then blank them both as I leave.

I am out of that house at last. I collect my bike from the garage and head to school. I am going to get my mark in registration, do lessons till lunch, and then get over to Caroline at the college.

Fucking pushbike! I hate this thing!

I have told them repeatedly that I need a new bike. A 125cc Yamaha will get me about, and it costs like a thousand pounds. But will they buy it for me? No. They want me to get a job. Be a Golden Arches worker. A Golden Arches worker? Me? Do they have no pride in themselves?

I leave the drive and start peddling to school.

Peddling again, every day I am peddling this stupid damn bike. I should be driving, cruising, if it wasn't for those two… tightwads!

I hope they die in a car crash on the way to their stupid dance lessons!

Three minutes after leaving home, I am at school.

It's Wednesday. I have drama, maths and English lit. before lunch. It's the only reason I am here today, as I like two out of three of those lessons. I put my bike into the bike rack and head to class. The corridors are full of kids, proper kids, all giggling and looking stupidly at each other.

I hate them all.

No, that's a little harsh, there is the odd doable girl in the hallway, but they don't look at me and I don't look at them.

No, I have changed my mind again, I hate them all!

I wouldn't do them anyway. They are too young for me. Still want candy hearts and French kisses behind the bike shed. Not like Caroline, she is a real woman. With a real body. I am too much man for any of these kids.

The drama classroom is on the other side of school from registration. I make my mark at registration and head over. Miss Walker is the drama teacher. Now, she is very doable. More than very doable, twenty-eight years old, long dark hair. She is the perfect woman. Everything about her is perfect. Caroline's a close second, but she is not Miss Walker's standard. Nobody is Miss Walker's standard. God, there is something about dark-haired girls. Petite dark-haired girls. Ones you can fit your arms around. Pick up and throw around the bedroom. Miss Walker is the perfect size for that. I can imagine that. I do imagine that. All the time. I sit in the front row so she can see me. She enters the room and smiles at me.

I would do you senseless, Miss, senseless.

I am sure she smiles at me on purpose. She starts to talk to the class about posture and pronouncing the words properly… The three Ps she calls it. All I can think about is her on her knees in front of me. Undoing my trousers and pulling them down, that smile on her face. The smile that tells me exactly where her mouth is about to go…

"Edmund."

On her knees slowly working me up and down, up and down…

"Edmund…"

Up and down...

Fuck is she talking to me?

"Yes, Miss."

"Lost in your only little world, aren't you? Was it nice where you were?"

"Sorry, Miss." I stand up. Why am I standing up? Did she ask me to stand up?

"I was saying that I wanted a volunteer and you are never shy of being centre of attention, are you, Edmund? And as you are already standing." The classroom chuckles.

I hate them all! I hate them fucking all! Why the fuck did I stand up?

"Read lines with me, Edmund, and then we can discuss how we can improve the context afterwards" She hands me a book and it's open on page twenty-seven.

"So, class, Edmund and I are in love. He is a young stable boy and I am the daughter of the Earl of Essex."

There is a chuckle from the class. Don't know what for, it's very believable. I will be very believable anyway. I am a great actor. In fact, I have this exact film under my bed. I am sure I do and you end up... Stop! I need to get that out of my head. Especially in front of this lot.

"Edmund, do you want to begin where I marked on the page?"

I look down and there is a section highlighted in yellow. I can do this. I would be an amazing actor. She knows that. Probably why she chose me. I am so talented. I should probably be one of those pin-ups you see in girlie magazines. I start to read.

"But he doesn't need to know anything."

"He is my father, he knows everything."

"It will be our little secret." I speak softly to her as I look her directly in the eye. That's real acting.

"I want to, I really do, but I am scared."

She is looking back at me. I mean really looking back at me. In the eyes and everything. She could be an actress. She would make an amazing actress.

"There is nothing to be scared about, everything we have been doing has been leading to this point. The walks by the river, the secret meetings in the barn, just to talk, to read to each other. I love you. I want you."

She has a sparkle in her eyes. She likes what she is hearing from me. I couldn't have written this better myself.

"But what if he finds out?"

That smile on her lips is definitely for me. I am going for it. I move closer to her. There is a sigh from the class. They wish they had my skills. I have them all engrossed in what I am doing, including Miss Walker.

"Trust me, nobody will ever know." I raise my hand to her face and touch her cheek. She isn't expecting this, but she doesn't pull back.

"We belong together. Your father will, in time, come to realise what we have is real. What we have, you and I; This will last a lifetime."

I am sure she just nuzzled into my hand. She knows what we have is real. This attraction is real. It always has been. I am going to go off script. Let's see what she does. I hold my hand firmly on her cheek.

"I love you. I know we haven't said the words before to each other, but I love you. I love everything about you. The way you walk, the way you talk, the way your hair dances as you do. I can't sleep at night for fear of never seeing you again. You are my life and I am going to be yours. Tonight is only the start of this." She is looking at me. She is still looking at me.

Fuck it, I'm going in.

I lean forward as if to kiss her. This brings her back to reality with a jump backwards. There is laughter in the room. They followed me, they knew I was off script. She turns to face the blackboard. To compose herself, no doubt. Really had her going then. She turns back to the class.

"I think, first of all, class, we need to teach Edmund about appropriate improv." She walks back to her desk. She places one hand on the desk. Steadying herself. Weak at the knees.

She is thinking about fucking me, I know it. She can't concentrate now.

"So what was missing from that scene, class?"

"A stable and some dodgy music in the background, Miss." As I sit down I turn and see Carl Carnegie at the back of the class laughing to himself and his group of cronies.

I hate that kid, I hate that kid above all others!

But he is not wrong. Me and Miss Walker in a stable full of straw on a rainy afternoon. Now, that is a plan. I had her and she knows I did.

I sit down. She can't look at me and carries on with the class. All about the three Ps. I can hear her, but I don't care any more. I have had my fun. My mind stays in the stable with her. Class is over and I leave. The whole hour went past without another look from Miss Walker.

She will be at home playing with herself tonight thinking of me. Thinking of Edmund the stable boy. She knows it is just a matter of time until we do it.

The maths class wasn't much fun and is over before I know it. Mr Smith, the teacher, he is OK. I only came for the two classes of drama and English lit. but that class was in the middle. It's too far to pedal home in-between them. But if I had a motorbike. If I had a motorbike I would just do the classes I wanted to do. If I had a bike.

I fucking hate my parents!

I head towards English lit. Mrs Palmer. Older woman type, a bit more round but still doable, I do like to read a good play. Must be the fantastic actor in me. Always ready to read any script, or go off script to mention that. We are reading about the adventures of Baron Bolligrew. Strange book about a baron, a dragon, and a hero type who isn't the hero.

Oblong Fitz Oblong, Carl Carnegie got that part, dick!

Obadiah Bobbleknob is the real hero, but the idiots in class haven't read that far ahead. That's my part. Share the limelight with a talking magpie, but it's OK. I do love a good play. I understand it's all make-believe.

Mrs Palmer is hot, not Miss Walker hot, nobody is Miss Walker hot. She is always touching me on the shoulder. Calls me Edmund, her little star. I sit at the front so she can see me. She smiles like she wants it. Husband probably hasn't touched her for a while. Looking for something a little younger and fitter, no doubt. I am the fittest one in this class, for sure.

Fuck I would do her too.

At last we are starting Act Two, they are going to know who the real hero is now.

Carl Carnegie is going to be pissed. Twat.

We carry on reading. The dork Oblong Fitz Oblong gets hypnotised and is useless. I have the watch now, to hypnotise the baron and the dragon. Should have read ahead, you dickhead. You would know what is about to happen. That the little old egg painter is the saviour of the town. Enter the hero. Me. Wait, did I miss my cue?

"Come on, Bobbleknob."

I really hate that kid. I wish he would just die.

I didn't really think this through, did I? I get back on track and carry on reading my part. I read to the end of the play before anyone else, that's why I chose the part. It's funny and smart and in the end he is the centre of attention. Didn't think the name through though. Bobbleknob. Should have known better. Should have thought of that.

FUCK! He is going to be calling me that for months.

OK, enough reading, just want out of the class now. Mrs Palmer talks us through the end of the play and the meaning behind it all. I've switched off again. The bell goes for lunch at last. I am out of here. I take one last look at Mrs Palmer, yeah I would. I bet it's bouncier. The bigger, the bouncier. I leave to see Caroline.

I hate this bike.

I have to cycle home. Caroline doesn't need to see me arriving at college on a BMX bike. She is never going to believe a nineteen-year-old student of drama is going to do that. I drop my bike back home and get the bus over to her college. It's about twenty minutes, but I said we would meet for lunch and then back to mine.

"Hi."

I didn't see her coming up on me. I was lost in my thoughts of Miss Walker and this morning. She knows it is coming. She wants it as much as I do.

"Hi, wow, you look amazing, Caroline."

"You always say that, Edmund."

"It's always true." It is always true.

Fuck she is so hot, almost Miss Walker hot. Almost.

"How were your classes this morning?"

I don't really give a crap, just want you back to the house and naked as soon as possible. But I ask, as it's the right thing to do. She needs to think I am one of those caring types. Girls like that shit.

"Another day, another lecture on Freud and his theories on life, love and whether or not he should have slept with his mother and killed his father."

Wait a minute... Fuck, I am Freud! Never thought about that...

"Yours?"

"Good, it was good. Work on the three Ps in drama and still working on the play in my English lit. class." I am careful not to mention any teachers' names as she probably would know them in this school. I cannot believe she has fallen for this for months.

"So my little egg painter, where to? Lunch? Walk in the park? Or an afternoon at Chez Edmund's?" She is laughing at me now. There is only one place we both want to go. She links her arm under mine and we are already walking. We take the bus back to my house. A real afternoon session... especially as they won't be home until eight o'clock.

On the ride over she plays with the inside of my thigh… practically did the job for me before we got home.

As soon as we are off the bus and in the house the clothes start coming off. Should have made sure nobody was home first, but who cares?

Upstairs on the bed and going at it like rabbits on heat. It was good. Well, I think it was good. Not really sure what she thinks. Don't really care either. Worked for me. Looking at her, she is probably just grateful she got to sleep with someone as hot as me. I think I would prefer it if she told me that once in a while. She needs to earn her place here.

"Juice?"

"Yes, please." I walk downstairs naked to fetch some drinks. Realising I missed lunch, I make a couple of sandwiches too. I did take a look in the fridge, she had made me some food, but it was lasagne.

I hate lasagne; she should know that… bitch!

I grab a tray and bring the food and drink back to the room. Open the door and she is putting clothes on?

What the fuck?

"Bastard, you lying cheating fucking kid!"

Fuck, something is up here. I can tell. She knows, doesn't she?

I put the tray down on the side.

"What are you talking about?"

"What am I talking about? You have the front to ask me that..." She is up, loud and mad. Is it bad that I am horny again now? I like this look in her eyes. Gives them a sparkle.

"What the holy crap is this, eh? What is this?" She hands me a photograph: it is of me and my mother.

23

"A picture of me and my mum?"

Act dumb, for Christ's sake, act dumb.

"A picture, turn the fucking picture over." I do as she asks although I am having a flashback of what is on the other side.

Crap, oh crap, that dozy bitch...

"That's the date and the age, isn't it? Me and Edmund, two thousand, aged four, four! What does that make you now, fifteen? Sixteen? For fuck's sake, you told me you were nineteen."

All the screaming is giving me an erection. I am harder than ever. Who knew she had this fire in her? This is a great look for her.

"How old are you, Edmund? How fucking old are you?"

Yep, a full-blown fucking erection. God, that's good.

"Sixteen... well, nearly sixteen."

"Oh my god, you are only fifteen years old!" She is hitting me now.

Fuck that's turning me on even more.

I am trying to grab her hands but the blows keep coming. She is screaming now. I am not listening to the words though, just watching her actions. It feels good, the heat, the passion of it all. Who knew this would be a turn-on.

Fucking wished I had pissed her off ages ago.

They are getting harder, I like it, but they are definitely harder.

"Enough!" I shout back at her, but she is still coming. I push her backwards towards the bed.

If she lands on her back I am fucking her whether she likes it or not.

She did, no, wait, she didn't, she is falling off the bed...

Fuck, she has hit her head!

Ouch that had to hurt. She is down on the floor and not moving. She is still not moving. Not sure what I should do now.

Holy crap, I've fucking killed her.

"Caroline, Caroline!" I lean over her and pull her back from the bedside cabinet.

All I can see is red. My nostrils fill up. There is a smell, it's strong, it's sweet. It's punched me harder than she did. It's making me dizzy. It's intoxicating, what is it? I lean closer, it's her. She smells, she always smells but not like this, there is something else. Something else is drawing me towards her. I lean closer.

Fuck, my cock, it is so hard it nearly bent in two then.

I pull back, lean it to one side and then go in again.

The smell, I can't get over the smell. It's the blood. The blood that is coming from her hair, it's amazing it's leaking fast from the cut on her forehead. I lean closer.

I can't stop sniffing it. Fuck, it's great.

It has my eyes dancing all over the place. I lean in and place my tongue on it. It tastes, it tastes like, like heaven should taste. I lick her. I lick her again. It's the best goddamn lollipop I've ever had. It's in my mouth. On my teeth, my tongue is swishing the taste around my mouth.

Fuck, I want her.

I pull her back to the middle of my bedroom and mount her. She is still wet from before, as hard as I am, I slip right in.

I can smell it. It's spurring me on. That taste in my mouth. She is amazing.

Harder and Harder. I must be fourteen inches by now, either that or my dick is going to explode inside her... Fuck!

She is not moving. It's amazing, this is all about me. Not her, me. Move here, a bit to the left, a bit to the right, none of that fucking nonsense. Me. I can do whatever I want to her. Wait, I can do whatever I want to her. I pull out and flip her over. Tell me I can't put it in there will you... BANG! It's yours.

I'm on top of her and my hand is in the back of her head pulling her hair. The blood is coming through the hair and on to my hands. I pull my hand back and lick it. As I lick it I place my hand full on my face and smear the blood across it. It's amazing, the smell is sweet and rich and dark and I am dark with it.

"Mmmmm."

Wait, was that her or me? Who was making that sound then?

What the fuck? She is moving! She is moving.

If I thought she was pissed at the photograph, she is going to be pissed at the fact I am mounting her up the bum covered in her blood.

I am not putting up with that shit! This is my moment. It's all about me!

I lean over her and grab the lamp from the nightstand. It's heavy, but it will do the job. I strike her round the back of the head again. As I do the blood almost squirts directly into my mouth. As it does all I can think about is when you put a spoon in a grapefruit and it sprays back at you. That spray makes you wince, but this spray. It's amazing.

I do it again. Oh my god, again it sprays at me.

Again. Again. Again… I am almost covered in it now. The blood is everywhere, the smell is everywhere.

I'm Coming! I'm Coming! Holy FUCK!

I finish and come out of her. I lean against the bed. I can't believe how good that was. I can't believe that for the past three months I had been having boring sex with this girl! Now that is what I call lovemaking. She must have come like a dozen times, I am sure of it.

"Wow, Caroline, that was amazing. Why haven't we been doing that all the time?"

She must be knackered. She doesn't answer. I lean over her, she is out cold. I am not surprised, I am a great lover. She is always tired afterwards.

"Sleep, Caroline, after that you deserve it. You were really good."

I was better. I stand up and catch a glimpse of myself in the mirror. I look like an Indian warrior covered in war paint. I look like a hot Indian warrior covered in war paint, to be fair. Is there no look I can't pull off? Think I am developing a six-pack. I run my finger over. Yeah, it's definitely in there.

"I am starving. I am going to eat your sandwich too, OK? I am so hungry. I will make you another one when you want."

I sit and eat the food. It's the best damn sandwich I have ever had. The blood from my face is mixing with the white bread. I will never look at tomato sauce the same again.

I devour both of the sandwiches and both of the drinks, and lay on the bed.

I am a stud. I knew I was, I just never knew how good I was. Women are blessed I am on this earth. I lay there staring at the ceiling.

"You know, I haven't said this to anyone before, but I think I love you. I will admit I wasn't sure, but after this afternoon, I think it is love."

She still isn't answering me. Normally she doesn't shut up after sex, but today quiet as you like. Probably the shock of me saying the words first. But I am a New Age man. I am in touch with my feminine side. Not like gay, but aware of a woman's needs. And women need to hear those words.

Exhaustion and excitement is taking over me. I can feel myself falling into a calmness that I haven't had for some time. Everyone and everything tends to wind me up but now as I lay here, for some reason I am calmer than I have ever been.

"Sweet dreams, my baby." I fall asleep.

"Edmund."

"Edmund, we are home."

Oh, that woman's voice. It's so irritating. I lift my head. It's eight p.m. I must have slept for like five hours. That's amazing. I look at the pillow and it's covered in blood from my face.

Fuck, this room is a mess. If they come in here and see it, there is no fucking way I am getting my bike.

"I will be down in a minute, Mum."

"OK, I will start with the dinner."

Chapter 2

"Look at this mess, you are going to get me in so much trouble." She still lies there and does nothing.

She is pissing me off a little now. I knew it was too soon to say the L word to her. I pick her up and place her in my bed, and cover her over. I am never going to get this cleared up tonight. I go to my door and open it.

"Be down in fifteen, Mum, just having a quick shower."

"OK, love. I am warming the lasagne for you."

"Thanks, Mum it's my favourite." I jump in the shower. Can't believe I have to clear this mess up. You would have thought Caroline would have made a start as I slept. Fifteen minutes later I am clean and back downstairs.

"How was your day, dear?"

Amazing. Fucking amazing. And, Mum, the sex, oh my god. You wouldn't believe the sex.

"It was OK, nothing special."

She places the lasagne down in front of me. With salad.

I hate fucking salad. She knows I hate fucking salad.

"How was the dancing?"

I don't care. I don't even know why I asked.

"It was great, thank you. Your father is becoming quite the little mover."

She walks over and kisses him. He brushes his hand over her bum as she does.

"Quite a mover yourself."

NO, NO, NO! I just had an image of them having sex... that's wrong, so wrong. Yuk!

"That's good."

I am still eating my dinner. Dad has finished and Mum isn't eating. Weight Watchers or some nonsense like that. She is always on some kind of diet.

"Edmund, we want to talk to you about this bike."

I nearly choke on my salad. They are buying me a bike.

"Your mum and I have agreed to pay half towards it, if you agree to get a part-time job."

There is a smile on his face. Does he think he is doing me a favour?

What the fuck is it with them? They just want me to work my fingers to the bone.

"Thanks, that's very generous."

Is it fuck generous? They just want to hear that shit.

"What if the job is the other side of town? How will I get there?"

Didn't think about that, did you, you moron. They just look at each other. I can't walk to a job, can I?

"If that is the case, Edmund, we have discussed loaning you your half of the money so that you can get the bike, and you can pay us back over a period of time."

Fuck, they actually looked chuffed at that idea...

Loan me the money… Loan me the money! I am your son… You give me the money. No point waiting till your dead for me to get it, is there?

"That's a great idea, thanks, Dad. Thanks, Mum."

She comes over and takes my plate. I lean over and kiss her on the cheek. It has to be him. She would give me the money, I am sure of it, but he is full of ethics and lessons to be learned. Edmund, this builds character. Edmund, you will thank me when you are older. I am already a man, how much older do I need to get?

"Want some ice cream, love?"

Ice cream, what am I, twelve! Maybe it is her. Maybe it's her bossing him around that I don't see. Still treating me like a kid all the time. Here is your pack-up, Edmund. Make sure you drink lots of water, Edmund. Do you want ice cream, Edmund?

"Yes please, Mum."

She is over in the freezer pulling the ice cream out.

"We only have strawberry or chocolate."

For fuck's sake, are you trying to piss me off?

"Strawberry, please, Mum."

She scoops out the ice cream into a bowl and places it in front of me. I just give her the look. The look as if to say what the fuck is this?

"Sorry, sauce." She takes it back and puts strawberry sauce on top.

I eat the ice cream in silence. Dad's already up and at the TV. That's him for the rest of the night. Mum is washing up.

"Going to study, Mum. Don't come up as I am going to have my headphones on and in the zone. I have so much to do."

She turns and comes towards me. Kisses me on the head.

"Night then, love, I don't think we will be up late either this evening." Dad hears that, turns and smiles at Mum.

No, no, it's back in my head. Mum, Dad, early night, Yuk! Yuk! Yuk!

I go back upstairs and into my room. It is still the same. The rug on the floor is soaked in blood and it's all over the bedding, and the bed.

"You could have at least attempted to clear it up?"

Still nothing. She must be out of it. I was good though. I am not surprised how tired she would be. Probably never had it that good before.

I lay on the bed next to her. Still with the job. Don't they think I have enough to do with all the schoolwork and chores they make me do? Their bank account is full. I know, I have seen the statements. They both work and this house is paid for. I am their only son. I'll get it all one day, it may as well be today.

It may as well be today! It may as well be today. They are old, they have had a good life and all that.

Now that thought is all I can think about. What would life be like if they weren't here? I would get my bike. No more peddling. I would be damn sure there would be vanilla ice cream in the fridge and I wouldn't have to eat salad again. I can't think of a single bad point.

"I think life would be better, don't you?" I turn and look at Caroline. Still nothing. The smell of blood is back in my nose as I am so close to her. But she has been a bitch all afternoon. Not saying anything. Not cleaning this mess up. I can feel myself getting harder, but she isn't getting it.

"No, if you aren't going to help, then you are not getting any of this." I turn back and face the ceiling. That will teach her.

I can hear them walking up the stairs. Early night. They practically followed me upstairs.

Fuck, door…

I jump off the bed and bolt the door. Just in time as they try the handle as they go past.

"Goodnight, Edmund." She can't get in. I don't answer as I said I would have my ear phones on. I go back to the bed, and lay facing Caroline.

"Fuck, that was close." Still nothing.

Shit, forgot I wasn't talking to her.

I turn and face the wall. She will get the message that way. The real cold shoulder. She needs to put a bit more effort in with me. I think she is trading on her looks too much.

It may as well be today! That is all that is running through my head. It may as well be today. Well, it may as well be tomorrow.

I fall asleep with those thoughts going through my head.

"Edmund."

"Edmund."

Every fucking morning, the same noise. It's better if she isn't here. It will save her screaming at me.

"I am up, Mum. Taking a shower and will be down."

That will hold her. I do need a shower. I am covered in blood again. It's not the same now though. The smell isn't the same. In fact it's starting to stink in here. I pull my arm from under Caroline. I am not sure how I ended up cuddled up with her after the lack of anything from her last night.

"Think you need to leave, love." Still nothing. Why isn't she talking to me?

She is pissing me off, can't believe I let her sleep with me.

I get in the shower. All I can think about is an accident. Car crash? Robbery gone wrong? Fire? They are always the best stories.

Fuck me, fire is a great idea. I don't have to clean up then.

They will find her up here though, wont they? They always do. I swear if everyone in the world just watched *CSI* or *Criminal Minds* they would know how to get away with stuff. It's like Murder 101 on there.

I get out the shower and dress for school. I am not going but they don't know that. I head downstairs.

Déjà fucking vu.

He is reading the paper and she is at the stove. She puts a sausage sandwich in front of me. I hate sausages. She knows that.

"Morning, sunshine."

"Morning."

Can't grunt to her on her last day. I grab the brown sauce, put it on my sandwich and eat it.

"So, Edmund, any plans for today?"

Fuck, does he have that written behind that paper so he can ask me every fucking day!

"Nothing new, Dad, just the usual. School, homework, that sort of thing."

"That's good, that's good."

34

Prick… I don't know why he bothers to ask.

I finish and walk over to the TV and put it on.

"No classes, Edmund?"

"No, Mum, ten thirty is my first one today, and I have everything ready. I was up till one a.m. studying."

I could lie for a living. I don't know what type of job entails that, but I could. I am great at it and everyone believes every word that comes out of my mouth. Politician maybe? They lie about everything.

"Good boy."

"I was thinking after dinner tonight about running down to Maccy D's to see if they have any job application forms?"

Dad puts his paper down at this. Now I have your attention.

"Well done, Edmund, nice to see you are taking this seriously."

Oh, I am, Father, I am.

I sit staring at the morning news on TV. They both finally leave. At last, the house to myself. I walk upstairs and back to my room. The smell isn't like yesterday. In fact it is starting to annoy me.

"Caroline, I don't mean for it sound bad, but you stink." No response.

We are so fucking over, nobody treats me like this!

Can't believe I have to clear some of this up. In those *CSI* programmes that I watch, they can detect blood even after a fire. Those people are amazing. Maybe I should do that as a job? I would make a good CSI person. They are not detectives, though I would be good at that too, they are more like scientists.

"Aren't you even going to help?" Nothing.

I am going to have to get her out of here.

"Caroline, if you are just going to lay there and not talk to me then I will just dump you. In both senses of the word." She must be agreeing with me in her head as she isn't responding. Probably heartbroken at that statement. She must have felt like she won the lottery when she met me. If so she should know it takes effort to keep me.

I pull the rug from under the bed and off the floor. Grab Caroline and roll her in it.

Fuck, it's a good job I like small petite women. Imagine if I tried to dump a fat chick. I wouldn't have a rug big enough for that?

I have Miss Walker to thank for that. She is the perfect woman. I guess I look at every woman and benchmark them against her? I am going to have to wrap this rug in plastic or something. Blood will leak all over the house and it's bye-bye bike. Well, for now. I walk downstairs and start rummaging through the cupboards for bin bags.

Why even have a mum if she isn't going to clean your shit up? I find the bin bags and selotape, go back upstairs and start to wrap the rug.

Fuck, this is hard work!

It's done. I've done a good job.

I am talented even at wrapping ex-lazy arse girlfriends.

I carry Caroline down to the garage. I need to take her somewhere.

But she isn't going on my BMX. Nobody but me rides that. I don't want blood spilling on my gold mags. The wheelbarrow will do.

Who the fuck chains a wheelbarrow to the wall? Do we have a world-renowned crime wave for fucking wheelbarrows?

My dad is a moron. I grab the key hanging next to the chain, undo the wheelbarrow, and place Caroline in it. I then chain her to it, and open the garage door.

Close the garage, close the garage!

I can see someone's feet go past as I look down at myself. The garage door closes.

I look like a fucking butcher.

"You stupid tart, look what you have done to my school uniform. My mum's going to kill me.

"I will take another shower then, will I? I am so glad my time with you is over. Good luck getting another boyfriend like me."

I go up and shower and change. Coming downstairs and into the garage I notice she still hasn't gone.

This time I open the garage and push the wheelbarrow into the street and then close the garage door. Nobody is around so I start walking. As I do I notice the widow Mrs Green coming out of the house in front.

She is a cougar. Would fuck me if I let her. I would let her too.

"Morning, Edmund."

"Morning, Mrs Green."

"Now, Edmund, you can call me Cynthia, you know that."

I bet I can

"What are you up to on this lovely day?"

"Just helping my dad, whilst I have a few classes free."

"Ah, you are turning into a fine young man, Edmund. I will have to get you round to help me with a few chores." She touches my shoulder.

Fucking you wouldn't be a chore, Mrs Green, would do it for free.

I smile and carry on walking. I turn my head, she is checking me out and still smiling. That's a sign that she wants me right there.

I am going to do her. Maybe not today. But I am going to do her.

I cross the next few streets without seeing anyone, and turn left towards the canal. Why are people always walking their dogs here? Don't they have like dog parks and places they can go? That's nearly ten minutes of walking and all I can see is people walking their dogs. I wait until they all disappear. One big push.

Bye-bye, bitch!

Was that too harsh? She let me do her. And up the bum. It's always how you are treated in the end you remember though, isn't it? Not the good times.

No, stunk the house out and made a mess. Bitch, it is.

I walk the back way to the house, and go in through the back garden. Don't want the cougar asking me what I did with my dad's wheelbarrow. I sit down on the sofa.

How to start a fire?

CSI always detect accelerants. Even ones from fireman. Why is it in at least one episode, it's always the fireman starting the fire? You know it is, and they still make the episode. Do they think we are stupid? No, accelerants aren't the answer. Cooking fire? Na, never going to work. She would notice.

Fuck, this is hard work!

And all because they won't just give me the money for a bike. Unbelievable. Gas leak! That's the one. Cut the pipe and wait for the spark. They will be out cold from the fumes anyway. Makes you go to sleep, I think. That will be nice for them too, an early night.

That's it, our fire. It's one of those old ones you need to hold the button down on. And it keeps clicking till the gas kicks in. I go over to it and look for the pipe and the button.

Where the fuck is it?

I keep searching. It doesn't have it.

What the fuck have they done with it? I start this fire all the time. It was right fucking here!

They have taken it off. They know how mad I am at them. They were expecting it. I bet they were expecting it... I sit back on the sofa. I realise I was thinking of my nan's house. We have an electric fire. My nan's house is the one with the gas fire.

The cooker is gas.

I walk over to it, it is, and I can get to the pipes. I am a genius. Takes a light switch or a phone ring just to ignite once the room is full, and that's what I will do tonight. Pretty clever for a kid who hates school. I walk upstairs and back to my room.

Fuck, forgot all the mess.

I take the sheets off the bed and wipe the floor with them. Her blood has soaked through the mattress. Mum would kill me if she ever knew.

What if the CSI find blood in my room? Going to have to do something. This isn't getting cleared up completely. It's soaked into the floorboards. Can't even bleach it. They always have that light that detects the blood.

And that lazy bitch isn't going to help me clean it up, is she?

Only one thing for it. I go downstairs, grab a knife and go back to my room.

I need to cut myself and then they will think it was my blood on the floor. I pull the knife across the top of my forearm.

FUCK!

That hurts. But as soon as I do, I can smell the smell. It's not as sweet as yesterday's but it still gives my head a buzz.

I am dropping my blood all over the floor and trying to mix it in with hers. I can't concentrate. All I can think about is yesterday afternoon.

Fucking her, licking her, tasting her. I love her. She was amazing. The taste, the smell. My hands are down my pants. I am hard, I start to tug...

FUCK! I cut the wrong arm. Cut the wrong arm. That's my wanking arm. I am a dick!

I sit back on the bed. I swear I want to cry. Think, Edmund, think. I try the other hand, it's all awkward and bumpy, just don't get the grip. I pull my bleeding arm closer to my nose.

Fuck, that's good.

My other hand gets rhythm. The blood is spurring it on. I smell it again. I taste it again. No, it's not as sweet as Caroline's, but still has the taste of heaven in my head.

That's it, that's it, that's it… Fucking Mrs Green, Fucking Mrs Green. Miss Walker, Mrs Green, Miss Walker, Mrs Green… God, yes!

The sperm goes further than the blood. I bet I could make a lot of babies with my sperm. It's super sperm. I lay back on the bed. That shot like three foot.

Fucking blood!

I realise it's all over me again. I swear at this rate I will be showering six times a day. Sick of it. I get in the shower and clean myself up, get dressed and go downstairs.

Fuck it, the room can stay as it is now.

Some *Xbox* and an afternoon on the sofa. I deserve some quality me time.

Chapter 3

"Edmund."

"Edmund."

What the F...

Oh, yeah, she is waking me up on the sofa. Controller in one hand and...

Shit hands down pants, hands down pants!

I pull out. She doesn't notice.

"What have you done to your arm, Edmund?"

Shit, didn't mean her to see that.

"It's just a scratch, Mum. I was getting a kitten out of a tree and it scratched me for the pleasure."

I am a fucking hero.

"Ah, you are such a good boy. Come on, get yourself up, I am making dinner."

She is off to the kitchen. Kitten in a tree, god, I can make some crap up on the spot, can't I? I get off the sofa and head over to the dinner table. She is at the stove and he is reading the paper.

I swear there must be nude pictures or something in that paper. Some days I am sure that is all he ever does.

"I am making homemade steak and chips." She smiles as she turns.

I hate fucking…

No, actually, wait a minute, I love steak and chips.

"With salad."

Bitch had to ruin it.

"So, Edmund, going to get your form this evening?" His paper doesn't move.

"Yes, Dad. Nightshift manager gets in at ten so going to do it then."

I lie. They will be on the sofa cuddled up by then. I need an excuse to get out of here. She serves up my dinner. I eat it. We all retire to the living room.

CSI is on. It's on every channel, every day. What is it with people and murder? They are obsessed. We watch it. I watch it, they are talking about dancing lessons and some other boring shite. I am not really listening to them.

"It's nearly ten, I am going." They both turn. They look surprised.

Been fucking lying here all night you know…! Not that you two noticed!

"Do you want a lift, Edmund?"

"No, thanks, Dad, I am taking my bike."

I get up and head to the kitchen. I quickly pull a knife from the drawer and slit the pipe at the back of the cooker. Not in half, that's how idiots get caught. Just a nick, and then I am out of there. The adrenaline is huge. I am at Maccy D's in like ten minutes on my bike. I will be here in like three when I get my motorbike. I can feel myself trembling with excitement. I go to the counter.

"Big Mac and chips and a vanilla milkshake."

"Sorry, no vanilla." I just look directly at her. I should shoot her. I should just buy a gun and shoot her where she stands.

No fucking vanilla milkshake.

My excitement has turned to rage.

"Chocolate then, please."

She disappears. The tall spotty lad with the stars on his shirt is walking around behind her as if he is god of the fryers.

"Excuse me, do you have an application form for a job?"

He turns to smile at me.

I couldn't work for you, you prick, if my life depended on it.

"Sure."

"Thank you." My supper arrives and so does the application form. I go and sit by the window.

What if they are dead already? What if it exploded as I left the street? What colour bike am I going to get? I like red. It will remind me of the blood. I eat my food. Why do they insist on putting salad crap in a burger? A burger should be a burger. With maybe the pickle, cheese and the sauce, but none of this lettuce stuff.

Sirens!

The noise is filling the streets. Is it them? Is it time? I look out of the window in the direction of my house. I can't see a fire, I can't see any smoke. The sirens pass going the opposite way to home.

Fuck! Why am I so unlucky?

I finish the burger, chips and chocolate shake. I didn't want the shake, but you need to drink something with a burger.

I put the application form in my pocket. Been thirty minutes. Is that enough time to fill a house with gas and blow it up? No idea. Should have watched *CSI*. Or googled it. I am sure they would tell you online, but then they check my Internet history. They always do that in the programme. There must be a way to delete it, I mean, I am sure porn doesn't stay on there. Does it?

I need to ring them to spark the gas.

It will at least get them to walk into the hall and answer the phone. Maybe turn the hallway light on. I take out my phone.

Hate this fucking phone!

Blackberry. Why couldn't they just get me an iPhone. Everyone else in the world has an iPhone now. When they're gone I am getting one! I ring home. It's ringing. Would it still ring if the house was on fire?

"Hi."

Fuck, it didn't work.

"Hi, Mum, just letting you know the manager is running late so will be about thirty minutes."

"OK, baby, be safe. If you want your dad to come get you, let me know."

I hang up the phone.

Where the fuck do all these lies come from… I am a fucking machine.

Seriously, how long does it take to blow up a house? Twenty? Fifty minutes? I can't just sit here. Need to go for a ride, it will be more believable. I get up and go for a ride. Down through the town and back to the canal to see if Caroline has got out. Nope, no sign of her or my dad's wheelbarrow. He

45

is probably going to be mad about that. And Mrs Green saw me with it. She won't tell him. Mum doesn't like him talking to her.

It's been forty minutes. I am just a few blocks away and nothing. I don't think I cut it enough. Either that or they have found the leak and turned the gas off. They would do that, wouldn't they? Just so I don't get my bike.

Fuck it, I am going home!

I start to cycle back. I can't believe they haven't turned on a light or anything. Just lying on the sofa all cuddled up, I bet. Or worse, gone for an early night. Even before I get home. Yuk!

Useless, they never do anything I want!

Wonder if I cut it enough. What if it goes off when I am in the house? Not going to be happy. I can see the house. Lights are on. No flashing blue lights outside. It didn't work.

Fuck!

There goes my bike and I am going to have to clean my own room. Suppose I have to go in, tell them I can smell gas, get them out, and get someone to come sort the house. Going to have to think of another plan… I suppose I will be a hero for smelling it. Maybe that will get me my bike. No, he won't see it like that. Saving his life isn't a lesson to be learned.

For fuck's sake!

Mrs Green is at the window as I pass her house. I am too angry to do her now. I give her a little wave just so that it's on the back burner for when I need it. I reach the bottom of our drive.

BOOM!

What the fuck! I'm on the floor. The explosion has knocked me off my bike. Fuck, it went up like a hot air balloon. Fuck, I've cut my head, I can smell the blood. Shit, this is not a time to get a hard-on.

The house is a fireball of flames. I like it. I am trying to get to my feet. All the lights in the street are on. I honestly feel a little dazed about it all.

Shit, here comes the widow… do something, Edmund, do something.

"What's happened, what's happened, Mum, Dad?"

It is a good job I am an amazing actor. I get up and head towards the house, slowly as I need to be stopped. Mrs Green is holding me back. She was like a lioness on a zebra, how did she get here so fast? I can smell her perfume, but I don't turn around. I am in shock and grief, that's what it needs. CSI always has shock and grief. I know it's too late but my shock won't admit to it.

"Calm down, Edmund, you can't go in there. Are your parents home, Edmund?"

"Yes, I just left them. Let me go, I need to save them!"

She is still pulling me back. Her grip is firm around me. She turns me into her, and my head is in her chest.

Fuck, move your arse back, Edmund, or else she will be feeling something on her hip.

I do, but the thought of my parents and Mrs Green's perfume aren't helping. I can feel that my jeans are far too tight. They just don't make that area big enough for people like me.

Horny as fuck now!

Definitely a red bike.

There is a crowd now. They are gathering. I know people will have called the police and fire brigade. To be honest they can probably see it from the other side of town. It's raging. Someone has put a blanket round my shoulders.

As if I am cold. I am standing next to a towering inferno, for fuck's sake.

The sirens are coming. I can hear them in the distance. It's been about ten minutes. That's quicker than I want. Can you survive ten minutes in a burning down house? Hope not. Last thing I need is for them to be OK. After going through all of this.

How the fuck do I have a chair and a cup of tea in my hand...? Where is this all coming from? Some marshmallows and I will be at camp.

Firemen are struggling to get into the house. It is proper burning down. I hear a crumbling. The roof has caved in. Fuck, that didn't take long.

Job done. That will cover up Caroline's mess that she made of my room.

Where has time gone? Everything seems to be on fast forward.

No firemen go in. The flames are put out from the outside. Mrs Green has one hand on my shoulder as a copper comes over to speak to me.

"Sorry, young man, Mrs Green informs me that your parents were home."

"They are." Tears are running down my face.

I am a fucking talented actor.

Miss Walker would have been lucky to do me. Will be lucky to do me. When she sees me pull up on my new bike.

"Then, I am sorry for your loss, son." He pats me on the shoulder also.

"It's a miracle you weren't home too."

"It is, Edmund." Mrs Green leans in and kisses me on the cheek.

Fuck, she smells good.

I am sure she has changed since I have been sitting here. I am sure she wasn't wearing that dress. It's for me and the fireman. I know that much.

"Do you have anywhere you can stay tonight?"

"He can stay with me, officer, and we will sort the rest out tomorrow."

Yeah I can, fuck, that is a great idea.

Stop, I can't do Mrs Green tonight. Will be too obvious that I don't care. Like when mobsters rob a bank and then go and buy lots of new stuff. Have to be sensible. Play it cool, get the money and my bike.

Fuck yeah, I am getting my bike. And a new iPhone.

Press have started to turn up. News vans and newspapers. I can use this. This is great.

Become fucking famous.

I keep my blanket on and walk closer to the fire. I can see the front page of the paper tomorrow already. I would make a great reporter. I can visualise a headline out of anything.

"Edmund, you need to stay here."

"I just want to say goodbye, Mrs Green."

I just want to milk it for maximum exposure. Cash and fame, what a night.

I will get laid like a fucking prince if I play this properly.

I am standing at the end of our path. The fire is all but out and the press are gathering like vultures. I put on the waterworks.

"Mum, Dad, why, why, why?" They are lapping this stuff up. I fall to my knees. It's started to rain.

I could be in a fucking boy band video, I look that good.

The sobbing continues as I lean forward and stay in the praying position. I can hear the cameras and people around me. Mrs Green is picking me up.

Fuck, what is she doing?

"Come on, Edmund, this isn't the time or the place."

The press know my name. All I can hear is Edmund, Edmund, I love it. I am horny again. I am so glad this blanket is round me. People chanting my name. That's what I was put on this planet for. For people to worship me.

"It's OK, Mrs Green, I can handle it." I stop in my tracks and turn my face to the cameras. A couple of people are filming and some are taking photos.

"Edmund, were your parents home?"

"Yes, yes, they were." I choke a little as the words come out.

Fuck, that was a nice touch

"Do you know what started the fire?"

"No." I look around as if to look for a fireman. I am not really looking for a fireman. Want to give that expression of hopelessness that sells the news.

"I was down the road getting a job application form. I only left them thirty, forty minutes ago. They said if I get a job they would buy me a motorbike. I was just trying to fulfil their wish."

Cue the waterworks, big time. If that doesn't get me a bike, nothing will. Probably won't even have to pay for it.

I am a god amongst men. The world will know that one day.

"Edmund, where are you going to stay?"

I look at Mrs Green...

"He is staying with me, and he has had enough for one night. Now leave him alone to rest."

Perfect.

I bury my head in her chest and we walk back to her house followed by the press. We go in and she locks the door behind her. She takes my blanket off and hugs me so tight.

She fucking must be feeling it in her side, it is huge.

"Do you need a drink? Some food or something, Edmund?"

Dropping to your knees would be good for a start...

No, sadness, remember, sadness! She needs to see you at the low point for the press and the news reporters.

"I just want to sleep, Mrs Green. Just sleep."

"Sure you do, my dear, come with me."

She leads me upstairs to one of her spare rooms. It's a big double bed with en suite. This will do nicely. For a minute I was sure she was taking me straight to her bedroom.

"Take a shower, love, and if there is anything you need I am just down the hall." She hugs me again. I am sure she can feel it.

She closes the door. I wait and then lock it behind her. I am knocking one out before the bolt slides across.

Fuck, that was amazing. The fire, the adrenaline and Mrs Green's boobs right in my face… Fuck, I should just go down that hall and—

"Let me know if you need anything, Edmund."

She is almost begging for it!

"I will, Mrs Green."

Ahhhhh, I spurt like a volcano.

I walk into the en suite and look at the shower. The smell of the fire is still on me and so is the faint smell of blood from the cut on my head. I don't want to shower, I am enjoying it too much.

I go back and lay on the bed. Kick my shoes off and lay at the headboard.

What an amazing couple of days. I have never enjoyed myself so much.

If you told me a couple of days ago I was going to have the best sex ever, get rich and get my bike in the next two days, I would never have believed it. But, here I am, ten feet away from the town bike, parentless and rich. Can't get any better than that, can it?

I fall asleep within minutes. Miss Walker on my red bike was my last thought before I did.

"Edmund."

"Oh, Edmund."

That fucking woman.

Wait, that's not her. Oh, yes, she is gone. That's Mrs Green calling me. It's daylight outside. I look at the clock on the wall. It's nine a.m. I slept like a baby.

"I am coming, Mrs Green."

That's not the last fucking time she will hear that.

I head downstairs. She is in her kitchen in her night-robe.

Fuck me, that's hot. She is doing that on purpose. Just a little bit of the teddy showing and a side boob.

"Oh, Edmund, you didn't clean up."

Fully intend to get down and dirty, that's why.

"Sorry, I must have fallen asleep."

She walks over and kisses me on the forehead again.

"That's OK, but we are both going to have to clean up if we are going to face that today."

She looks over at me and then at the window.

I walk over to the window to see what the fuss is about.

Fuck me, there are hundreds of them.

"They have been arriving since around six a.m., Edmund. I heard them setting up."

"What do they want?"

I know what they want, they want the same thing you do, Mrs Green, a piece of this!

"They just want to make sure you're OK, Edmund, people care about you."

She is standing by me again now. Not sure how I am going to keep from banging her brains out. I look back out the window to distract myself.

I am a fucking celebrity.

I am trying as hard as I can to keep the smile off my face. But it's true, I am the biggest, hottest property in this little frigging town. I look all over and there are the papers, the TV channels; there are three vans from the BBC alone.

Edmund Carson, fucking famous.

Wait is that a motorbike with a bow on it! No way, wait it's blue.

Fucking blue. Morons!

Chapter 4

I can't believe it's been a year today. A year. That has gone so fast.

A year since they fucked off and left me!

And what do I have to show for it? Nothing, that's what. Sure it was good for a couple of months, but now, nothing. Where are they all now, eh...? I will tell you where they are, off covering another shooting in an American school or some soppy story about the Prince and his new baby.

Maybe I should do a school shooting. Fuck knows my classmates deserve it. Especially Carl.

I can't believe it's been a year and nobody cares? After the explosion, king of the world for at least a month. Press release every frigging day and now... I couldn't get recognised walking down the street.

Maybe I should do something today? Maybe I should go back to the house or something, maybe a press person is going to do a piece one year on... I would. Look at me now, I can grow designer stubble, been working out. I could be one of those male models, without a doubt. I should be back in the paper, that is for sure.

Maybe I should do a calendar or something, like those pop stars do for Christmas. Birthday in two days, Edmund the orphan at seventeen, I have got to be in the top ten world's hottest seventeen-year-olds. Especially with my backstory. That shit sells newspapers.

I get up out of bed and stand in front of the mirror. Naked.

Damn, I am hot!

Six-pack, big dick, long hair, not too long. Long enough to be cool but not a grebo… I would so do me.

I go to the bathroom and knock one out. Miss Walker is in my head. She is always in my head. I need to be in hers. I need this to be in her.

"Edmund."

"Edmund."

Fuck, not now… Miss Walker, Miss Walker, Miss Walker… Yes!

I tell you the last thing you need is your grandmother calling you when you are knocking one out.

"Be down in a minute."

Be nice to the old girl, she is giving me the card in two days. Two days!

Can't believe I have had to wait. It's my money, it's not like they left it to anyone else. She won't even tell me how much I am going to get.

I bet it's a fucking lot!

They were minted before they went. The house must have been insured for like what, three hundred and fifty thousand? There was at least two hundred thousand in the bank account and if they had life insurance, I will be a goddamn millionaire.

I get dressed and walk downstairs. Can't believe I live with my nan. I would have stayed at Mrs Green's house. God, I could have had some fun with her, but no, the law says I am a minor. A minor? Me?

I am a fucking major… Wait, sergeant fucking major.

"Morning."

"Morning, handsome, what can I fix you for breakfast?"

"I am fine, Nan."

"Come on, you need to eat something. I know it's going to be a hard day for you, so I don't want you leaving on an empty stomach."

I love my nan, proper love my nan.

Never been anyone else in my life like her, she so gets me. And she trusts and respects everything I do, that's why I am getting the money early. She believes in me. Why wouldn't she? I am awesome. She knows I am.

"Just a sausage sandwich will do."

"Coming right up."

She goes over and starts preparing breakfast.

Yes, maybe I should do something today. It is an anniversary and all that. I wonder if I should go past the house and lay some flowers. That's the kind of thing you see on the news or at the roadside, don't you? It will get some attention. I wonder how long I need to sit there to get someone from the press to arrive. See little old orphaned Edmund which they have forgotten about.

You can call the press, you dick!

Crap, why didn't I think of that already? That's the plan. Go to school, tip off the press, and let's see who bites. I still have all those cards from a year ago. I am sure one of them will turn up and cover the story. I can give the old sob story about how hard it's been. How much I miss them. And how I am doing now. The boy has become a man. Back in the limelight Edmund, back in the limelight.

"There you go, my dear. Just as you ordered."

I love my nan, but sometimes her cooking leaves a lot to be desired.

"Thanks, Nan"

I eat the sandwich. It's better than usual.

"Nan, can I have some money? I would like to get some flowers today."

"Of course, my dear, that's a wonderful idea. Would you like me to come with you?"

I think about that for a moment. I love her, but the doddery old girl could probably upstage me. Na, just me.

"Think I would like to do it alone, if that is OK?"

"Of course it is, I was going to the cemetery whilst you were at school anyway."

Cemetery, is that better than the space where the house was? Na, doesn't make it real; everyone goes to the graveyard. Besides, don't like it there, every time she makes me go I imagine my parents' hands coming out of the grave and trying to pull me under. I have watched those films too, many times. Back to the house, that's the place to go. Edmund Carson, one year on.

I kiss my nan and get on my bike. My bike, the coolest in school. That's because my nan bought it for me. Fuck yeah, I remember that blue bike the press guy brought me, what a hunk of junk that was, but this is the real deal. Has got me laid no end. I knew it was going to.

57

"Be careful out there."

Every morning she follows me to the garage to say that, every morning.

"I will," I mumble through my helmet and head to school.

The day passes before I notice it. There are days with Miss Walker, and days without Miss Walker. This was a day without her, so don't even remember what happened.

I walk out and get on my bike. Amy Bunting walks past me. I don't acknowledge her as she does. She is there on purpose. Buttons undone. Short skirt. The boots. I love the boots.

She wants fucking again.

She wasn't bad, but not worth doing twice. Well, I say she wasn't bad, she was a virgin when we went out. Took me six weeks to get her to open her legs. Six weeks. I mean, look at me, girls drop in hours for this. She did try blowing me first though.

So fucking funny!

The dozy mare blew for the first five minutes before I knew what she was doing. I laugh inside my helmet as I start the bike up.

None of them have been worth doing twice. Not since Caroline.

Caroline. Been a while since I have thought about her, what is wrong with me? She was the best ever. Haven't seen her around for ages. What's it been, like a year or something?

Fuck me, I have had seven girls now!

And not a sniff at any in the last five months. That thought stays in my head. Fucking famous people get all the pussy. I need to be back on top and fast. I drive my bike off to the flower shop. I park my bike and walk in.

"Be with you in a moment." The shop is empty. I look at the flowers. What do you get dead people? It's not like they can see them, is it? I mean, why spend all the money people do on flowers? It doesn't make sense, but everyone does it. Is it for the dead people or to show the world how much you cared about the dead people? People are morons.

Need to spend a lot of money on the flowers!

The more I spend the more they will think I care. The more I care, the more sensitive I am. People like that.

I turn and see the shop assistant coming from behind the counter.

Fuck, she is hot!

Small, dark-haired, looks like a young Miss Walker. Not that Miss Walker is old, she must be like what, twenty-three, twenty-five.

I take my helmet off. As I do she is fixated on me. Yeah, I am hot too.

"Afternoon, sir, can I help you?"

Sir. That is a sign she is trying to impress me. She has that twinkle in her eyes, she wants me. Time to turn on the story.

"Hi, yes. Sorry, not really sure what I am doing here, I am looking for some flowers?"

"OK, and is it for a special occasion?"

Cue the sob story.

"Special occasion. I guess it is really. They are for my parents." I pause as if to clear my throat. I have used this story so many times.

"When I say my parents, my late parents. It's been a year since they passed, and I just wanted to do something to remember them by. You know, just to show that I am still thinking about them. Every day. Still thinking about them every single day."

And here come the soppy eyes and the tilt of the head.

"I am sorry for your loss."

I have her, and I am going to have her.

"Thank you, it's fine. But as I said, I don't really know what I am doing, I have never bought flowers before. Apart from for my grandmother who I live with and take care of now. It was just the anniversary and everything."

I am an expert at a quiver in my throat. Lonely orphan, caring grandson. I know exactly what I am doing. Little boy lost is such a turn-on to girls.

"OK, let me help you." She takes my hand. She wants me.

"How much do you want to spend?"

"It doesn't matter." She smiles back at me. She starts pulling different flowers from around the shop. She is talking to me, but I can't hear a word. All I can think about is what she looks like under that apron. Before I know it she has made an arrangement. It's wrapped and in front of me.

"Wow, that's beautiful. You are so talented." She smiles back at me. I check out her name badge.

"Thanks, Sophia. Thanks for helping me."

"Any time. Do you want a card?" She pulls a box from under the counter.

"A card?"

"Yes, sometimes people like to leave a card. Just some words that you would like to have said or want to say."

I have to think for a moment. Should have bought me a bike when I asked springs to my mind. Thanks for the memories? Don't think either of them are going to get me laid tonight.

"OK. Just... Mum and Dad, there isn't a day goes past without me thinking of you, missing you, loving you. I would give everything I have to have you here with me. Love, Edmund."

She writes it down. I would. I would give everything I have today. Not everything I will have in two days. Well, I say everything, not my bike.

"Edmund Carson?"

And there goes the fame card. Nice to know some people still remember me. I need to be a star again. That look in her eyes. They all looked at me like that.

"Yes."

"I thought I recognised you. I can't believe it has been a year." She walks around and hugs me. I am hard within seconds.

She walks back over and fills in another card.

"If you would like to grab a coffee or something, here is my number."

Fuck, she does want me!

"Thanks, Sophia."

I grab the flowers and leave. If I leave her wanting more, she will bend over on the first date. She needs to be in the 'will he, won't he?' call frame of mind. Then bang... She will spread like butter.

I take the old business cards out of my pocket that they gave me a year ago and start to ring the numbers of the press offices.

"Excuse me, sir, that young boy, Edmund Carson, he is sitting on his parents' lawn with flowers, crying. I thought you would want to know. I think it has been a year or something."

Five minutes later and I have called ten different newsrooms, which should pique their interest. Just need to get there now. That's why I love my bike. In and out of traffic. I am at my old house in five minutes. Nobody is here yet. Great, I made it before them. I place the flowers down with the card pointing upwards and wait. Wait, what should I do? Be on my knees or standing? You never know which photo they are going to use. So I have to look good in all of them. I will be mad if they use the one of me in the blanket again.

For fuck's sake, they are going to be using the one in the blanket again, aren't they?

Look at me, do I look like that kid now? I am like a supermodel now. Better than a magazine wannabe. I sit here on my knees. Staring at the house. I wonder how much the insurance was really worth. Should I rebuild it with the money? There is definitely a story or front page in that. Plaque to Mum and Dad and all that. Could be some kind of a shrine.

I wait. I still wait.

What the fuck, it's been fifteen minutes at least since I made the call.

Wait, I can hear something. No, it's a car. One of my stupid neighbours. Wait, not even the neighbours are bothering to come out. This is hurting my knees: I am lying down. I pull my iPhone out of my rucksack and stick on some tunes. I guess the prince has had another baby or something. They will definitely be here soon. This is front-page stuff. I am front-page material.

I wait. I wait some more.

"Edmund."

I open my eyes. Mrs Green is standing over me.

"Edmund, darling, are you OK?"

She is leaning over me and I can see straight down her blouse.

She must fucking know that!

"Hi, Mrs Green, I was just, thinking, you know."

Wait, how fucking long have I been lying here?

I look at my watch.

A fucking hour and a half!

"I know, Edmund, must be a hard day for you today. I did think about you this morning."

I bet you did. Wait, stuff that, where is the press? Not a single van, not even a reporter? Nobody cares it's been a year since I was left alone? Nobody? What do I have to do to get some attention around here?

"Thank you, Mrs Green. That's very kind of you."

"That's fine, Edmund. I hardly recognised you at first, how much you have grown and filled out, Edmund."

She is looking at me now. She is thinking about jumping me as I lie on the ground, I know it. I stand up. No, nothing, not a press reporter or photographer in sight. I can't believe that not one of them came.

What the fuck is this world coming to?

"Edmund, you have grown so tall, and is that a beard I can see you are growing?"

Not fucking one… Wait, is Mrs Green coming on to me?

"Yes, Mrs Green."

"Edmund, we have said this before, you don't need to call me Mrs Green"

"Sorry."

"Now, why don't you come back to my house and I will fix you a drink. I am sure we could squeeze to the odd beer or two without your grandmother knowing. Especially today."

Fuck, she wants to get me drunk and do me.

If there is no press, then that is definitely the best option.

"Thank you, Mrs, Cynthia."

"That's better."

She links my arm and we walk down the street to her house. I can see curtains twitching as I walk. The neighbours think she is a cougar. That's probably because that is exactly what she is. But why the fuck not? We walk into her house. I am fine with people knowing I have done her.

"Take a seat, Edmund."

I do. She is up at the fridge and she grabs me a beer.

"I am sure you could use one of these today, couldn't you?"

"Yes, thank you, Cynthia."

"So, how have you been Edmund? How is your nan?"

"Fine, just fine. I like living with my nan, she is a lot of fun and she looks after me. Too well, if I am honest."

"I am sure she does. She has turned you into a very handsome man."

She is looking directly at me now. There is only one thing on her mind.

"Oh, Edmund, what must you think of me? I have been in the garden all day. You drink your beer whilst I just sort myself out."

She disappears upstairs. I drink my beer as I walk around the house. Lots of pictures of her and her late husband still on the sides and coffee tables. Probably shagged the poor bastard to death. To be fair, that isn't a bad way to go if you have to go.

Poor woman just misses a good fucking, that's all!

I stand looking out the window. Why didn't the press turn up? I told them I was there... I am special and they have said that. The public adore me, so, why wouldn't they turn up? I keep looking out of the window, but nothing.

"I am sorry about that, Edmund, let me get you another beer."

I turn around. She has a red robe on, that is all. There is nothing else under there. Her hair is wet from the shower and she is half drying it with a towel, and her skin is glistening. She is smoking hot for an old girl.

I am harder than a lead pipe as she walks into the kitchen. All I can think about is Edmund in the kitchen with a lead pipe. That fucking kids' game.

Fuck it, I am following her.

She hears me as I follow her into the kitchen. Her head slightly turns. She is making sure I am behind her. I will be behind her.

"Won't be a minute, Edmund, now where did I put that beer?"

She bends down in front of the fridge. Her robe pulls up so you can see everything below her waist. I can see the beer on the top shelf. There is only one reason that she is bending down.

Fuck it, let's find out…

I walk over behind her and place my hands either side of her hips. I can feel the pelvis bones and they feel like handles. I pull her back towards me. She doesn't say a word. She just moves her arse up and down on my dick.

That's enough of a signal. One hand still around her waist I unbutton my trousers, pull down my pants and I am in her within seconds.

Fuck, that's hot, my dick plunges in her and it's wet and hot inside. She has been strumming herself upstairs getting ready for this.

"Oh, Edmund."

It is Edmund, didn't expect a dick this big, did you, Mrs Green?

I pull her head out of the fridge and bend her over the table in the kitchen. The wet hair reminds me of Caroline, without the smell. My fingers are running through it as I keep pumping her.

I can make the smell… It wouldn't take a lot.

I look around, there is nothing on the table. Nothing within reach. I am fucking her so hard now…

Fuck, I might fall in at this rate…

I need the smell. This is good and god, she is moaning as if she had never had sex before... But no smell. No smell… It's not the same.

I look down. She is over the table, the robe is on the floor and she is loving every minute of it. I pull at her hair as I enter her over and over again… She carries on screaming my name.

I like that she shouts my name. Shows she is really into it. Caroline never shouted my name. Not even the last time when I know she must have come like five times. She pushes back hard and I am out of her. She turns and sits on the table and pulls me closer to her. I am harder than a Trojan Horse now and I enter her with ease.

Fuck, she is close to me...

Her arms are all over me, her mouth is kissing my neck, she is moving up, she is trying to kiss me.

Fuck, I don't want to kiss you, you're like thirty-five or something.

I push her back on the table and she lies there as I bang her like a jackrabbit. She keeps screaming. The whole neighbourhood will hear her. At least they will be hearing my name around here. Damn the neighbourhood. They saw me come in here, nobody else came over to see me. Mrs Green deserves this.

I am not going to get the smell, not today. I keep at her... And at her. She could go on all night.

Fuck, will she never come...!

I am not coming first, I am holding this back. You will remember the time Edmund Carson came for a beer. And when I am famous, you will want to tell everyone.

"I am coming, I am coming."

Thank fuck for that, thought I might backfire if I hold it in any more.

She screams as if someone had stabbed her. I come inside her. It's warm, pulsating. But not Caroline. She lies back exhausted, her hand brushes my thigh. I pull out. Still hard but relieved. I look out of the kitchen window. The lad that lives down the street, want to say Oliver, is standing about eight feet from the window... I bet at twelve that's the first time he has seen that. The look on his face is one of horror. I pull my trousers up and stick two fingers up at him and he disappears. As he does a BBC van drives past the window.

Fuck! Fuck! Fuck... Bitch cost me my fame.

I pull my trousers up and try to get out of there as quickly as possible. Have to promise to come and see her again, but need to see if there are any more vans out in the street.

There aren't. I hang around for another ten minutes, but nothing. Fuck!

Chapter 5

"Happy birthday to you, happy birthday to you."

"What the…"

"Happy birthday, dear Edmund, happy birthday to you."

Oh yeah, it's my birthday. I open my eyes and she is standing there with a cake in her arms and the candles still going.

I go to push the covers back and quickly remember I am naked. Easier for night-time self-indulgence. I pull the covers around my waist, get on my knees, and blow out the candles. The cake is made into a one and a seven.

"Oh, Edmund, happy birthday, sweetie."

"Thanks, Nan."

"I just wish your mother and father were here to see what a great boy you have turned into."

She had to bring them up, didn't she? Nobody cares about the Carsons any more. I bet that van wasn't even there for me. Just passing.

"Now, get dressed and come downstairs, I have made you a special birthday treat."

She leaves with the cake.

Seventeen, fucking seventeen, today I become a millionaire...

Well, rich, but I reckon there has to be a cool mil in that bank... What with the house insurance and all that. Driving lessons, I need driving lessons... Real ones not what Nan has been teaching me. My hand goes immediately under the covers... nope I am even too excited to do that. I am up, in the shower, dressed and downstairs within fifteen minutes.

Nan has laid out pancakes, bacon, eggs, the full works on the side for me and her. Party hats and everything and a banner with seventeen on. She is amazing. Nobody has a nan like mine.

"Thanks, Nan."

I go over, hug and kiss her. I sit to eat.

"We are going to the bank after school, Edmund, so you come straight home. No chasing girls just because it's your birthday."

"I will, Nan. And you're the only girl for me."

Damn fucking right I will. I will even pretend to like school today.

I go to school. The day just disappeared in front of me. Saw Miss Walker at lunch, she smiled in my direction. I don't think things have been the same since that day in class a year ago. I think, I know, I must have got the old juices going that day. Must be hard for her to keep her distance. Seeing how I have filled out and matured and all that. I can tell she has the hots for me. Probably waiting till I leave school. That would make sense. For her, it makes sense. For me, the sooner we get it done, the better. It is so going to happen. The bell goes and

I am out of there and heading towards the bank. Meeting Nan at four sharp.

I arrive and she is waiting on the steps for me. She is never late that woman. If she says she is going to do something then she is going to do it. She is like some kind of superhuman.

"Did you have a nice day, dear?"

"Lovely, thanks." I kiss her on the cheek and we go in. We sit awaiting our appointment for four fifteen with a Mr Lawley.

My god, he is fat.

I guess you don't have to be fit to be a bank manager. I bet that is because he has a day job. Sitting behind a desk all day long makes you fat and lazy. I couldn't do that job. We follow him back to his office and sit down. He offers Nan a tea or coffee and soft drinks for me. Does he think I am a kid? I must be an important customer though. I can see all the normal chumps still out there dealing with people at the counter.

"Now, Mr Carson, how may we be of assistance today?" I look at my nan. Surely she is going to sort this.

"Well, Mr Lawley, Edmund and I have come to an agreement with regards to his money. I am going to trust my grandson with his money as he has turned seventeen today and he needs to learn how the ways of the world work."

He doesn't look happy. But my grandmother has already told him that this is what is happening today. He is just testing me, I know it.

"That is indeed a lot of trust, young man, that your grandmother is showing in you. I hope that you live up to that."

It's my money, Fatty. I can do what I want!

Just because his job pays like a hundred a week or something.

"I know, sir, I would never let her down."

She holds my hand, I hold hers back. Touching, Edmund, very touching.

"Now then, all we need to do is set you up with a card for the account, sign a few documents, and it will be open for you to use."

He starts tapping away on his computer.

Fuck, I am excited. I haven't been this excited since... Well, since Caroline.

"Now, what would you like for a daily limit from your account?"

Limit? Limit? It's my money, can't I just take as much as I want?

I look at my nan.

"Well, Edmund, my limit is five hundred pounds. I am sure you will want the same, won't you?" She is smiling at me. I do love her.

"Yes, Nan."

Am I happy or sad about that, I am not sure? Five hundred a day is more than the five-pound a day I get at the moment. But I am minted now. What if I want more?

"Sir, if in the next couple of months I want to buy a car or something, as I am taking my driving lessons, will I have to take five hundred pounds a day out for like a month to pay for it?"

He gives me a look. One that screams you're an idiot, my son. I know that look, my dad gave me that look, a lot.

"No, this is only the card limit. Should you require more than this, then you can come into the bank and as long as you have ID with you, you can take up to twenty-five thousand pounds out per day."

Fuck me, I can have twenty-five large a day!

"Oh, thank you, sir."

I notice I am still holding hands with my nan. I have to move our hands over to her lap as I just got a damn erection at that.

He carries on typing away.

"If you will both bear with me I will fetch Edmund's card that we have sorted for him and then collect the papers."

He leaves the room.

"Now, Edmund, you are going to be sensible with this money, aren't you?"

"Of course, Nan, there isn't really anything I want or need at the moment. It is just good to know it is there."

Going to party like it's 1999!

Not sure why they say that. Must have been a great party in 1999.

"So, what shall we do after this? It is your birthday after all?"

"How about I treat you to dinner? There is a little Italian at the end of the street. I can test my card out."

"Sounds perfect, Edmund." She squeezes my hand a little tighter.

The door opens and Fatty walks in. So does…

OMG, I can't breathe!

I can't believe I used the letters OMG in my head. Who am I?

"This is Melanie Epsom. She will be your personal banker, Edmund. Anything you need she will be here for you."

I need a blow job, I need a blow job… Fuck, she is gorgeous.

For a moment, just for a moment, she is Walker gorgeous.

"As Mr Lawley said, anything you need, Mr Carson, here is my card."

She hands me a card. My hands are almost trembling as I take it. She is Miss Walker league. At least the second prettiest woman in the world.

"Thank you."

Fuck, struggled to get those words out.

"Now if you can just sign here, here, here and your grandmother signs here and here, we are good to go." The papers are out in front of us both and we both sign.

"Well then, Mr Carson, you are good to go."

"Thank you, sir. When will my card be activated?"

"It is already, just stick it in the machine and away you go."

"Thank you."

We get up and leave. Melanie throws a smile in my direction. It's a Miss Walker smile. This girl has everything.

"See you soon."

Oh my god, yes you will!

We walk out of the bank to the machine on the corner.

"Well, Edmund, do you want to give it a go."

"OK." I rip open the piece of paper Fatty gave me and it has my pin number on it. Two seven zero three. I put my card in the machine and pin the number. Do I want cash or to see my balance?

What is my balance!

I look over my shoulder and my nan is watching the people in the street. I press balance.

FUCK ME!

I think my fucking heart has stopped. The numbers start to blur in front of my eyes. One comma nine eight four comma two three four dot nine eight. I focus again, is that right? I have nearly two million in the bank…

FUCK ME!

I quickly come out and push £500 quick cash… My hands are shaking as I take the money out. I grab my nan's hand and we start to walk down the street.

My parents must have loved me. But why didn't they want to buy me a bike? They were minted!

I am stunned, literally stunned by all this. We walk down the road in silence. I don't know what to say to my nan. We pass the flower shop I was in a couple of days ago. Before doing Mrs Green. My mind flashes back to her bent over the table. I would do that again. But I need the smell. The smell and my name being screamed out. How fucking great would that be? Then my mind wanders to the shop. The hot shop girl. I pull my nan into the shop. Sophia is in here.

"Twice in a week, Edmund, so nice to see you again."

She remembered my name. She wants fucking, without a doubt.

My nan is looking at me and smiling. I smile back at the both of them.

"Hi, Sophia, I have brought my nan in and I want to buy her some flowers."

"Oh, Edmund, you don't have to."

"Shh, Nan, I want to." She is smiling at me. They are both smiling at me. I must seem like the cutest guy ever. Nothing like playing the old nan card, a loving grandson. Honestly, I was made for this stuff.

"That's lovely, and what are your nan's favourite flowers, Edmund?"

"Orchids, Sophia, white and pink ones." How impressed is she that I know that. The fact my nan keeps them all over the house is a pretty big clue. Sophia starts to make up a bunch of flowers.

"Is the Italian down the street any good?"

"Mario's? Yes, I think it is, I hear they make a great Spag bol." Sophia is smiling at me.

"Thanks, I love Spag bol. I am just taking my nan to dinner."

"He is such a good boy, it is his birthday and he is taking me to an early dinner." I smile at the both of them. I must be coming off as a saint.

"That's a lovely gesture." She continues to wrap up the flowers.

"Do you need a card, Edmund?"

"No thank you, dear. I know that he loves me." My nan kisses me on the cheek. Played her part down to perfection. Best wingman a man could hope for. I hand the flowers over to my nan and she smiles at me. Sophia hands me a card as I am leaving the shop. We walk down to the Italian and go in.

"She seems like a nice girl, Edmund?" I think I am blushing in front of my nan. She must know that I liked her.

"What was in the card she gave you?"

My god, that woman doesn't miss a thing, does she? I swear she has hawk eyes.

"I don't know, I haven't opened it."

"Well, go on then." She is smiling at me.

I open it. It simply says *Call me later and we can really celebrate your birthday.* I am smiling at the paper. What a day, my birthday and I become a millionaire and now I have a hot girl for a date tonight. I am the luckiest guy alive. How can this day get any better?

I know how this day can get better.

"She wants a date with me."

My nan laughs. She has a funny laugh, still all sweet and innocent as if she was a little girl herself. We sit and have dinner together. It's a good time. I have the Spag bol so I can tell Sophia about it later. Nan does like to talk about my parents though, as if I am ever going to forget them. They gave me like two million quid. After we eat, I push my motorbike home whilst walking with my nan. She walks everywhere that woman, so fit for, what, a sixty-year-old or something like that. We arrive back home.

"Now, go and take a shower, and call that young girl. I will iron you a nice shirt and you can go out on a real date, not one with your old nan."

I kiss her on the cheek and go upstairs. I ring Sophia and we decide to go to the movies. Going to call a cab and pick her up at eight. I get into the shower. Melanie's face keeps appearing in my head, and now Sophia's, and now both of them and now both of them and me. And fuck me if Miss Walker doesn't join in as well. Before I know it I have knocked one out in the shower leaning against the shower wall.

What a day!

I am dressed other than my shirt and I head downstairs. My nan has ironed a new shirt for me that she bought for my birthday, Ralph Lauren.

"Thanks, Nan, but you should not waste your money on me."

"Nonsense, who else do I have to waste my money on? Now let me look at you."

I twirl for my nan. I know how hot I am, although this shirt does make me hotter, if that is possible. Sophia is in trouble.

"Handsome boy." She kisses me again. There is something about being kissed on your cheek by your nan. You don't really want the kiss, but also she wouldn't be your nan if she didn't do it.

"Now, did you call that nice girl from the flower shop?"

"Yes, Nan, we are going to the movies."

"Not on that bike, I hope, girls don't like that sort of thing on a first date?"

"No, not on my bike, Nan, going to pick her up in a cab."

"Now, there is a good boy."

We sit and chat in the kitchen. Nans are great listeners, and they always have like a million stories to tell you. Never really got why parents aren't? They do turn into nans and paps. My cab arrives and I leave. The drive to Sophia's is about fifteen minutes, and she is waiting outside when I get there. Nice big house though so her parents must have some cash. Good to know. Now I am upper class, can't be seen with the lowlifes. She gets into the cab, and we head to the cinema.

It's almost silent the whole journey till we get to the cinema queue.

"What did you want to see, Sophia?"

Please don't say chick flick. I do like them but it doesn't make me look very cool on a first date. I have to give my softer side away slowly. That's the trick.

"I don't know, what type of movie do you like? Funny? Horror? Comedy?"

"Shall we go for a comedy?"

"Let's have a look what there is: *Abraham Lincoln, Vampire Hunter, Twilight Saga, Dark Shadows, The Master, Taken 2* and *Ted.*"

We both look at each other and at the same time say:

"Ted." Must be kismet.

All I can think about now is vampire movies. What is it lately with this? Vampire movies or zombie movies. That is all that is on at the flicks. The world's fascinated about blood and lust and killing, it's sick.

We order popcorn, salt and sweet, and drinks and take them to our seats. I booked the premium double seats. The closer the better. We go in and find our seat. There is nobody near us. Good, I hate it when people are next to you in the cinema. Nothing worse than someone munching nachos in your ear hole.

The movie starts. It's funny as fuck. Talking teddy bear that has all the traits of an alcoholic womanising stud. We both laugh at the movie. I move my hand over to hers, she doesn't pull away. Twenty minutes into the movie we are holding hands. For the rest of the movie we are wrapping each other's fingers together as we play. We are the last to leave the cinema, and I push her up against the wall before we walk out of the doors and kiss her. It is a hot and passionate kiss, her hands are wandering all over me. She can feel that I am hard and she just goes with it. Two minutes later the door opens and some spotty kid walks in with a torch.

We stop and laugh and walk out holding hands. That was hot.

"Shall we stop for a drink?"

"Yes, why not."

Fuck why did I say that?

Wasn't thinking straight, she had me all tied up in emotion. What if they ID me? I am only seventeen, which clearly she doesn't know. Or does she? She said she knew who I was, if she did, she would know my age.

"There is a pub on the corner. Let's go there."

We walk out of the cinema and five minutes later I am at the bar ordering drinks. She wants a large glass of Pinot Grigio and has disappeared to the toilet.

What the fuck am I doing here?

I have never walked into a pub before. What do I ask for? The barman comes over. He looks grumpy. He must know how old I am.

"Yes, mate?"

"Two large glasses of Pinot Grigio"

"Want the bottle, mate?"

What!

"Pardon?"

"Want the bottle for a tenner?"

What? He is going to make me carry the bottle for an extra tenner? What the fuck do I want with an empty bottle?

"Yes, please."

The barman comes back and gives me a bottle of wine and two glasses. I hand over a twenty. He returns and gives me a tenner back. Get what he meant now. He was probably grumpy as he was just a barman. Not a great job, I imagine. Sophia is back and we sit in a booth.

"So, Edmund, how was the dinner with your nan? And how is your birthday so far?"

I smile at her. She is hot. She is smart and hot. Not Miss Walker or Melanie, but as a date on your birthday goes, she is hot.

"It was perfect, Spag bol was great and my birthday has been great."

You could make it so much better if you want to though!

"How is your first legal drink? Or, sorry, did you have one with your grandmother earlier?"

She thinks that I am eighteen. I will take that. She must be roughly the same age.

"No, this is my first." She is still smiling at me and grabs my hand. We sit and finish the wine. She tells me about her job, her family, Mum, Dad, little brother, all the normal chitchat women like to talk about. All I can think about was that kiss in the cinema, and what I really want to be doing right now. After the pub we walk back to hers. It's cold so I give her my coat and we talk the whole way home. We reach the doorstep. She turns to look at me.

"I had a lovely evening, Edmund. We should do this again sometime?"

There is a pause. Why is there a pause?

"Well, goodnight."

No, not goodnight. Surely you're going to ask me in?

"Goodnight, Sophia." I lean in and kiss her. It's a long lasting kiss and then I pull to turn away. If that doesn't get her all hot and bothered nothing will.

"Wait, I haven't given you your present."

Knew it, she is gagging for it. I turn and she is smiling at me.

"Be quiet though as my parents and brother are asleep upstairs."

Now you are fucking talking!

She grabs me by the hand and leads me into the house. We are silent. She takes me into the first door on the right. It's her bedroom.

Fucking great, a bedroom downstairs.

As soon as we are through, she locks the door behind us.

"Don't want Mum or Dad checking up on us, do we?"

No we fucking don't!

She pushes me up against the door and starts to kiss me. Hard. With one hand she has my head and the other is frantically trying to undo the belt of my jeans. It's undone and my trousers and boxers are down. And now so is she. She is sucking like she has been starved of it for months. Oh, she is good at that. It's not the first time she has done that. Definitely not her first time.

I survey the room as she is down there. On the side, next to the door, there is a big shell. Looks like something you get from a beach, but her name is carved into it and the year two thousand and ten. I pick up the shell and smash it across her head.

FUCK! My dick is in her mouth... my dick is in her mouth!

82

Her jaw comes down on it. I want to scream, but I know it will wake the house. I smash her head again and she is down and on the floor. I am on my knees in pain, but surprisingly I am still hard as a rock. As soon as she is down I check it with both hands. Thank fuck for that, all ten inches are still there.

Chapter 6

What the fuck do I do now!

My dick is sore, but the blood has my head in a fizz. I am all over the place, I don't know whether to shag her or scream at her. And she is just lying there. But the blood, oh the blood, it is actually like a fountain out of her head. The shell must have been hard and sharp.

Fuck it I have too.

I lean down. The smell of blood is stronger the closer you get to it. It's hot, sweet, and rich. I push my face into it as it continues to spurt. I have her undressed and on the floor in seconds.

Fuck, this is going to hurt.

I enter her. She was wet for me. At least that is a benefit. I start going at her. She is still spurting blood, but not as much as before. She is good though. Oh, she is good, and considerate, not like Caroline. She isn't waking up as I do this. The blood is strong, there is so much of it. She must have like a dozen pints of the stuff just in her head. I feel the back of her head and there is a fuck off hole in it. Never noticed that in the cinema.

Oh, this is good, so much better than Mrs Green. She was all like needy and clingy, wanting to kiss me and stuff. Who wants to kiss an old bird like that?

I did like the name-calling though. I whisper in Sophia's ear.

"Shout out my name, go on, it turns me on."

I wait and wait but nothing, maybe she didn't hear me.

"Shout out my name, go on. If you don't want your parents to wake up, just whisper it in my ear."

Still nothing. She must be lost in the moment.

Or not fucking enjoying it?

Don't be stupid, how can she not be enjoying this. I am a god. A sex god. I keep going at her, harder and harder. The pain from my dick is just making it even better. I spurt like a champion and fall on top of her. That was good, but god, it was silent. Never done it with other people in the house before. Kind of plays things down a bit. I think that's why she didn't call my name when I asked her to.

"Is that what it was? You didn't want to wake anyone in the house?"

Still nothing.

"You should have said, I would have gone and taken care of them first so that we could both really let go. It's better when you both get into it."

Makes me think about Amy Bunting. She was really into it. Made her decade, a night with me. She really enjoyed herself that night.

I should do that now, take care of them, and then I can spend the night with Sofia!

"Should I do that? Give us another go? We can both really get into it then?"

I look at her. I know her answer, she doesn't have to say anything. After the seeing-to I have just given her, it is not surprising that she is exhausted. I get up and unlock the door. The house is still silent. In front of me I can see a kitchen and to the side what I presume is an open living room/study and another bathroom.

Maybe a knife is the way to go. I head to the kitchen. I am thirsty, my god, all this lovemaking takes the fluid out of you. I go to the fridge and fix myself a drink. Oh, a sandwich. I remember the sandwich I ate after Caroline. It was the best tasting sandwich ever. I fix myself one. Ham and cheese out of the fridge. It's the blood, I am sure of it. The way it drips on to the bread just makes everything taste so good. It was as good as I can remember. They should bottle this stuff and sell it.

OK, I am getting hard again now. Let's take care of everyone in the house so me and Sophia can go and have some more fun.

I grab a chopping knife out of the rack and head upstairs. The first room I open is clearly a spare room.

Why wouldn't Sophia like it up here more? I need to ask her, but it's a good job she didn't, that may have woken her parents.

The next room on the right has a sign on the door. It says 'Carl's Room Keep Out'.

Carl, I fucking hate that kid.

I go into the room. I nearly trip over the damn Scalextrix lying on the floor. Why doesn't he keep his room tidy? I stand above Carl. He is sleeping.

I swear the kid is turning into Carl Carnegie as he turns over, still asleep.

It is him, it is fucking him...

One swift motion, the knife goes across his throat. I lean down and smell the blood and whisper in his ear.

"Eat that, Oblong Fitz Oblong."

I walk out of the room. That's for all the times he has called me Bobbleknob! There is one door left. It has to be Sophia's parents' room. I push the door and they are both fast asleep. I move to the right-hand side of the bed and I can see her mother.

Fuck she is hot!

Hotter than even Sophia. Her dad must bang her silly. I am hard just thinking about it. Makes me want to do her. In fact, I am going to do her. Sophia will never know, she is probably asleep downstairs by now. Look how it took it out of Caroline, she barely was awake the next day, I am so good. She will be out for a while yet.

With one quick motion I slit her throat. The blood spurts back at me.

Fuck, she is convulsing.

She is jumping around. He is awake. He jumps out of bed, and I run around towards the door.

"What the fuck is going on?"

He looks pissed at me.

Fuck, he is coming at me... Fuck that hurt...

He smacked me round the head. We are on the ground. I have no idea what has happened to the knife, but he is punching me hard.

What the fuck is his problem?

I am still a kid, you know! I punch back, and it hits him square on the jaw. His head moves backwards.

Wow, never really punched anyone before. That felt good. We start proper fighting now as we are rolling around on the floor. He is even pulling my hair. Think he is screaming at me. Can't understand him. He may be Scottish or something. Certainly doesn't sound English.

"You bastard, what have you done?"

Oh yeah, got that. He is English. Just must have misheard him.

Why is he calling me names? What have I done? You're the one punching a seventeen-year-old kid, you freak! You can get arrested for that, you know!

Wait, is he crying as he is hitting me? What kind of bloke does that? I raise my knee and must have caught him square in the bollocks as he winces in pain.

"Fuck me, your wife and son didn't put up this much of a fight." He stops moving. Wait, did I say that in my head or out loud? I am guessing by his actions, out loud. Crap, sorry, didn't mean to say that. Not tasteful.

I can see the knife, I can reach the knife. He still isn't moving. In one motion I pick it up and bring it down on his head. Well, in his head. It's pierced straight through his eye.

Fuck, he is convulsing now!

What's the problem with these people? They're like dying fish.

They can't just keep still. The smell of blood is really strong in this room. I can feel myself getting excited even more by it all. I can hardly even feel the bite marks any more. The blood's probably pumped it so big, it has filled them in. I stand up. Sophia's mum has stopped moving and her dad is barely twitching now.

"Wow, that was good, you two, wow. I really, really enjoyed that, but to be fair, Mr, you nearly had me. You nearly did, I can't believe it. I really need to start working out, if I am going to do something like this again."

I am so going to do this again. I was born for this!

I look at Sophia's mum on the bed. The covers are half off her, and I can see one side of her body.

Fuck she is fit.

I pull the covers back to have a proper look. Wow, is all I can say. I thought Mrs Green looked all right for an older chick but wow, wow, wow. I am naked, stark naked, within a minute and on top of her.

I go in like a hot knife in butter. They must have been having sex tonight she is still warm. Feels so good. Better than her daughter. Wait, I did think that in my head, didn't I? Not out loud. That wouldn't have gone down well. She isn't screaming at me, so I think I am safe. Fuck, almost forgot he was in the room till then.

"Why wouldn't you? I think I would have sex every night?"

"Don't blame you... Your wife is so hot."

I am going at her, she starts to whisper my name on her lips. I think she is trying to keep it down for his sake. Sophia's dad just won't shut up about it. Think he is just mad because he is still on the floor.

"Sorry, did you want to watch us as we make love?"

That should shut him up. Wait, what?

"You do?" Jesus, this is getting freaky, but I must admit I am more turned on than ever. I get off Sophia's mum and walk over and pick her dad up off the floor.

I place him in the chair in the corner, and go back to the bed. We are at it again. There is something about the older woman, shapelier, more comfortable. It's the love handles, not fat but hippy, kind of gives you something to hold on to. And the breasts they are amazing. Firm, big, and round. It's like they are full size compared to Sophia's and Caroline's. I bet Miss Walker's are amazing. That gets me going harder and faster, the thought of her. Calling my name is getting louder, but he is still talking. He is not mad at what we are doing.

"For fuck's sake, we are making love here."

I get up again and walk over to her dad. He is moaning that he can't see everything. I remove the knife from his eye.

Fuck, the eye has come out! The eye has come out.

"Sorry, sorry didn't mean to do that." I pick it up off the floor and put it back in.

"I said you can watch, so you can watch. See, how is that?"

That's better he can see now. I go back to Sophia's mum. She must be well pissed off with her husband, keeps interrupting us like that.

I am back and we are in full-on mode. The bed is rocking. Any louder and Sophia is going to find out, and I am guessing she is not going to be happy about it. But my god, she feels good to be inside.

"You must love this part." I can feel myself building up to come. She is begging me for it... I take out my dick and come all over her face. There is so much of it, even in the dark I can see the white and the red all mixed together.

I turn around. Sophia's dad is still in the chair. I swear if we knew each other better he would have been jacking off at that. Hell, I am going to be jacking off at that for the next week or so.

I lay back on the bed. The smell of blood is still filling my nose. The exhaustion of sex, twice in about an hour, is making my body tingle.

This is what I was born to do…

"You both must admit, I am good at it."

"I don't know about best. I would keep your voice down, your husband is still in the room. It's not very fair to him."

"Oh, you agree. She has never been done like that before. Thanks. I am only glad she got to experience it too."

"Well, I am a little younger. And your daughter, she was as good as your wife."

"Wait, too far? I am sorry."

Probably shouldn't have said that. Wouldn't have liked to hear that about my daughter when I have one. There is a little silence.

"I am sorry about that. You see, my head is all over the place at the moment. My mouth sometimes engages before my brain."

"I guess I am in a little bit of a crisis. You see, I love doing this, it's fun, exciting, exhilarating even, but I believe I was destined to do more. People adore me. I was born to be famous. I had a little taste of the limelight a year ago and I can't seem to get it out of my head. I can't work, you know, like a normal job for a living or anything like that. I was destined for the spotlight."

They are both silent now. I know they agree with me but how can I do this and be famous.

"Wait, really? You reckon I could do that? Be famous for this? I consider it more like a hobby at the moment. A bit of fun to relieve the pressure. I have been thinking about doing more of it, but I never get the time."

I could, I really could be famous for this, but I would need to do something special. Not just another person. I would need to become the best.

"Wait, let me get my phone and see who the competition is."

I run downstairs and into Sophia's room. My phone came out of my pocket when she pulled my trousers down.

"Sorry, I will be back in a moment, I am just talking to your mum and dad."

I run back up the stairs. Sophia didn't say anything, but I know she would have been pissed as I forgot to get dressed. I jump back on the bed and google: *Famous people that do this*.

"OK, let's look, there is a doctor in Manchester. Officially high teens, but as many as two hundred. But not proven… Not proven! That is the point. And then, they are down in the teens anyway. A cook, some bloke from Yorkshire, a couple. That's a bit odd, a couple, and then old Jack, we learned about him in school. Now, that was fame. Even made a song about him and his associates. Think I can be that good? Think they will ever make a song about me?

"Thanks, I think I can also, but I could do so much more. What's the one thing that these people haven't done? Eh?

Don't know? I will tell you. Advertise. Look at them, all of them. They skulk around in the shadows and never want to be seen. Why wouldn't you want to be seen and famous for what you do? I was saying just the other day that if you wanted to do this for a living, you could, and get away with it. Just watch all the programmes, the *CSI, Criminal Minds,* that sort of thing and do the opposite to all the morons on the show. I tell you, I could keep away from the police and in the public eye forever."

I could fucking do this!

These two are amazing. They are so full of encouragement. Sophia must love having parents like that. Nothing like my parents.

"I don't know how I can thank you people enough, this has made the best birthday ever. Actually, wait, come over here."

I get up and pull Sophia's dad on to the bed with us.

"Don't panic, it's not some weird threesome thing. I just want a photo of us all together, when we came up with this. You have really helped me set my sights to a goal."

I lie down and take some selfies with them.

"See, that's better, you're a great family, great kids and well just great. I wish I had had a family like yours. Bet you do all sorts together, don't you?"

"See, I knew it, bike rides in the country, game nights, and dinner together. I would have loved to see that."

I would love to have seen that! That's fucking it! Famous starts here.

"Why don't we do that, eh? A game downstairs? Scrabble or something like... No Scrabble is perfect, fucking perfect. I can leave clues and everything. I can't announce myself to the world, the world needs to come looking and then, BAM, here is Edmund Carson. Fucking great idea."

I get off the bed. This shit is really flowing now. It's all coming to me.

"I will meet you downstairs. I will just go and find the Scrabble."

I leave them lying on the bed, still tired I expect. It's been such an exciting day. Best day ever. I go downstairs. Sophia is still in her room. She is not going to be impressed about the mum and dad thing, I just know it. I head into the living room and, there, underneath the coffee table… Scrabble. Scrabble, the word game of champions.

"I could just spell out some clues and they would be able to realise it's me."

I open the box. I pull the tiles out and start to place them on the board. I spell out orphan. I use the O for alone. The A for gas and then the S from that for superstar.

Fuck, the N now has NU, that's not a word.

I take superstar off the board. Son. I can put son and no. Cool. And use the N for naughty… Naughty, alone, orphan, son. That will get them on my scent.

Where is everyone? I seem to be setting this up on my own.

"Come on, it's game time."

I look down at the tiles. I could use the U for Edmund. Surely that makes it too easy for them… They don't seem to be moving.

I get up and walk into Sophia's room. She is still on the floor. And pissed at me I can tell.

"Come on, I was just talking to your mum and dad, they have helped me come up with a great plan."

"Because, when you fell asleep, I spilt a drink down myself. I was just washing the clothes."

She doesn't believe that. I pick her off the floor and take her to the living room. I sit her on the floor next to the coffee table and leaning up against the chair.

"See, some nice quality family time. I would have thought you would have loved for me to meet your parents? So I have, and we will be best of friends."

She still isn't speaking, she is mad at me. She will get over it.

I go upstairs and bring down Carl. I don't really want him to play, but it is a family thing.

I then go back to Sophia's parents' room.

"I can tell by the looks on your face you have been up to no good, haven't you?"

"Ha ha, I knew it was going to get you going, sir, seeing me and your wife all up and at it. A dream come true, I bet."

"Twice? Really? No wonder you two are too knackered to come downstairs… here, let me help you, it's the least that I can do after what you have done for me this evening."

I help Sophia's dad downstairs. He must have been knackered he could hardly walk.

I go back upstairs to see Sophia's mum lying on the bed. She didn't follow us downstairs, I think I know why. I walk over to the bed and kiss her. I can still smell the blood and it has my heart pumping. But, no.

"No, not now, I think three to four times in a night is enough, don't you?" She is smiling at me now. I swear she is insatiable. Imagine what Sophia is going to be like at her age.

I help her downstairs. Not sure how she thought we could have sex, her legs are already like jelly. The three of them are already around the table playing Scrabble, but there are only four of those tile holder things.

"Think you should probably fix some drinks and snacks for us as we play? Yes? Good, sounds good, no butter on mine though."

I help Sophia's mum to the kitchen and put her on one of those stools to start making food.

I go back to the table and we start to play Scrabble. This is what a real family does. I take my phone out and take selfies with everyone, to remind myself of the best birthday ever.

"Shit, it's two a.m., where has the night gone?"

"Sorry, you are right, I shouldn't swear. My nan is going to kill me, I have totally lost track of time."

I get up, run upstairs and get dressed. I swill my face in the bathroom and head back downstairs.

"No, it will be fine. I will shower when I get home. Look you can hardly tell in the dark, can you? You guys are always looking out for me."

"I know, I know... I have said it and I am going to say it one more time. Best birthday ever."

I leave by the front door. The shirt my nan bought is a bit messy. Going to have to hide it or wash it or buy another one. I am loaded now.

I take a selfie at the door as another reminder, and then start the walk home.

I can't believe how great today has been, nothing could top it. I have money, I have direction, I have had some of the best sex ever and with a mother and daughter. That's what dreams are made of. This is what dreams are made of.

I keep walking towards home when a car pulls up next to me. Think someone is shouting at me, but I keep walking. Who is going to be shouting at me at two o'clock in the morning?

"Edmund."

They are definitely trying to get my attention.

"Edmund."

Flashbacks are in my head. I know that voice, I have heard that voice before.

I turn to see a dark-haired woman leaning across from the driver's side.

"Edmund, why are you out this late? Jump in, I will give you a lift."

I can't breathe. Is this really happening?

"Edmund, jump in."

Fuck me, it's Miss Walker! Fuck, fuck, fuck... Best birthday ever!

Chapter 7

"So, Edmund, what has you out at this time of night? Shouldn't you be tucked up back at home with your nan?"

"It is my birthday, Miss Walker."

It is my mothe- fucking best birthday ever, Miss Walker.

"Wow, Edmund, eighteen already? Where does the time fly? I guess being legal has had you out drinking, amongst other things?"

Not eighteen, seventeen, but what the fuck, she will think this shit is legal…

I just smile back at her. We carry on driving. I notice she hasn't asked me where I live yet… Why is that?

She hasn't asked me where I fucking live? Where are we going?

We turn a corner, this is my way home. She must know where I live.

"What has you out at two o'clock, Miss?"

She smiles over at me. Is that a naughty smile? Or a none of your business smile? I can't tell.

"It was my leaving do tonight, Edmund. I am moving schools to London in a couple of weeks, and I was out with some of the other teachers. I am going to Preton High School for girls, just outside of Wimbledon. It's an amazing school for gifted older girls."

She is leaving? She is leaving. I am lost for words. I just sit looking at her as she drives. Miss Walker is leaving me. That is not the plan. Not the plan at all. This has just turned out to be the worst day of my life.

"I must admit, I will miss you all terribly, but it is the right time to move on. Driving, on the other hand, probably wasn't the right thing to do, a couple of glasses of wine too many, but it's not too far to my house."

She is drunk and driving to her house, and she is leaving the school. No, worse, she is leaving me. We were meant to be together.

"You're only the next street, aren't you? OK if I drop you off at mine and you walk round the corner? It will save the one-way system, and the less I drive the better."

Miss Walker lives around the corner from my nan's house! I didn't know that. Why didn't I know that?

Fuck me, I would have been at her window months ago.

"Thank you, Miss Walker."

We keep driving in silence. My hands are shaking. This is Miss Walker, she is drunk and walking distance from my house. Surely, if I am ever going to have a shot, it is tonight. She is leaving in a couple of weeks. Leaving, and I am never going to see her again. I can't just let her go without her knowing. She would regret that for the rest of her life. This could be something. She knows it and so do I.

"Miss, won't your boyfriend think it is strange you getting out of a car with someone at two thirty in the morning?"

Smooth as fuck, I am smooth as fuck. She is quiet as she keeps driving.

"I don't have a boyfriend, Edmund, so it is fine."

She knows why I asked that question, I am sure of it. That's why there was a pause. She knew I was fishing, and she took the bait. Owned up to being single. Knew she had to stay single until I was eighteen.

"How about you, Edmund? Which young girl has had the pleasure of your company till two a.m.?"

Fuck, how do I respond to this? If I say someone it might put her off... If I don't, where the fuck have I been all night?

"No girl, Miss Walker."

That should do it, damn! She is looking at me ... does she think I meant it was a boy... does she think I am gay!

"What I meant was, I got a little drunk and fell asleep on a friend's sofa."

Silence in the car again. We pull up at her house. Damn, I pass this house every day on the way to school and never knew she was inside of it. How did I miss that?

"Seems we have both had a drink too many then?"

Was that a question or a statement? Is that a line? That's what you say when you have no control about what is going to happen.

Fuck, my head is frazzled at the thought of it.

"As you said, Miss Walker, it's legal now."

Fuck, where did that come from? That's a line and a half.

Wait, no, it's not. She didn't say that. Sophia did, in the bar. All she said was happy eighteenth. Fuck, I must look like a prick. She gets out of the car. Did she hear me? Is she just ignoring me? I have blown this? What do I do now? I get out of the car. She starts walking up the driveway. I can't just let the love of my life walk out on me. Not me. I am fucking Edmund Carson. She isn't even acknowledging I am here. I turn to start walking home. This is going nowhere. Worst day ever! I hear the door close. I turn and look at it. It seems like I am looking at it forever. I have lost her? I am not going to lose her. Not her.

"I suppose, Edmund, if it's legal I should fix you a nightcap."

Thank you, fucking god!

"Thank you, Miss Walker, that would be lovely."

I walk back up to the house and we go in. I switch on the hall light and the light to the room on the left. I am in Miss Walker's house.

"Edmund, fix us a drink? G&T? Whilst I sort myself out."

"Sounds good to me."

What the fuck do I know…?

Never had a G&T in my life. But I am in Miss Walker's house, drinking at two thirty in the morning… On the best birthday ever! The best day ever.

She walks into the living room. I have made two drinks from the drinks trolley in the front room. Who still has a drinks trolley? I do like it though. She is wearing a short black dress. I didn't notice in the car as she still had her coat on.

She is so hot.

I have dreamed this moment for years. I place the drinks on the table to the side of the sofa. There is a big white rug on the floor in front of the sofa and it's in front of one of those fake fires.

She looks at me, and then at the fire. I walk over and switch on the fire. It's a man's job, and I am her man. I have had this dream... I have actually had this dream. The fire makes a glow in the room.

"Don't want us to get cold."

She sits next to me on the sofa. I turn off the lamp and pass her a drink. I take a sip. God it's awful, but I pretend to like it.

"Too much gin?"

"No, just how I like it."

I would drink just about anything to be here. She takes a drink. A big drink.

"So, Edmund, I have a confession to make." She is smiling straight at me.

Oh my god, she is smiling straight at me.

This can't be happening. Her confession can't be what I want it to be... Not today. She is a dude, or a chick with a dick... or a lesbian. Has to be something like that. Not today. God doesn't love me that much.

"That drama class we had, about a year ago. I haven't been able to get it out of my head. The way you went off script like that. Said those things to me. The look in your eyes they, well, I am embarrassed to say. Turned me on so much."

Fucking hell! It's real! She wants me. God, if you let me fuck her I swear I will become a vicar or go to church every day. Anything, anything you want.

I take her drink off her, and place them to the side. I move my hands to the side of her face like I did at school.

"I meant every word."

Smooth as a fucking blender... This is my dream.

We are kissing. I am kissing Miss Walker. I could come here and now, I know it. Wait, she is pulling back a bit? Her head moves to the side and she whispers in my ear.

"Not too hard, Edmund, soft and slow. Let's make this moment last."

I am now harder than I have ever been. Just the fact that she spoke in my ear would have been enough. I am worried that there is no blood left in my body, it's all throbbing in my dick. I may pass out. Don't let me pass out.

We stand up and slowly our clothes disappear to the ground. She is conducting every move I make, with her hands over mine. I am standing in front of her naked by firelight. She is naked in front of me. It's everything I ever dreamed of. She is perfect, there isn't a blemish or a scar. Her skin is perfect. She is perfect. There are ten inches between us, but there won't be for long.

"Edmund, you have some dried blood on your body..."

Fuck, I look down, there is quite a bit of it.

"Thought I had it all, I had a nosebleed, Miss."

She is looking back at me. She doesn't believe me, I can tell in her eyes. She is still looking directly at me.

Fuck, this is about to go so wrong! God, please, I swear to you. I will join a monks' house.

How long has she been looking at me? Like an hour. She whispers back in my ear.

"You can call me Emily."

She is going down. Miss Walker is going to her knees in front of me. Did she just lick the blood on the way down? She licked the dry blood on the way down and—

"OOOOHHHHHHHHHH!"

I CAN'T BREATHE! I can't breathe... I am blinking like a lunatic.

With every intake she has of me, I can't breathe. I swear, I am going to faint. I can't just stay here else I will be coming in seconds. I pull back from her and drop to my knees. In one smooth motion I have her on her back, and I am now the one on top of her.

I return the favour and go down on her too. It tastes sweet. There is still the taste of blood in my mouth from before, but she tastes sweeter. I lick inside and outside. When I come up for a breath I nibble at the inside of her thighs and then return to the sweet stuff. All the time I am doing this I can hear softly in her voice my name being called. That is such a turn-on, my name out of Miss Walker's mouth. A mouth I have been in, a mouth that my dick has been sucked by. It's everything I have ever wanted. I have gone off the licking now. I need the real thing. I need her.

I move up and start to kiss her body on the way, past her belly button. On to her breasts. Oh, the times I have dreamed about these. They are perfect. Small enough for the mouth, big enough to roll around my tongue. I spend some time there as it's always been one of the places I wanted to see. I then move my way up to her mouth and kiss her. As I do, I enter her. There is a huge sigh from both of us as I do. The build-up was amazing, and now down to the real work. I just want to thrust and thrust. I start to hammer her like a jackhammer; both her hands grab my bum and slow it down.

"Slow, hard, and deep." Those words are whispered in my ear. I do as I am told. I am playing them over and over in my head. Slow, hard, deep. She is still calling my name over and over again. This is what sex was meant to be like. This is how you do it properly.

Fuck, this isn't going to last long! I can feel myself coming.

I pull out to save some time and return to her breasts. She isn't having any of that. She pulls me back in. I need to take my mind off coming. Need to think about something else. I start thinking about shopping, at the fish market, with my nan. Nope not working, Father Andrew in the church… Me at the church, I promised God. Father Andrew and me at the church with the nuns praying for the orphans…

Nope, fuck, the nuns are now naked apart from the stockings and suspenders they have on under their robes. Fuck, why are nuns so hot.

I am doing everything, but look at her. She knows it. Slow, hard, deep. Slow, hard, deep. She reaches down and grabs the bottom of my ball sack.

Fuck, that hurt!

Wait, I don't want to come now? Slow, hard, deep. I keep going at her; she is still calling my name nearly every time I enter her. The sweat is pouring from both of us. I look down at her, her eyes are closed and she is lost in the moment. I watch as my name falls off her lips over and over again. This is where I was meant to be my whole life. Slow, hard, deep is all I can think of. Slow, hard, deep. Her eyes open and they are looking directly at me.

"Are you ready?"

Ready? I could have come an hour ago!

I nod at her.

"Then harder, and faster."

She doesn't need to tell me twice. I am at her like a bull in a china shop. She still has hold of my balls. I didn't know that would work. Her screaming is getting louder. My name is getting louder. She releases her grip of my balls and her arms are out holding my arms as hard as she can. I can feel the come mounting again, it's building faster and harder just as she had asked for. This is getting harder. Harder and faster, we are fucking hard, we are fucking like rabbits. If we were on a table or a bed we would have fallen off by now. I can feel her nails digging into my arms. She is screaming. I am screaming. The intensity is amazing, it's wild and hot and everything that I have ever imagined. I swear we are almost off the ground at times, it's so hard, so strong. She is ready, I can feel it, I am ready… one last hard…

"Yes!"

I pump her as hard as I can a few more times to ensure what she has it multiple. But she is spent, her arms are by her side now and eyes open looking directly at me. I smile at her and she is smiling back. She is exhausted.

I collapse on the side of the fire and we are both laid out looking at the ceiling. Takes ten minutes for either of us to even talk.

I turn on to my side and look directly at her. She is still smiling at me.

"I am not your first then, Edmund, am I? That was amazing."

"No, Miss, not my first. And thank you."

"Emily."

"Sorry, Emily."

"Have there been many, Edmund? Many before me?"

What kind of question is that? Is it a trick question? Does she want to feel special? Fuck, what's the answer?

"Just one, Miss, sorry Emily, about a year ago before my parents' accident. Since then, I have struggled to be able to connect."

I knew the orphan card would get me out of the conversation. We kiss, full-on kiss as if we were in a long-term relationship. This feels so natural. This is the woman I am meant to be with. I have always known that.

"Stay here and sleep with me a while."

I cuddle up behind her. I don't reply. I was never going to say no to her. I can feel the fire on my back and Miss Walker in my arms. This is as close to heaven as I am ever going to get.

Shit, should have never promised the church thing!

I can't be a vicar, it's not in me. I am sure he will understand that tomorrow. It was just in the heat of the passion tonight. I can feel her heart beat as she falls asleep. Or is that mine? Still pumping so hard.

My nan's is going to kill me. What am I going to tell her? I was with a teacher all night? The clock on the wall is turning four fifteen.

Fuck, four fifteen? How long were we at it?

She must think I am a god. I bet this has been her fantasy for a whole year. Every night looking at the fire and the rug, and wishing I was here. I lay there cuddled up behind her. I do believe this is the end of a perfect day. I close my eyes and fall to sleep also.

Six twenty, fuck!

My nan's alarm goes off at two minutes past seven and I need to be home for that. I slowly pull my arms from Miss Walker. She doesn't move. I stand up, gather my clothes and get dressed. She doesn't move, she is sleeping so soundly on the rug.

Shit, the rug!

It's covered in blood. Must have been the sweat and the heat of the fire taking the dried blood from my body. And the damn rug had to be white.

Shit, looks like there has been a murder here.

I can't clean it, it will wake her up. I just need to get out of here. She is never going to believe that is one hell of a nosebleed.

CSI, Edmund, fucking CSI, I need to learn better...

She is still not moving on the floor. I must have done a great job in satisfying her last night, she looks dead to the world.

I sneak out of the house. Not a soul is in the street and I run like the wind to my house. I use my key and go in through the back door. That way I don't need to pass my nan's room. Upstairs, in my room, yes. I strip and put my clothes in my school bag. Nan won't look in there. Then I jump in the shower. I look down at myself before turning on the shower. There is a lot of blood on me. How didn't Miss Walker go mad about it? Didn't it freak her out? I get out the shower and look at my nose in the mirror. It's a regular size. She must be a little silly in the head if she thinks that much blood came out of there. I get back in the shower, and turn on the water. I just stand there as the water hits me. The events of yesterday replaying in my head. The money, the date, the conversations with Sophia's parents. Good people. Miss Walker.

Miss Fucking Walker, Edmund!

It feels like the stuff fairy tales are made of.

"Edmund, are you up?"

Must be three minutes past seven, she always shouts me first thing.

"Yes, Nan, in the shower, will be down in ten minutes."

I finish showering, get some clothes from my wardrobe, and head downstairs. Nan is at the cooker making breakfast. That's the perfect sight to start my day.

"I was thinking full English this morning, Edmund, what do you say?"

"I say, I love you, Nan, just what I wanted." I walk over, kiss her on the cheek and sit at the table. I am starving. I am knackered. All that exercise and no food. Must remember to eat more. I always forget.

"So, whilst I am doing this you can tell me all about your date with the young girl from the flower shop. Sophia, wasn't it?"

Holy crap! I forgot my nan knew where I was last night! CS fucking I, Edmund.

How the hell am I going to be famous if I tell anyone and everyone where I am going, and then leave DNA everywhere? Including a teacher's house. What kind of nutter am I? I need to be better if this is going to be my job.

"Nothing to tell, Nan, she didn't show."

She stops cooking and turns around.

"She didn't show, Edmund?"

"No, I tried ringing her and even went and knocked on the house, but nobody answered. Think she may have been teasing me… I ended up going to the pictures alone. Watched *Ted*, was a good movie. Very funny."

She stops cooking and walks over to me. Gives me a big hug and a kiss.

"Then that's her loss, my darling. You are an amazing young man, Edmund."

She goes back to the cooking. Smells great.

"A nice breakfast will sort you out, Edmund. Then I am off to my Saturday job at Oxfam, and what are you doing with your weekend?"

"Don't know, nan. I will cut the grass back and front this morning and do the hedges, maybe have a lazy afternoon with the TV."

Her head turns and she smiles at me.

"You are a good boy, Edmund, always helping your nan. Watching those detective programmes, no doubt?"

"No doubt, Nan." I smile back.

Too right, no doubt. I need to brush up on my skills if I am going to be world-famous. Because at this rate, any idiot would catch up with me.

Chapter 8

Two minutes past seven, I can hear Nan's alarm go off. Three minutes past seven comes the call, 7.03 comes the answer. The weekend is over. I have watched at least twenty episodes of *CSI/ Criminal Minds* and *Elementary*. Lucy Liu is so hot. She would definitely get it. Small, dark-haired... definitely get it.

I take the notebook from the side of the bed. Kept a log of the ways to avoid the capture. It all seems pretty straightforward to me. I am not sure why they seem to get caught in forty-three minutes every week.

I get dressed and head downstairs. My nan is at the bottom of the stairs. She looks sad. She gives me a big hug and asks me to sit down... Don't like this, my nan is never sad. Something has happened to her. Or she knows something.

"Oh, Edmund, it's horrible, I just switched on the news and that girl, Sophia Merson, and her family, they have been, oh, it's too horrible to say."

She is all welled up? Don't know what's up with her, they were playing Scrabble when I left them.

"All of them, Edmund. Sophia, her mother, her father, and her five-year-old brother. Must have happened before your date, that is why she didn't turn up. They were all killed, Edmund. Killed."

I sit there in shock. She must be able to read it on my face. Carl Carnegie is not five? He is the same age as me. They must have got it wrong.

"Oh, Edmund, I am so sorry. Poor family. I know you liked her. I am so glad you are safe though. Imagine if anything had happened to you."

"It's OK, Nan. There are some horrible people out there. What do I keep telling you? You need to keep safe, as there are horrible people in this world. Do they have any clues who would do such a thing?"

You know, other than the ones that I left them. I am regretting that now though. Clues are one thing, but if I am going to be number one, I have to get my numbers up.

"All they said was that someone was helping them with their enquiries."

What the fuck!

Someone was helping them with their enquiries. Who would be doing that? I am right here? And, I have already helped them. I gave them the clues. Too many clues. They haven't come for me?

"It is so sad, Edmund. I just wanted you to hear it from me. Come on, I will make you some breakfast."

She kisses me on the head and we both walk over to the kitchen.

Someone is helping them with their enquiries, what does that mean? I know what it normally means on TV, it means that we have the person, but we don't have the evidence. Do they have the person? Do they have a person?

I eat breakfast in silence. I can see my nan looking at me all the way through it. I wasn't going to go to school today, but I think I need to act normal.

I am scared now that I haven't done this right. I haven't planned enough. I have let this get out of control. Too much evidence, too much DNA. Too sloppy, Edmund, far too sloppy. If I were on TV I'd be caught today.

I get on my bike and head to school. My head is in a spin. I need to start to make a plan about all of this. I screwed it up. I screwed up, now that is bad.

After registration I head to Miss Walker's class. My head is in such a spin I almost forget about Friday night until I see her name on the door. I walk in.

Carl Carnegie!

Maybe my nan got it wrong. He is sitting at the back of the class. My head is all over the place. He can't be here, can he? It was him, wasn't it? But he has another sister, I am sure of it.

This is going to be awkward, I can tell. What do you do with a teacher that you have banged? Do you still call her Miss? Do you kiss her when she comes in? Do you even acknowledge her? I wouldn't be upset if she told the class how good I am. It's a good thing and a good thing for them to know their teacher is getting a good seeing-to.

I walk in, but instead of sitting at the front of the class, as I would normally do, I get a seat at the back by the door. Head down as if I am reading. I knew I should have popped around and seen her over the weekend. Get all the awkwardness out of the way. I thought she would have contacted me.

"Morning, class."

I look up and it's Mrs Whitaker taking the class.

"I will be taking your class today, Miss Walker hasn't showed today."

She hasn't showed? Shit, is Miss Walker the person helping with the enquiries? Have they matched all the blood on her carpet with the blood in the house? They always have like traffic cameras and stuff in the *CSI*. They will have seen her car driving down the road. Maybe picking a person up? Tracking back to the house. Are they on their way to see me?

Fuck, I am never going to be famous! I am going to be like one of those chumps who is caught in the act. Nobody will ever remember me. Fuck, there go the songs about me!

I can't stay here. I need to get out and make a plan. I put my hand up.

"Yes, Edmund."

"Can I go to the bathroom, Miss?"

Miss Whitaker just nods at me and I grab my bag and I am out of there. Jump on the bike and get home. Nan is at her Monday job. I swear that woman has a better social life than I do. I get on to my computer in my bedroom and look up today's news.

They were discovered on Saturday. The one thing the Internet does well is give you all the stories related to a single event. Between this and social media you can be worldwide in days. I read all the stories. All say that a man in his early thirties is helping with enquiries.

What the fuck!

Are the police getting it wrong or is someone purposely trying to steal my limelight? I sit back in my chair. I can't decide if this is a good thing or bad thing? I spelt it out in the tiles. Surely they picked up on all of that? I go downstairs and grab a Coke from the fridge; I need the sugar rush.

All in all I decide it may be a good thing. Besides I have the photos. When I am famous I can prove I spent the night with the Mersons. Mersons. It can't have been Carl. His name is Carnegie.

I have pictures of us playing Scrabble! I will come clean when I am ready.

They will probably tell the police it was me anyway. Unless... Unless they are protecting me? That's what it is. They are throwing them off the scent. I knew I liked that family. Miss Walker is nowhere in the reports. She isn't helping them, I am sure of it. She just believed the story about the nosebleed, I am sure of it. That was close. I need a plan and I need one fast. I know what not to do. I get my notebook and open it.

Page one has the obvious on it.

How to get caught by Edmund Carson

1. Bank (Always deal in cash)

2. DNA. If they have it they can trace you (Don't have mine)

3. Car. Change vehicles as much as possible. (Get a car)

4. Cameras. Streets, shops, traffic, office blocks, government buildings. (Change clothes, hide face, dye hair)

5. Technology. Burner phones, IP addresses, GPS.

If I cover off the top five that's a start. Need to work out how much money I need and what I will leave my nan. I run upstairs again and get my calculator.

I start typing in numbers. Hotels £100 x 7 x 52 = £36,400. *Fuck me, thirty-six large just for hotels a year!*

How many years do I want to be doing this for? At school they said Jack the Ripper only did like three to four, 1888 to 1891.

I should do five. Then I will be like twenty-two or something. That's pretty old so I will have to start settling down by then. Family, kids, all that stuff. Maybe little Walker-Carsons running around. Carson-Walkers sounds better. I think she would definitely be up for that.

OK, hotels. Food, the same, say, a hundred a day. Clothes: hundred a day. Going to need some decent clothes for the press releases and stuff. Bits and pieces: bags, hammers, knives, a gun. Do I want a gun? Isn't that like too easy? Oh, and some tools: rope, that sort of thing, another hundred a day. Technology: phones, Internet, etc., etc. Hundred a day. That's my limit, that's 500 quid a day from the machine.

Fuck!

I can't go to the machine. That's number one on the frigging page. Think, Edmund, that's how they catch you. They trace the card. I need to get the money out of the bank.

Melanie Epsom!

She is so hot, the only woman I have ever seen that is Walker hot. Well, ninety-nine per cent Walker hot. But after Friday night, I doubt any woman will ever be Walker hot again. Concentrate, Edmund. I am going to need some help from her. I type into my calculator.

116

500x7x52x5 = Fuck Mm! £910,000

No wonder they thought old Jack was royalty. He must have been to keep going for four years. I am never getting that out without the bank kicking up a fuss to my nan. That's without cars and stuff. I am going to need to change my car every couple of months at least. Well, when I have one.

Maybe I just do this until I am twenty? That's three years. Just set a challenge to myself, to be bigger than Jack in three years. He didn't have the CSI on him or anything, surely that makes me better. And if my numbers are good, then that is what really counts, surely? What was there? Like half a dozen women in his song? I want my song like that Beautiful South one. The one with all the names in it. Maybe I should try for every girl's name?

I sit at the table in the kitchen. That's still six hundred thousand I need to get out of the bank. Without anyone knowing. I take out my wallet and pull Melanie's business card from it. I call the number.

"Middleton banking services. Melanie speaking how may I be of assistance today?"

She sounds hot even from the phone. I would pay for this call on one of those pay as you go porn lines. She could definitely work on one of them.

"Hi Melanie, it's Edmund Carson from the other day."

"Hi, Edmund, what can I do for you today?"

"I was wondering if I could get a meeting, to discuss some money? And my grandmother?"

"Sure, I am your personal banker, Edmund, and available to you twenty-four-seven. Head to the bank and we can talk whenever you like."

Available twenty-four-seven. I need to test that!

"Okay, thank you. I will be leaving in about ten minutes, if that is OK?"

"That's fine, Edmund, see you then."

I hang up the phone. I only have one card left to play with this. Sweet little orphan Edmund, let's see what that gets me. I jump on my bike and head to the bank. I ride past Miss Walker's house on the way. Her car is still there, but she was not a school? I think I need to stop past and see her at some point. I don't like the way I left her, sleeping on the rug. She probably doesn't realise how much I love, wait, like her. That was close. That word nearly slipped out. I am not ready for that kind of commitment. Not yet.

I get to the bank and they take me straight through to the back room. Melanie is waiting for me.

"Hi, Edmund, please take a seat. Is there anything I can get for you? Tea, coffee, soft drink?"

I can hardly look straight at her. She could be Sandra Bullock, I swear.

"Coffee, please."

I don't like coffee, but figure it makes me seem more grown-up. She nods at the girl closing the door and she disappears to make the coffee.

"So how can we help you today?"

Here goes, been working on this one all the way over.

"It's my grandmother, I want to do some things for her, now that I have access to my accounts. She has been so great to me since the fire and I need to ensure that she is OK for now and for her future."

118

"Okay, like what kind of things were you thinking about, Edmund?"

"Well, this was my plan. There is an auction next Wednesday for a house in the village just outside ours, and I want to buy her, her dream house. Every time we drive past this house she always says what a lovely garden it is. Thing is, it costs five hundred and fifty thousand pounds. I also want to transfer some extra money into her account to ensure that she is comfortable for the rest of her days."

Need to slow down my speaking. All of that came out a little fast. I think she is buying it though; there is almost a sad look in her face. Either that or it's a confused one. Her eyes are so bright it's hard to read what she is thinking. It's like she can see straight through me.

"That shouldn't be a problem, Edmund. Transferring into your grandmother's account can be done any time as she is your guarantor. There is no limit on that. And we have a perfectly good mortgage advisor who can help you with the house."

She is smiling directly at me; there is a sort of twinkle in the corner of her eye now. It reminds me of the school and the read-through with Miss Walker. She had the same look in her eyes. I am sure she must be thinking about me. Me and her. Edmund the millionaire, and her. She wouldn't have to work another day in her life if she was with me. Really with me.

"Edmund, did you hear me?"

Fuck, lost myself there for a moment!

"Yes, sorry, I was miles away. That is good about the transfer, thank you. But, you see, the auctions are cash auctions and I need to have the money to be able to pay there and then? I am not sure how that works. Is there any way we can do that as I don't want her to lose her dream home?"

There is an innocence to my voice. I know, I put it there. I am so talented at acting. She is quiet. She pulls up her laptop screen on her desk and taps away.

"That shouldn't be a problem, Edmund. If you bring your grandmother in, we should be able to sort something out between us."

She closes the laptop. She is smiling directly at me now. I just need to stop thinking about doing her, and start thinking about selling myself to her.

"The thing is, Miss Epsom."

"Melanie, Edmund, you can call me Melanie."

"The thing is, Melanie, I want it to be a surprise. I am going off to university very shortly, and I want to leave my grandmother set for life. Can I tell you what my plan was? I think I should have probably started with that."

She nods her head and smiles at me.

"My first plan was to go to the auction next week with the money, but I am also worried about losing out to someone. So I was going to walk up to the house on the Tuesday and make a deal with the owner before the sale. It is a cash auction, but if I turn up on his doorstep the night before with fifty thousand above his price then I am sure to get it. Once I have the house, my plan then was to ensure it's prepared for my grandmother. I need it to be safe for her whilst I am away. I am sure you know I lost both my parents in a fire and she is all I have. If it weren't for her I would have been left in a foster home or something until now. She deserves the world, and in my own way I want to give it to her."

I pause and wipe away an imaginary tear from my cheek.

"Once the house was ready, on one of our weekly drives to the market I was going to ask her to stop and look at the house. My plan was to knock on the door and walk in. At first she would be shocked, but once inside I would have the house full of white and pink orchids, her favourite flowers. I could then explain what I have done for her. It will never compare to what she has done for me, but she is the last of my family."

She isn't moving. I lift my head to make eye contact with her and her eyes are welling up. That sparkle looks so much bigger with tears in her eyes. I have her. In that moment she is Walker hot.

She opens her laptop and starts to bash away at it. She hasn't spoken so I am not sure now whether she is going to fall for it or not. She looks up from the screen and smiles at me.

"Edmund, I think I know a way, but there will need to be some safeguards with regards to making a cash purchase outside of an auction. We will need papers drawn up to show the money has been exchanged, and a witness from the bank at the time. I can do this myself as your personal banker."

"Okay."

Does that mean she is going to give me the money? She is still tapping away on the computer.

"The bank account we set you up with, Edmund, can be linked to three other accounts. Each of these accounts can be set up with a withdrawal limit of twenty-five thousand pounds. This means that you would be able to take out one hundred thousand pounds per day. Now this wouldn't normally be allowed without your grandmother's signature but given the circumstances I think we can make an exception."

Fuck me, I am good.

I am looking directly, attentively at her. Trying to look as I am hanging off every word that comes from her lips. I am hanging off every word that comes off those lips. Those lips, I can just imagine them round my...

"Edmund, that means that you can take twenty-five thousand out today, then Tuesday to Monday you can take a further five hundred thousand in total, and on Tuesday, before we go to see the seller, you can take a further seventy-five thousand out. Should cover everything. I will sort all the paperwork, and set up a meeting on Wednesday with our insurance people so that we can get the property insured."

She closes down the laptop.

"Give me your card, Edmund, and I will go and make the first withdrawal for you. Then, every day, come and see me, and we can sort the others together. Do you have a safe at home, Edmund?"

"Yes."

I don't have a safe. Who am I, a mafia boss?

"That's good, as there will be a lot of cash sitting around at home by next week. The other option would be to put it in a security box in the bank. Something you have unlimited access to."

"The safe will be fine."

I want the money out of the bank, and as far away from here as possible.

She disappears out of the room and closes the door behind her. I sit there in disbelief that she just bought it until all of a sudden, my legs make me stand up. I push the chair back and I am jumping in the air. Punching my fist upwards.

I am going to be fucking famous…

I want to scream it from the highest mountain. I am still jumping as the door starts to open. I stop and stand still.

"Sit down, Edmund, we haven't finished yet, still need your signature on this."

She hands me a piece of paper and a pen. I sign my name and then she points to the seat. I sit back down.

She starts to count the money out in front of me. Somehow I thought twenty-five large would be bigger. It's not as big as I thought it would be.

"Twenty-five thousand pounds, there you go."

She hands me over the money.

"Now, Edmund, I have to ask. As your first trip alone to the bank, how did you find it?"

I nod my head at her.

"Good, very good."

"That is excellent news, and is there anything else that I can do for you today?"

"No, thanks."

"OK then. Then, we will see you tomorrow and let's see if we can get all this sorted for your grandmother in the next week. It's a wonderful thing you are doing for her, Edmund."

She stands up, so do I. I put the money in my backpack, shake her hand, and she walks me out of the bank. I am outside standing on the path with twenty-five large in my backpack.

I think this is what shock feels like. All of a sudden reality kicks in.

Blow job!

How didn't that come into my mind when she asked me if there was anything else that I needed? What is up with me?

When a beautiful woman asks you 'is there anything else you need from me?' you reply with a blow job. Always a blow job.

I head over to where I parked my bike and then head off. I am sure I caught a glimpse of her at the window as I did. She wants me even more now. She has to be thinking I am some kind of saint. And good-looking people are always attracted to good-looking people, it's just nature.

I ride back towards home. Before I get there I go to Miss Walker's house. I park my bike at the bottom of the driveway and walk up and knock on the door.

Nothing. I knock again. Nothing. I am sure I don't know the protocol for what has gone on, but her car is still there. Is she mad at me? Embarrassed that I am a student? In love and thinking about not leaving to go to that Preton High School place? It can't be as good as our school. Why would she want to leave me to go there? What do they have that I don't? I leave. I don't want to think about her leaving for some crappy school. She is mine. We are meant to be together. We both know that. Time to get this money home.

When I arrive back home I take the money straight upstairs. I have an old Umbro cricket bag which is big enough to hold my pads in so it will be big enough to hold everything I need. I put the twenty-five thousand in there. Then stuff it under my bed. I pull my notebook out of my bag. Number one in not getting caught, done. I need four and five now I have cash: clothes, lots of hoodies, hats, that sort of thing. And burner phones, pay as you go. I can use my laptop for starters until they discover me, and then, when I am discovered, I will ensure I change IP addresses. Oh, and a car, I need a car.

Chapter 9

"Edmund."

"Edmund, dear."

Seven, 0 fucking three…

I won't be missing this next week when I am out of here. I lie on the bed and look at the ceiling.

"I am up, Nan, be down in fifteen"

Friday already. Where did the week go? I jump out of bed and pull the cricket bag from under the bed. It's all still there, three hundred and twenty-three thousand, a dozen phones and some clothes, all black. I push it back and lay back on the bed. No need for a shower, had one last night. Haven't been out all week. Not with the money in the house. I am staying close to it.

Still can't decide how to start. The Merson case is still going on, but they have no idea I was with them that night. Caroline hasn't turned up either. Have to be bolder, more outrageous. I want a cool nickname like Jack's… Edmund the Slasher, Edmund the Evil, Evil Edmund, I am not sure I like Evil. Sounds too bad. Edmund the Mighty, Edmund the Necromancer… Don't know what that means, but I think it's something to do with a lover and a fighter and I am definitely that. Although Miss Walker still seems to be keeping her distance. Been a week today. I get up, dressed and downstairs for breakfast. She is waiting for me at the counter, and has a serious look on her face.

"Now, Edmund, I want you to tell me the truth before we eat. What have you done?"

What! Where is this coming from? Fuck, I hope she hasn't been under my bed. She is never going to believe they are not my magazines. Surely all teenage boys have them. It's online anyway?

"Sorry, Nan, what do you mean?"

"At the bank, Edmund, what have you done?"

Fuck she has been under my bed, she knows about the money! Act dumb, act dumb...

"At the bank, Nan?"

She walks over and kisses me on the forehead.

"Yes, the bank, sweetie. I know you have transferred money into my account. You didn't need to do that. I have my pension and my savings, I am OK. I don't need a lot of money."

Thank fuck for that, she was only on about that quarter of a mil.

I smile at her and kiss her on the cheek. She wanders back to the stove to make breakfast.

"It's just a little money so that I know you are safe when I am away, that's all."

"A little money, Edmund? I nearly had a heart attack checking my balance this morning. I don't need your money, my dear. All I ask for is a little company every now and again."

"I know, Nan. Let's call it just in case money."

"Besides, are you planning to go somewhere? And leave me?"

Now there is a question. Am I? I think if I am going to be famous, I need to be where the action is. And I am pretty sure the action isn't here. It's far too quiet.

"No, Nan, not going to be leaving you any time soon."

She shoots a smile back at me and is back on with my sausage sandwich. I really need to decide my next steps. I have been watching *CSI* all week, there is no way they are catching me once I start, but how to start? Whatever I do needs to be able to be converted into a cool nickname. Or I give the press a cool nickname. Now that's an idea. I could be like that Milk Tray advert. Leave a calling card with my name on so they know who is responsible. You can make like business cards in those booths… hundred for like a fiver.

"Edmund, earth to Edmund."

She is standing right in front of me with my sandwich. I couldn't even see her.

"Sorry, Nan."

"You was away in your own little world then, wasn't you?"

"Yes, sorry, Nan. I was thinking about Mum and Dad."

That always keeps her happy. I always know just what to say. It's a gift.

"OK, eat your breakfast and get off to school. I am at the WI this morning and I won't be back until teatime."

She kisses me again and disappears. I eat the sausage sandwich. I go back up and lie on the bed. No school today. There is no point in going back there if Miss Walker isn't going to be there. She hasn't turned in since our night together. Nobody knows anything. Probably already off at her precious high school and forgot about me. I still can't believe that she would pick that school over me. We have something. We have always had something, ever since I went to that school. I am not finished, we are not finished yet. It will work out. I need to work on a plan for that too. I need to pick up the money from the bank, and then I need to start working on my plan. Time is moving on.

There is a knock at the door. Nan must have forgotten her keys. I walk downstairs and open the door.

Fuck me!

Miss Walker is at my front door. Actually at my front door.

"Morning, Edmund. Can I come in?"

She doesn't look happy at all. That twinkle in her eye almost looks like it could stab me. She is still in a little black dress. She must know how much I liked it the other night. At least she is making an effort after ignoring me.

"Sure, Miss."

Do I call her Miss now? Something about the way she was looking at me told me to at that point. I step to one side and let her in. I close the door and as I turn to see her. SLAP!

"Ouch! What was that for?"

She slapped me straight across the face.

"That is for fucking lying to me, Edmund."

She slaps me again and again and they are turning into punches. I have nowhere to go, I am pinned in the corner. I grab her hands and move her backwards.

I think, she thinks she is hurting me. She should know the only thing this does is give me a hard-on.

"Woo, what is the matter with you? Miss, what are you doing?"

"What's the matter with me, Edmund? You lied to me, you lied to me about where you were the night we met. You lied to me about how many women you had slept with, and since then you didn't even have the decency to call me to apologise."

What the fuck is she on about!

"What? Who said I lied to you?"

"You know you did." She is still proper shouting. I am going to need to gag her in a minute.

"You know you fucking did. I picked you up outside their house, Edmund, their fucking house, and you have the cheek to come up with some story about being drunk… You were in there having sex with them, weren't you? A mother and a daughter at the same house. That's disgusting, Edmund. Then you make up some other cock and bull story about only ever sleeping with one woman. What was that for? To impress me? To make me fall for you?"

She isn't fighting as much now. She seems upset more than angry now. Wait, did she say fall for me? Miss Walker has fallen for me?

"I thought our night meant something to you, Edmund. Not that I was the third girl you had that night. How many more, Edmund? How many more girls have you slept with? I want the truth!"

Is that a trick question? I have seen enough TV to know you never tell a girl how many women you have slept with.

"Six. Six more…"

Fuck it, she is angry already!

I hold my breath and wait for the response.

"Six? Six? So I was what like number ten, sorry, eleven? Edmund, when you make love to someone you tell them the truth. You don't lie and break their heart."

Wait a minute she is mad that I lied to her, not that I have slept with other women? How the fuck does this stuff work? Women are so confusing.

"If you must know, I haven't slept with anyone since you, Miss. I can't get that night out of my head."

She has stopped fighting. I think that is actually what she has come around here for. She doesn't hate me, she likes me. Use the right words and this will turn in my favour. Just like Nan.

"Besides, you said you were leaving. I thought you were just using me as a one-night stand before you went. To get that vision out of your head. You are leaving me, remember, for some horrible school for gifted girls. You could have stayed here with me."

I am probably not staying here either, but a little guilt is a good thing. She is smiling now. I am not sure I like it as much as the shouting.

"Edmund…"

Her hands come up to my face. I lean back a little just in case it is another slap. It's not. She takes my face in her hands.

"Edmund, when you are in a relationship like ours, you need to be honest with each other. I am only going to London, it's like forty-five minutes from here. It will hardly be a long distance relationship, will it? We, together, are going to make this work."

Relationship? What the fuck? This is getting weird.

She pulls me in and starts to kiss me, slowly at first and then stronger. She has one hand on my belt, now two and my trousers and boxers are on the floor and so is she, sucking me like there is no tomorrow.

"Oh, Edmund, it's magnificent."

She is at it again, harder and faster. I love the blow-by-blow commentary. She knows exactly what I dream about without me telling her. She is amazing. All I can hear are sounds as if she is having an orgasm herself. The speed in which she is doing this is outstanding. This isn't her second time, I am fucking sure of that. Should I ask her the question? Or is that going to end all this? Not that I care about the answer. I build up and up and I grab the back of her head pulling it closer to me. I exploded inside her. She is still going, like every single drop of me is needed inside her. She stands up and kisses me. My first instinct is to pull away. I don't want to kiss her, I know where she has just been. Would be like doing it myself? And I can't do that. I have tried.

"Come on, Edmund, we need to talk now."

She walks off into my house. Did she even know my grandmother was gone? Because if she didn't, that's some kind of freaky, isn't it? We walk into the house and into the kitchen. She wanders over and puts the kettle on as if she lives here.

"Shall we have some tea?"

"Okay. Sit down, I will make it, I know where the stuff is."

She does. I go and pull out the tea bags and the cups and make us tea and we sit at the breakfast table.

"So, what are we going to do about our situation?"

This is another test, right? I kind of want to make her mad, because, fuck, she is hot when she is mad. But then, she is hot when she is not mad.

FUCK! I don't know the answer…

"I love you."

I don't know why I said that, I just figure that women want to hear that every now and again. She is not moving. Think I have made her mad. Wait, is that a tear in her eye? She comes from round the table. Shit, don't know whether to defend myself or hug her. Or just run. I may have to run.

"I am always the one who says it first. Edmund, I am so glad you said it first. I love you too."

She is kissing me everywhere. This L word has a strange effect on women. When I told Caroline, she never spoke to me again, and now Miss Walker can't get enough of me. Wait, what does she mean she is always the first one to say it? How many people has she loved? OK, she has stopped kissing me and is sitting back down again.

"I am only forty-five minutes to an hour away so we can see each other all the time, and when you leave school… When is that by the way?"

"Next week, Miss."

I am not lying, it is actually next week, although the school don't know it. But she should. She knows my class and she knows I am not really eighteen. I think she just couldn't wait any more. It is understandable.

"Edmund?"

"Sorry, Emily, it's hard to get used to that, but I guess I will have to."

I smile at her. That twinkle in the corner of her eye is back. I am a natural at this shit.

"That's great, and what do you want to do as a career?"

Now there is a question… Not sure I can get away with telling her that answer, but I have seen what lying to her does also. The punches are good, but the downtime isn't.

"I don't know, Emily, I am going to take some time to find myself. My parents left me some money, so I am OK for a while."

"That's perfect. Then you can come and spend some time with me in London. The centre is just a tube ride away from the school, and you will love the school, Edmund."

London. London, that is not actually a bad idea. I need to be where the action is and that's where old Jack did all his best work. Maybe that's where I should be doing mine? Whitechapel, somewhere like that. Make a district my own. Like he did. Lots of famous people have their own sections in London. Baker Street for Sherlock. Buckingham Palace for the Queen. Yeah, maybe a part of London for me.

"I think that is a great idea. Will need to split some time between here and London, because I still have to look after my nan."

I am sensing that was the wrong answer, the twinkle it's turned a little red.

"But more time with you, obviously, just need to check up on her as she is old and stuff. She has lots of friends to look after her too…"

Waiting, waiting and the smile returns. So this dating game, generally I am realising that if you are a bloke, tell the woman exactly what she wants to hear. Do what she wants and, if you have to lie, for fuck's sake don't get caught... Simple really. I don't see what all the fuss is about. Second date and I have it nailed. Maybe that's just me though.

We finish our tea, she tells me all about her new private school for girls. It's a big old stately home, run by a mixture of nuns and teachers. I am not really listening, all I can think about is that I have Miss Walker eating out of the palm of my hand. Is there anything I can't do? I am not only going to be famous, but, it would seem, a god amongst women. When good-looking women see you with good-looking women it like attracts them too. They think you must have something. I am going to be worshipped.

Wait, she is standing up. What the fuck was she saying?

"So we are agreed, Edmund? I am so happy."

Fuck! No idea what she said...?

"Of course we are agreed..."

"I will see you Friday then in my new place. I have written the address down for you. It's a little village just outside of the schools grounds."

We are heading towards the door, so I guess she said she is going somewhere in that conversation.

"Thanks, Emily."

She turns and kisses me. Hard.

"I love it when you call me Emily. I am looking forward to seeing you Friday. A weekend in bed sounds perfect."

Wow, did she say a weekend in bed? I really should listen more. I open the door and she is gone. I close the door behind me.

Miss Walker fucking loves me!

Who saw that coming? I go back to my bedroom and lie back on the bed. I spend the next ten minutes wondering whether that really happened or not. Miss Walker loves me and wants to be in a relationship with me. You fuck a girl, you don't call her for a week so she comes round, gives you a blow job, and asks you to spend the weekend with her? This shit really happens? Surely this is the stuff that dreams are made of? Then my life is probably the stuff that dreams are made of. Not everyone can be me.

I clear my head and go back to the task ahead. How am I going to start this? Where am I going to start this? London does seem like a great idea. I like the idea of making something my own. An area of London that will always be associated with me. That makes you famous. Maybe something to do with the tube? Not like those loonies. Something classic. Classic like Jack. Tube Terror is a great headline. District line disaster, Metropolitan line Murderer. Piccadilly Psychopath. Could be any of them. The tube it is. Need to google just to make sure someone else hasn't done this before, but I like it. I spend the next hour thinking out my calling cards and fall asleep.

Fuck! Seventeen minutes past four...

The bank closes at five. Need to get there to get the money out. I have some missed calls on my phone from them. Must be Melanie checking that I am still coming. I run downstairs, get on my bike and head across town.

Eight minutes to spare. Melanie is waiting at the counter for me, and we walk straight through to the room at the back.

"I didn't think you were going to make it today, Edmund?"

"I know, I was helping my grandmother and time got the better of me. Had to make my excuses real fast."

I don't even know where these lies come from.

She takes my card as before, and then disappears. Returning with a hundred large, and papers for me to sign. I sign.

"Would you like a drink or something before you go, Edmund?"

"Why not? Can I get a Coke or something?"

Melanie gestures to the bank teller and she disappears, reappearing with a Coke and water for her and then closes the door on us.

"So, how has your week been?"

"It's been OK. School mainly, but I leave in another week so that's nearly done."

Need her to know, I am not just a little kid. I can tell from her face she doesn't think of me that way. More a lust in her eyes.

"That's good, and any plans on what you are going to do once you leave?"

What is it, career for Edmund day today!

"Not really, think I will help my nan with her new house for a while, and decide some time after that."

What new house? What the fuck am I talking about? Almost give a little chuckle out loud. People just trust me. I have that type of face.

"You are a good person, Edmund. What are your plans for the weekend? Any lucky lady in your life?"

Wait, is that a come on? Why else would she be asking if there is someone in my life? She wants me, I am sure of it. It must be pheromones or something. Women are always attracted to men who have other women.

"No plans, and the only woman in my life is my grandmother. She is the most important person to me at the moment."

Yes, you heard, I am single and available, at the moment. Which means there is room for you. In the future. There is a shiver down my spine at the thought of Miss Walker hearing that though. I look over my shoulder, I don't know why, she isn't here.

"Well, I am sure you will find someone soon."

There is a silence. It wasn't a come on, was it? She was just being polite. I play it over in my head again. The emphasis was on soon, wasn't it? Soon meaning now. In front of you, Edmund. Yes, she wants me.

"How about you? Any plans with your boyfriend?"

Girlfriend, twin sister? Please, god, tell me it's a twin sister. The way my luck is lately she has a twin sister, and they like the same men.

"No, no plans for me. Not for the next two years. I have started an MBA in business studies, so no time for men or for partying I am afraid."

She is a lesbian. Who says they have no time for men for the next two years? Either that or she is preparing to become a nun of some sorts. There is silence again.

"Anyway, have to go. It's Friday and I have to pick up the fish supper for me and my grandmother."

I don't even know what I am saying now. I don't even like fish. These words just seem to float out of my mouth.

"OK. I will walk you out, Edmund, as it's time for me to leave also."

She grabs her coat and bag and follows me out of the door.

"I would offer you a lift but…"

I show her my helmet and point over to my bike.

"That's OK, Edmund, I live just around the corner. Have a lovely weekend, and I will see you on Monday."

She disappears around the corner. I walk over to my bike and push it in the same direction. When she says just around the corner I wonder how far she means. She is walking pretty fast, but I am just about keeping up with her. She turns to a doorway, unlocks the door, and walks in. I follow up to the door. Her name is on it. She is really just next door to the bank. Good to know.

Chapter 10

Quarter to seven. Tuesday. I get up, shower, and I am downstairs before Nan's 7.03 alarm call. When she gets downstairs I am cooking her breakfast for a change.

"Morning, my handsome boy."

"Morning, Nan."

She comes over and kisses me.

"You didn't need to get up and make me breakfast. You know I love doing that for you."

"I know, I wanted to. Besides, I am going to miss you when I go on the school trip."

"You will miss my breakfasts, or me?"

She smiles at me.

"I know, I can't believe I forgot all about it, Edmund, that is so unlike me."

She didn't, there is no school trip, but I needed to make something up so she didn't worry. I fully intend to be off, after tomorrow. At least a couple of weeks in London to get my future started. The sooner I am back on the front pages, the better. It will be good to have somewhere to come to keep away from the press as well. These things can get intense at the beginning.

"Sit down then, and I will bring over some breakfast for you."

I smile at her, and she wanders over to the table. I have made scrambled eggs and bacon for breakfast. We eat it and discuss the trip. Apparently I am off to Scotland for two weeks to tour the Highlands. Who knew? I certainly didn't until I made it up on Sunday. After breakfast she disappears to her Tuesday walking club. Eight o'clock every Tuesday. I am thankful of that today. I need to get to the bank early as I have a plan that needs execution and precision today. I guess it starts today.

As soon as she is out of the house I get on my bike and head across town. I park outside the bank and walk around the corner to where Melanie lives. I wait to see someone coming out of her building. It takes about ten minutes, but finally someone comes out. I grab the door as if to walk back in. The guy disappears. I pull out the resin I have in my pocket and stuff it into the lock cavity. Then I stuff in a couple of five-pence pieces, and try and close the door. It closes and opens.

Damn, I am good!

Now you don't need a key or a buzzer to get in. I try it a couple of times and then leave. I just hope no one notices it. Before I get to the corner of the street there is a call from behind me.

"Morning, Edmund."

It's Melanie. That was close. Another minute and she would have seen me at her door. I turn and walk back towards her.

"Morning, Melanie."

She is so hot, and first thing in the morning as well. Surely she can't wake up looking that good. I will find out one day, I am sure of that.

"You are an early bird today?"

"Yes, I thought I had better get a start on the day. Yesterday was a long one."

I smile at her and she smiles back. We walk around the corner to the bank. She lets me straight in and takes me to her office at the back. Within ten minutes I have the final seventy-five large.

"So, Edmund, what time are we meeting later to approach the seller? I am really looking forward to it."

We are not.

"I have already enquired and he finishes work around seven, so I thought seven thirty. I have a cab booked and my plan was that I can pick you up on route?"

"That sounds like a good plan, Edmund. I have all the papers ready to sign. My first house negotiation. Haven't even bought myself a house yet."

She is smiling at me as she pats a stack of papers on her desk.

"So, I will take them home with me this evening and you can pick me up from there. It is just around the corner."

There is a little more chitchat, but then, I am out of there. I stop outside the bank for a moment. My head goes back to my list. And the plan.

I have the motherfucking money! All of it!

It's all I can do but to give a little dance there and then. I stop myself. I need to focus. What I don't have is a car. I need

141

to buy one today. Second-hand. I ride home and go online. Needs to be close so that I can bus or taxi over and drive the car back. I start going through local second-hand car dealers and private sellers. Private is probably best, they won't ask me as many questions, I am sure. Money talks. Three thousand for a two-door Toyota Celica red. It's an old car, but it's an automatic. My nan has an automatic, and she taught me to drive in hers. I figure that is the best option.

I call them up and head over. It's about four stops on the bus. Some bloke in his mid-fifties takes me for a test drive in it. I only go around the block. Don't want him to ask too many questions about my driving skills. He hands over the service manual, and a lot of paperwork nonsense. Ensuring to tell me to register it? Not sure what that was all about. I give him the three large and he gives me the keys.

I drive it home. Never driven on my own before, always had someone in the passenger seat. It's quite scary. I can feel myself wanting to go faster and faster as I do. I am home within ten minutes, and park the car on the next street. Don't want my grandmother seeing it.

I am back in the house and I go through everything I have. I have packed a bag of normal clothes for my trip to Scotland for two weeks. Then I have my go bag. My costume and money. Then I have my tool bag. It's so cool. Bolt croppers, knives, rope, tape, hammers. I go through the bag again. All tools that I am sure I will need one day when I hone my craft. This starts tomorrow, in London, but that's not where this is ending. According to *CSI* I will escalate a lot. The more you become famous, the bigger and better you try and become. And I am going to be famous. Bigger than Jack. In three years.

I put my go bag and suitcase under my bed, but not the tool bag. Going to give it its first outing tonight.

It's only eleven thirty. I have the rest of the day to myself. Tomorrow is the start of the rest of my life. I get the box set *of Criminal Minds* out, and sit downstairs to watch a few episodes. I watch five. It kills most of the afternoon, but that's what happens when you need to research. I am like these actors, when they go and research a part in a movie. They go and live it for a couple of weeks. I am just doing that without leaving the house. They are so thick. Don't they know you can learn everything off TV or the Internet? Nan comes home and starts making our tea. I sit with her at the kitchen table.

"Nan, what did you want to do when you were my age?"

"I don't know, dear. I guess when I was seventeen I had already met your grandfather, we were already in love, and talking about getting married. I would say that is all I wanted to do. We had your Uncle George and then your mother. My life was pretty complete by the time I was twenty."

She settled down at seventeen? Who does that? I couldn't even think about that at my age. Although, that conversation with Miss Walker was odd.

"Why do you ask? Are you struggling to know what to do, Edmund? I thought you said about being a doctor? Or a lawyer? I can see you in a suit, Edmund. Very handsome."

No, I said that because that is what you wanted to hear, Nan I know what I am going to do. I am going to be world-famous. They will make a movie about me. A trilogy. Even songs. I think a TV series to start.

"I do think about being a doctor, Nan. I guess I am just not sure. The thought of operating on people does excite me.

143

Holding people's lives in your hands must be amazing, but what if I get it wrong?"

I am not kidding at that point. Life and death. How would you choose? By looks? You wouldn't save everyone, would you? That's what that doctor did. That's why he got away with it for so long. You wouldn't know, would you?

"You have plenty of time, dear, you are still young. Whatever you do, I am sure you will be amazing at it."

She places tea in front of me, and kisses me on the forehead. We carry on the discussion through tea. She tells me of her time with my grandfather and my parents when they were younger. She will be proud of me when I am famous. She just wants the best for me. After tea she starts on her quilt. She has been making that thing for nearly a year now. I tell her I am off out for a while. Whilst she is in the front room I go upstairs, get my tool bag, and I am out of the house.

I walk along the street to where I left the car and throw the bag on the back seat. One more loose end to tie up. If *CSI* has taught me anything this last week it's not to leave questions unanswered.

I drive across town. It's six thirty. The nights are still dark. I park next to the bank and walk around the corner. I push the door open to Melanie's apartments. It still works. Nobody has noticed. I check, the five-pence pieces and resin are still in there. I pull a screwdriver from my bag and flick it out. The door closes behind me.

FUCK, gloves!

I was going to wear gloves. I stand in the hallway. Do I clean it and put gloves on now or not? Gloves are generally so

144

nobody knows it was you, but I actually want people to know it is me. I am going to be famous.

I decide to leave it. Besides, the police don't have my fingerprints or DNA yet. They can't find out it's me because they don't know who me is. And when they do, they will need to link it all together so they know I am bigger than Jack.

I walk up to her apartment. I stand at the door. She has a little plant outside her door and in the plant pot is a little sign saying no place like home. She is too cute to be true. I press my ear against the door. I can hear the TV going, but also the shower. I know she is single, she is in it alone. That thought has me hot before I even start.

Fucking perfect!

I try the door. It opens. Wait, no, it stops. The chain is on. And like Mr Ben would say, as if by magic, the tool bag. Or was it the guy that owned the shop said that? I love those classic TV programmes. Never mind, I am a natural at this. I snip the chain and I am in. I close the door behind me. The shower is definitely running. She must be in there. The TV is on also, which is good as there is sound. My hearing is amazing. I am just the perfect specimen of a man. I place the bag on the floor, look inside, and pull out a hunting knife. I have seen this in a movie somewhere. Girl in shower attacked by knife-wielding legend. Now I am that legend.

The door to the bathroom is ajar so it just takes a little push and it's open. The bathroom is too cute too, ducks and hot air balloons fill the walls. I stand next to the shower curtain. It's white with ducks on it so nobody can see through it. I pull my knife back and strike. As I strike down it hits her on the shoulder. She falls. As she does I try to grab her through the curtain, but can't; she is too slippery. She hits her head on the front of the bath.

I pull off the curtain to finish the job, but as I do I can smell it. Even over the perfume of the shampoo. The blood is out. Melanie is laying in the bath, her head embedded in the cold tap.

"I am sorry, so sorry I didn't mean for that to happen. Fuck that looks painful."

That must have hurt her. I am shivering just thinking of it. Thankfully it's the back of her head that is in the tap. It didn't mess up her face. That would have been awful for her. Even laying there you can tell how beautiful she is. Wet and soapy. I have had that dream, a lot, since I opened my account.

She isn't talking. I look up and work out how to turn the shower off. It's stopped. I am soaked though. I pull Melanie off the tap and get her out of the bath. I have made a mess everywhere. It's soaking in here. I pick her up and take her out of the room. Again, I am so glad I like small girls. Fat girls must be harder to get around. I can see a bedroom behind the kitchen area, so I take her over to this and lay her on the bed. I then go back to the bathroom to clean it up, and myself. Grabbing a towel to dry myself off, and then dry the floor. She has been so good to me I don't want her to have to tidy up after me. I then grab another towel and take it back to the bedroom.

"You will catch your death of cold if you don't dry off." She is lying on the bed and I dry her body off.

Fuck, she is beautiful!

I really take my time drying every inch of her. Everything just as I imagined it would be, right down to the little landing strip. Her hair is soaking wet. I am not sure whether it's blood or the shower, and the smell isn't that strong now. I pick her off the bed, and take her over to the dressing table she has in the corner. Everything is laid out from hairdryer to make-up. That must be to save time. I grab the hairdryer and the brush and dry her hair for her.

"You know, my nan always says that you shouldn't walk around with wet hair. Look at mine. It's about the same length. She is always telling me I will catch a cold. I never have though. I guess that's because I always dry it. You have beautiful hair. You must use some kind of conditioner or something?"

She is still not speaking to me.

"Has anyone ever told you, you look exactly like Sandra Bullock? I mean exactly. You could be twins. And she is hot. Very hot."

That will impress her. Telling any woman they are stunning is always impressive. Especially if they look like superstars.

I think she may be a bit peed off about the bathroom. I stand and dry her hair and lay her back on the bed. Then, I just stand at the end of the bed looking at her. I can't get over the fact that she is so beautiful, and doesn't have a boyfriend. It's not natural. If I was a girl and looked like her, I would have a dozen boyfriends. And sex every night. Twice a night even. With different people.

"Are you a lesbian?"

She still isn't answering. Is there ever a good time to ask that question? Is she not answering because it was a rude question or that she still isn't speaking to me?

"Is this a game? Do you want me to find out?"

147

There is definitely a smile on her face now. That was it. She is playing hard to get. I don't mind a little game every now and again. They say it keeps the romance alive.

"OK, let's look through the drawers. Who lives in a house like this?"

That got a faint chuckle, I am sure of it. I open her wardrobe.

"Little black dresses, that's always a good sign in a girl, but wait, what are these? Dungarees? That's bad. They do look like you paint in them, but it's still a bad sign. Most lesbos have them in their wardrobe somewhere. Lots of make-up on the table over there. Good sign as lesbians tend not to wear a lot of make-up. Well, some do. Well, I guess that's not really a sign, as all the videos I watch of them they all do wear make-up, and are pretty damn hot like you. Let's ignore that clue. I am losing track there."

I walk over and start opening drawers.

"Black underwear, good sign. You know what they say? You only have black underwear if you want someone to see it… oh wait, some granny panties too? Proper size too. Like that girl movie. You know the one. Hugh Grant was the lover and the guy was Mr Darcy… Don't tell me, it will come to me. Surely you don't fit in these? You are far to fit for that."

The rest of her drawers are filled with jumpers and sweaters.

"So, the most telling of all, what does a hot personal bank manager keep in her bedside cabinet? And we have a winner."

I pull out a selection of vibrators. Not just one, she has about four in there.

"I am sure lesbians don't have these."

Her smile gets wider. And the sparkle is back in her eyes. That's the look. The look I have been waiting for. The Walker hot look.

"In fact, I am not sure what lesbians do have? Do they have like female ones of these? What would you do with it? Anyway, I sense from this, and the K-Y jelly and the… What is this?"

"Oh, you're talking to me now. I put that on, do I?"

"What, it vibrates for me? Why would you even have this if you have no time for men in your life?"

It's some kind of ring that the man puts on his bits. Never seen that before. Maybe she is kinkier than I imagined. I can't even imagine that mine fits in there. It's not that big.

"No, there was no house. I am going away tomorrow to London. I am going to be famous. I have a plan and everything. I just needed the money out to start on the process. The Nan thing was for her though. Needed to ensure that she was safe before I left. You will never believe how much it costs? You know, to become famous."

"Oh yeah, you know, six hundred large. Can you believe that? That is just for three years? I am going to use the rest of my money when I retire."

"Yes, this is our last day together."

She doesn't look impressed at that. I think she has been imagining more.

"I was hoping to, before I left? Is it something you want to do too? You were a bit quiet earlier so I thought you might have been a little mad at me? I cleaned the bathroom for you, and I am sorry about the whole tap thing. It wasn't my intention. I am so glad it didn't mess you up."

Her smile is intoxicating me. The way it lights up her eyes and the corner of her mouth. Next to Miss Walker she is the most beautiful woman I have ever seen. Better than Sandra.

"Since the first time we met, eh? Me too. I knew there was an attraction there. Well, I hoped. You kind of took my breath away."

That will seal the deal. Nothing a woman wants to hear more than that.

"I understand. Leave it with me, and I will see what I can do."

It's obvious really, she only gets to spend one night with me as I probably will be too famous to come back here. If she wants romance, I will romance the crap out of her. I escort her to the living room and leave her in front of the TV. I head back into the bedroom and search around. I find some music and a CD player. Don't see many of them around any more. I pick out a little bit of Michael Bublé, he always seems to get the girls going. Then I am back in the kitchen area, and underneath the sink.

Jackpot!

A bag full of tea candles. I take them back into the room and lay them all around the bed. Lighting each one before I escort her back into the room.

"Keep them closed, no peeking now."

I lay her back on the bed.

"I know, you said special. And as our last night together and our first, this is the best I could do. If I had a little more time, there would have been champagne and roses."

I lean over her. She is really smiling now. I whisper in her ear.

"Because Melanie, you are stunning. Stunningly beautiful."

There is a little nuzzle into my head. I can feel it.

"This is true. Sorry."

It's a fair point. Why am I still wearing clothes? I strip and lie on the bed next to her. I lean over and go back into the drawer.

"There is like two types, a red or a blue one… The red is for sensitive, got it."

The music is soft in the background. I follow her instructions and apply the jelly. Then we begin to make love. Soft and slow just like Miss Walker taught me. She is enjoying this. I don't think she thought I knew about all this stuff. Probably thought I was too young, and there is no substitute for the real thing. No matter how big or black it is that she has in her drawer.

"Wait, stop, just one moment. I love this song."

I jump off her and turn it up a little. Michael Bublé is singing *Mack the Knife*.

"I am going to be as famous as him one day. You won't believe it, but I am almost halfway there already, and I haven't even started yet."

"Thank you, yes, and a lot better looking."

"Yeah, I guess so, if they do write songs about me they will include all my ex-girlfriends like Suky Tawdry and Lucy Brown for old Jack."

That's a bit needy isn't it? I mean, she is hardly my girlfriend so why would she think she is going to be made into my song? The song finishes. We are back to making love. Slow and hard, slow and hard. Miss Walker's voice is running through my head. I don't seem to be enjoying this as much. Think it may be the needy thing? The fact that I know she is so clingy to me. She must feel so lucky to have me here. Is that it?

Fuck, wait, no, the blood!

I dried her hair, I think I dried the blood. I can't smell it, that's why it's not as good. I jump back off and go and get a knife from my bag.

"Just a nick in the neck, it won't hurt, I promise"

She consents, yes that's better. We are back at it. I lick the blood, and then again. The taste is sweet. Not as sweet as I remember it, but sweet nonetheless. We keep going at it, but it's awkward and bumpy. I don't really think she is putting a lot of effort into this. It just doesn't feel right. I finish. All in all, very disappointing. I didn't think sex could be disappointing.

"No, I am fine. Just didn't get my blood, boiling you know? Think it was all the prep work. The candles, the hair drying and all that. A lot of effort on my part. I tried to make it special for you."

Very little effort from you, Melanie, is what I am fucking saying.

"No, it's fine, I don't want to try again."

And that is so not like me. I am a five times a night man.

"I am sure you could, but the moment has passed."

"I know, sometimes these things don't work out, it's probably me, not you."

It's so definitely you, believe me, it's you. I get up and get dressed. I can totally understand why you don't have a boyfriend or time for one. They all packed you in, didn't they?

"Well, I guess that is that. I have your number, and I will call."

I won't call. As hot as she was. She just wasn't good in the sack. I am out of there. I am just about to leave the building.

Fuck!

The paperwork. I go back into her apartment. On the side in the living room are the documents for the house purchase, with my name on them. I am not in London yet so I don't want to be picked up before that. I don't have enough numbers. I am not yet number one. But I will be. I need to be. I need that cool nickname.

I put them in my tool bag. Should I leave some kind of calling card so they know it's started? If I do it's a change of the unsub's MO? As Agent Morgan would say. Maybe throw them off the scent a little?

I go back into the bedroom. She is still lying there. I think she has been crying. I don't blame her, she just probably lost the best thing that could have ever happened to her. It has to be hard on her.

"I am sorry. I was going to leave some kind of message. You know, for anyone who wants to know where it started. You know, like now I have worked out what my future would be."

"Yes, I suppose it will make you a little famous too, as you were here, at the real beginning."

Glory hunting bitch, you would think this was all about her. Everyone is going to want to tag their name to mine in some shape or form, aren't they? Maybe it is something you just have to get used to.

"Can I just borrow a little?"

She nods and I dip my fingers into her neck. It's cold already. A little bit like her. Maybe that's why it was so bad. Bit frigid.

Above the bed I write in blood: *It Begins*. Looks cool. I take out my phone and take a selfie with the sign. She also begs me to, so I take a couple with her. This is all going to look good on social media. When I am ready.

"Of course I will send them to you, I will, I promise."

I turn to leave. I don't think I have her number. Oh well. I quickly turn back.

"Bridget Jones, that was the girl with the big panties. Bridget Jones. Blonde but kind of hot. For a blonde girl. You can tell, not a fan of blondes."

I am out of there for real this time.

I start the drive home. Was that bad because she was bad, or bad because I am in a relationship? Am I in a relationship now? That's what she kept saying to me. Is it different in a relationship? Is Miss Walker playing in my head? Never really had bad sex before. Well, not bad sex, I had average sex with Caroline before we got into it for real that day. But am I off my game a little? Maybe the pressure of the bank, getting the money, all the supplies. I have been working hard researching what not to do. That can take its toll also.

I hear that sometimes when studying, people take like drugs and Pro Plus and stuff. Maybe I should get some, for when I am overworked. You hear about it all the time. Stars having breakdowns, drinking too much or taking drugs. I need to watch that as I become more famous. I am not ready for rehab yet. Not until I am preparing a comeback or something. That's when they do it, isn't it? All about the press. I am home.

I leave the tool bag in the car and the car in the next street and head into the house.

"Just in time, Edmund, I was going to make some cheese on toast. Would you like some?"

"Love some, Nan. Can I have some onion on mine too?"

"Of course, dear, go into the front room, and we can watch one of your CIS programmes together if you like whilst we eat them."

"*CSI,* Nan, *CSI.* Sounds perfect."

I am sure she gets it wrong to make me smile. I go in and put *Criminal Minds* on. Penelope is hot with brown hair. Like smart hot. Not hot hot.

Chapter 11

The Nan alarm wakes me up. I lie on my bed staring at the ceiling; I can hardly believe the day is here. This is the day that all my dreams start to become true. I almost leap out of bed. I am dressed and downstairs in under ten minutes. Nan is at the stove making sausage sandwiches. Perfect way to start the day. I walk up behind her and give her a big hug.

"Morning, handsome, are you excited about your trip to Scotland today?"

"Morning, Nan, I am. I really am."

I sit down at the table and wait for my breakfast. She brings it over with the brown sauce. She knows exactly what I want. When I want it.

"Now, don't forget to ring your nan whilst you are away, will you? I haven't been without you for a long time, Edmund, and I am going to miss you a lot."

"I won't, Nan. I will try and ring you every day?"

"Don't worry if it is not every day. I want you to be having fun with your friends, but send me one of those text things, and I will learn to reply to you on them."

I give out a little laugh, it's actually a real laugh, I am not faking it. I must be really happy today. This is the beginning of something. And I love the thought of my nan learning to text at her age. She is so cool.

"Do you want me to come and see you off at the school?"

"No, that's fine, Nan, I know Wednesday is Oxfam day. They won't cope without you."

"It is, but I am sure they won't mind."

"It's OK, besides nobody else's parents are going to be there."

Damn, shouldn't have really said parents, that might upset her a little to think about Mum? If it did, it didn't show. She just kissed me on the cheek and went back to the washing-up.

"Is there anything you would like back from Scotland, Nan?"

Let's change the subject. Quickly.

"Just you, sweetie, just you. Oh, and one of those Loch Ness monster trophies, that could be quite fun. I always wondered about him. Swimming around that big lake all on his own. Very sad really."

She is smiling over at me.

"He is definitely real, Nan, and I am sure he has a girlfriend with him. Both called Nessie. I will see if I can get a picture with him. Or the both of them. On a date like."

We both have a chuckle at that. I am going to miss her. But I will be back in a couple of weeks once I am famous, I am sure. She has washed up and is out of the house before I finish breakfast. I am not surprised, she gave me six sandwiches. Think she thinks I will starve when I am not here. I walk into the living room and stick on the BBC. No news about Melanie. In fact, no news about the Mersons either. That has really gone quiet, they must have done a right number in putting the police off my scent. They were nice people. I should visit them again soon. Maybe stay the night. She was great in bed, Mrs Merson. A true professional at that.

I can't get last night out of my head. I don't want to get a reputation for being poor in the sack. I am a god when it comes to the ladies. I think either Melanie was just that bad or Miss Walker has got into my head more than I care to think about. Either way I am not seeing any of them for a couple of days. Today I need to start my journey. For once it's all about me.

I turn off the TV and head upstairs. I check through the go bag. Nearly six hundred large, couple of black outfits, and some phones. I grab my laptop and place it in the bag. I go into the bathroom and empty all my toiletries into my suitcase for the journey.

That's it, I am ready. I grab both bags and head downstairs. I grab a bottle of water from the fridge for the journey, and then head out of the house. I walk down the road and then place both bags in the boot of my car. I then turn and return to the house. I forgot to leave Nan a note. She will like that. Knowing she was the last thing I thought of when I left the house.

I go into the kitchen and pull off a piece of kitchen roll.

I write *See you in two weeks, don't worry, Nan. Love Edmund Carson xxx* I then sign it at the bottom. That signature's going to be worth something one day so that's a nice keepsake for her. She will probably frame it and put it in the hallway for when her friends come over. I will sign one for her friends too when I return. Probably half price for them.

I head back out of the house and into the car. I can't believe how happy I am. I have a car, some money, and all the things I need to become famous. This is how movie stars must feel. The world at their fingertips.

I start the drive to London. It takes me about an hour, but then I am here. I pick a hotel in Leicester Square. It's easy for all the tubes, and has secure parking so I know no one is going to break into my car. They won't let me check in so I take a walk for a while. This place is so busy. At home I could walk down the street for ten minutes and not see a soul. Here, I can't move for people bumping in to me. Every nationality as well. Half the people I can't understand, but that's good. I can be famous in London and then worldwide very quickly. Everyone will be talking about me.

I need one of those secure places to stash some of the money. I am never going to concentrate whilst that money sits in the car. I get out my phone and google safety deposit boxes. There are lots: Metropolitan, Chancery Lane. All no questions asked. Must be a lot of dodgy people in London, that is all I can say. There is one within walking distance. I go back to the secure parking, and grab my Umbro bag. I walk down the street and head into the security box place.

Three large for eighteen months. Fuck!

You have got to have money, just to hide money. Access twenty-four-seven, that's a good thing. I stash four hundred large in there and a burner phone for when I need it. Feel a bit like James Bond. All spies have safety deposit boxes, don't they? Maybe I should have got a false passport as well. That's what they all have, don't they? Where do they get them from?

I still can't check in for another two hours. I head back to Leicester Square. I have time to start on my social network plan. When I am famous I intend to get more followers than the President of the United States. Need to keep them entertained so it's all about the selfies and the jokes. If I keep posting pictures about me, what I am doing, I will get even more famous. Quotes are good also. Those soppy loving ones. The girls will love them. They will all think they are about them.

But I don't start it until I am ready. I need the world to be watching all at the same time. Leicester Square is a perfect place to start. I go to the cinema in the centre. It is where they hold all the premieres. They are setting up for one. I take a selfie outside. Then over to M&M's World. Maccy D's, that one is for my parents. I walk down to the horses and Ripley's, believe it or not, I am probably going to be in there one day. People won't believe how good I am. How great I became overnight.

That gives me an idea and I head over to the London Eye and Tower of London. More selfies, even one with Jack. I could sense he was impressed. These are going to go down so well once I have launched myself. I will be posting every day so I need lots of them. Should have brought a change of clothes, how cool would have that been. They will never know where I am.

Fuck it's three p.m. already!

Time has flown. I head back to the hotel and check in. Hang my clothes in the room, plan is to stay for at least the two weeks. I am seeing Miss Walker, but I will just stay down there without checking out. I can get there on the tube from here she

160

said. Don't want to be checking in and out all the time. That will draw attention. I don't want that. Not yet.

I sit on my bed and go through all my selfies. There is nothing more of a distraction to the authorities than posting a selfie from somewhere knowing full well you are not going to be there when they arrive.

I pull my bag out and get my outfit: black shoes, black socks, black trousers and pants, black T-shirt and a black hoodie. I stand and look in the mirror. The hoodie is two sizes too big so it really drowns out my face. I go back to the bag and pull out the hunting knife that I bought. I spin it in my fingers as I look in the mirror.

"Northern line night of horror. Knife attacks kill seven. The subway killer."

No, none of them are right. I think I will wait and see what the press comes up with tomorrow, and then I need to run with that.

I place the knife in my pocket, and head out of the hotel room.

I then head back into the hotel room, take off my shoes, and sit on the bed to watch TV. It's four thirty in the afternoon. Hardly going to wreak havoc at rush hour.

Luckily the hotel has Sky. So *CSI*, *Criminal Minds* and *NCIS* are everywhere. The rest of the evening is back in research mode until it gets to nine thirty. That's when I head out into the night. Just like Jack. This is how he must of felt. This is so cool. My heart is really pumping.

Leicester Square is buzzing. With the amount of lights still going on, it could almost be daytime. I head over towards Chinatown and duck into one of the all-you-can-eat Chinese's.

Can't do this on an empty stomach. I watch as the hordes and hordes of people pile in and out as I eat my dinner. As soon as I am finished I head back down to the station. I jump on the Northern line and ride all the way to High Barnet.

I then take it back to Leicester Square. If I am going to do something tonight it will need to be at the latter end of the journey: Totteridge or Finchley or even Mill Hill East. The train empties more. Leicester Square is just too packed. I change platforms and head back to High Barnet. I walk up and down the sections of the tube waiting for an opportunity to present itself. By the time I get to Tufnell Park the train is basically empty, all bar three people. Now is the time.

There is enough distance between all three of them not to notice. The first is an Asian looking man. He has his headphones on his ears, the second is a woman who looks old enough to be my nan, and the third is another woman. Hot for an older woman. Not doable hot, but I am sure she used to be.

I walk past the guy with the headphones; I pull my knife out and slit him straight across the throat. He didn't see it coming, and his eyes were closed as he listened to the music. He grabs at his throat, but doesn't make a sound. The other two passengers are still facing in the direction of the tube so they don't see him. I carry on walking. I sit down next to the old lady, she turns to look at me, probably to say something, and I plunge my knife into her throat. I watch as she looks at me. I sense a thank you on her lips, but I don't hear it. The blood is now dripping down my hand from the knife. It's amazing how nobody on the tube looks at each other. That is two down and the woman at the front still hasn't moved. I turn my attention to her, the older once doable woman, and carry my walk up the carriage. Before I get to her the tube stops. We are in Archway, and she is getting off. Worse than that, there must be a dozen people getting on. Who gets on here? It's in the middle of nowhere. I need to get off. I can't be the only person left on the tube. I put the knife back in my pocket and get off.

Shit! Shit! Shit!

Got to get out of here before anyone notices. I walk fast up to the barriers and out. I don't want to run in case it draws attention to me. As the tube pulls out I can hear screaming. I don't think it's the last time I am going to hear that sound. It might be cheering?

As I get out of Archway, I decide to head back towards Leicester Square. Have to walk as I don't want a cab driver saying they picked me up. I walk back to Kentish Town. I skip out Tufnell Park as it's too obvious. I am back on the tube and heading back towards Leicester Square. I am not sure two is going to be enough as an introduction. Problem is it's a long way to Morden or somewhere like that. Unless I take a risk on a busy tube. Is two enough? It's hardly terror. More trouble or a disturbance. Maybe just one more and get in and out? I wait until I am back in the region of Leicester Square. The tube is back to being packed like sardines.

There is a bunch of women who have been out on some kind of hen party. On a Wednesday, who does that? Everyone is packed so tightly together I can hardly get my knife out from under my coat. I do, and I plunge it into the nearest girl as the doors open. There is so much noise you don't even hear a scream. I am off and up the escalators before anyone notices. I am out of the station and back towards the cinema in a matter of moments. Nothing. No one is following me and I can hear nothing. I stand by the ticket office just to check that nobody is following. They are not.

I go over to M&M's World and go down the stairs. I like M&M's but only the peanut ones. I make a bag up and take it to the counter to buy. I notice there is blood on my hands. I dry it against my hoodie, and then pay for the sweets. My treat to take back to the hotel. When I arrive back at the hotel I grab some water from the fridge and sit on the bed. I think the orange ones actually taste like orange, is that weird? Smarties are the same? Is it just my mind playing tricks on me or is it really orange flavoured? Odd.

I make that eleven!

If you include my parents. I grab my notebook. That's the same as Jack already. Day one. Four behind the cook and the doctor if you only take into account the true number. All these hypothetical numbers don't make any sense. He is also fifteen until someone proves to me otherwise.

Tomorrow I need four and I am equally famous on day two. Day two. Now, there is an achievement. I get undressed and lay my costume back in the bag and put it under the bed. I don't want room service finding it. I shower and lay on the bed and switch on the TV. *Wolf of Wall Street* is on. I have seen it, but I watch it again.

My nan says I remind her of a young Leonardo. Maybe they will choose him to play me in the movie that they make about me. He is good-looking enough. I don't think there are many that could be as close. Although the movie will be, what, four years away. He may be a little too old to play me then. Will need someone younger and hotter. More lifelike.

I wake up at three minutes past seven. How spooky is that! Must be some kind of internal clock thing that makes me wake up the same time as my nan. I grab my phone and text her *good morning*. That way she won't worry about me. It takes a few minutes, but I get a text back with *love you, handsome* on it. And a kiss. I love the fact that my nan now knows how to text. How cool is that. I pick up the phone and order room service.

Purposely not turning on the TV until I am set up. I want to remember my opening debut as a landmark event. I wait impatiently whilst my breakfast arrives. Once the waiter has gone, I set myself up on the bed with my breakfast, and Switch on the BBC.

The princess is having another fucking baby!

What are they, rabbits? I wait for the headlines to come up. Nothing.

Then the local London news. Finally. Stabbing on the subway. I listen to the report. They report for less than a minute. They have come up with two separate stabbings: the first believed to be gang-related as the Asian guy was part of a gang and they believed the older woman witnessed it, and the other a stabbing of a girl on a hen night out. Believed to be a robbery gone wrong.

What the FUCK!

They don't even mention the outfit. No nickname or anything. Not even made the main news. What is the world coming to when this isn't even a major crime? I am well pissed off. I flick through the other channels. Doesn't even get a mention on ITV. Sky News is leading with a piece on safety on public transport, but no mention of me or last night.

At least there should be a nickname, like the black hoodie. Not a person has even mentioned what I was wearing. I am like the third most famous person in the UK history, what is the matter with you people? That's put me right off my food. I switch off the TV and lay on the bed staring at the ceiling.

How did they even miss the costume? Surely, this is London, they will have at least had CCTV on the tube or in the stations. I knew three wasn't enough? It just didn't hit home enough. And four won't either. If they don't give airtime to this, then how am I supposed to become famous?

The fucking cards!

Maybe it's because I didn't announce myself? If I had left cards at both the scenes they would have known that it was the same person. That's what I need to do. That is what I said I was going to do, but I got overexcited about the day and forgot. I need to find one of those booths that prints like a hundred cards. I am sure there is one in Leicester Square. I passed it on the way to the Chinese. I eat a piece of toast, it's all I want now. I don't deserve scrambled eggs and bacon this morning.

I need to capture the momentum as I have started now. I get dressed and leave the hotel. Heading to the back streets near Chinatown where I saw a photocopy place. Yes, make your own cards. I stand outside the shop thinking about what they are going to say. I have no idea. I was hoping all those media types were going to help me with today's headline. But I am a not today's headline. I can't go in until I do. I walk about a bit. This place is so loud and so busy, how is a guy supposed to think and plan his future here?

Maybe I should have stayed at home and launched my career from there. You know local boy done good and all that.

It makes headlines. The Mersons are still headlines. But not in fucking London. I keep walking trying to clear my head.

How about just 'ONE' in big black letters. I will be number one very soon anyway. Then there is no mistaking it. I am the ONE. The Only ONE. Number ONE. ONE Man. ONE Crusade. ONE Master. There are so many puns that can be made about the Number ONE. Think they have already made a song about the number ONE. They will probably start to play it when they give press releases or talks.

I can play it when I start making videos for YouTube and stuff. I have my own background music and everything. Yes, that's cool. Number ONE is definitely the name. I head back to the photocopy shop and make my cards. I toyed with the idea of hashtag before the number ONE for a moment but I don't want to be limited to one social media. There are millions out there that need to hear and see my work. I need to be king of all social media.

I head back to the hotel. I am hungry now so I order breakfast again as it is on till eleven. I eat it in my room. There is still very little on the TV about the event of last night, but I blame myself for that. I didn't think it through enough. Tonight will be different. I will change the line, probably Piccadilly or something. Heathrow to Cockfosters, there must be plenty of opportunities on there. I lay back on my bed. Need to go out and do some more selfies around London. Maybe Buck House, Big Ben, that sort of thing. I am still a bit disappointed about this morning, but I need to get over it. There is a knock at the door.

"Room service."

I open the door and there is a cute little Spanish woman there with towels. My first thought is one of fun, but my second says I will have to check out. I let her in and head out. The day is spent taking selfies around London. Done it all. All the main tourist places. Then back to the hotel.

That's a point: I need to download all these pictures. I pull up my laptop and do just that. As soon as I am famous, going to have to go to burner phones. I download everything. I pull my bag from under the bed and grab my costume and my knife. I dress and stand in front of the mirror.

"Tonight, Edmund, you become the number ONE. The Special ONE. The Famous ONE. Just the ONE."

I hold the card up to the mirror and smile to myself. Never really thought there was a point to business cards, but clearly there is. People need to remember you, and I am not going to be ONE to be forgotten.

"Tonight is the night, the night I become a legend."

I leave my hotel room and head towards the station for the Piccadilly line.

Chapter 12

Three minutes past seven. I tell you, that woman has it ingrained in me. I lay on the bed. I am still fully dressed. I look up at the ceiling and smile.

Oh my fucking god! Last night, fucking amazing.

Five, five in one night makes me, wait for it, Number ONE. On my second day, number ONE in the charts. I kick my legs and wave my hands around as I lie on the bed. That is amazing. Imagine where I am going to be when I am like three years into this. Jack, the doctor, the cook, all now left in my wake and can't even increase their numbers as they're all dead or in prison. Me, I am out, and my number is going to be huge.

I need to start researching the biggest serial killers the world has ever known, because at this rate, I am going to be world number ONE. I am UK number ONE. I am a legend.

I order breakfast and jump into the shower. By the time I am out of the shower it has arrived and I place it on the end of the bed. The moment of truth has arrived. BBC News. Click.

Terror on the Tube are the first four words that come out of the TV. There will be more in the next bulletin...

Yes! Yes, fucking yes!

I stop dancing for a minute and sit on the end of the bed eating my breakfast. Oh, I love scrambled eggs and bacon. I am eating like I have never tasted food before. I get flashbacks to that sandwich I had with Caroline and the one with Sophia. They were amazing. I should have had more of them.

Food must taste better when you are happy. It must do. I almost wolf the whole thing down in less than a minute.

Here we go, here we go, main headlines. I turn the TV up a little.

"And back to our main headline for today. *Terror on London Tube lines*. In the past twenty-four hours London police can now confirm the death of seven people."

Seven, no eight, eight people, get it right. I am Number ONE.

"Wednesday, two people were killed and a third seriously injured whilst travelling on the London Underground. Last night, we can confirm that a further five people were stabbed to death in what is being called the biggest attack on civilians since 7/7. We can cross live to Chief Constable Adrian Moore at South Ealing tube station for the latest update."

It was eight, fucking eight, I am number ONE. I turn the TV up some more.

"Last night, between the hours of ten and eleven p.m., five people were brutally stabbed to death on the London Underground. These attacks were unprovoked. We are asking for anyone travelling on the tube at that time that may or may not have seen anything to come forward. We have these images of the assailant or assailants. Believed to be between five eleven and six foot one, young, athletic, and male Caucasian."

I am fucking six foot six feet. And there is only ONE of me. It's on the fucking card. What is up with these morons? I take a big breath. At least they got the costume this time. That's a plus point.

"We believe this to be the work of a gang calling themselves the ONE. They have left this calling card."

My calling card is on TV, that is so cool. Wait, did he say gang?

"It is early days, but I can confirm this attack is similar to a chain of murders on overland trains in Texas nearly three years ago. We will be working closely with the US authorities to catch these people. At this time we ask you to be vigilant, and only travel on the tube if it is paramount that you must do so. Any eyewitnesses who would like to come forward there is a helpline and a website on the bottom of your screens now. You will be treated with the utmost confidentiality."

FUCK! What the fuck is going on? I am not a gang. I am one person. For fuck's sake, I left you a card with ONE on it!

I can't believe this. I can't believe they got it wrong again. And what's this crap about like someone else. I am not like someone else, I am me. And the goddamn best at this. And what was it about seven. Yesterday I am sure they said three, three people. I am number ONE. I am the best. I couldn't have spelt it out any clearer.

Why is all this happening to me? It's like they don't give a fuck about what I am trying to achieve here or about me. How am I supposed to become the greatest that anyone has ever seen? It's not hard is it? I am putting all the work in here. I don't see anyone helping me.

All this is my own work, mine. Other people, they have entourages or something like that. People who help them. But me, no, I am doing everything myself. The bank, myself. The tools, myself, the fucking work, myself. Nothing, nothing from anyone. How can they think it is the work of a gang of people? Am I working too hard?

You can be assured as soon as I make it there will be people round the block trying to know me. They will all be wanting a piece of Edmund Carson, but fuck them, they don't deserve it. When the chips are down none of them deserve it, cause where are they now, eh? The press can go fuck themselves.

I lay back on the bed. I kick the tray off the bed and onto the floor.

Fucking gang. Where the fuck did they get that crap from?

There is a knock at the door.

"Room service."

"Not today, thank you."

"OK."

Like I want someone in here cleaning when my world is falling apart. What is up with the world? Why can't I just get what I want, when I want it?

I turn over and bury my head into the pillow. I am not happy.

Maybe I need a break. I have been working really hard lately. Not that anyone cares about that. Maybe I am burnt out. All the prep and everything takes its toll. You hear about stars being burnt out all the time.

It was eight, it was definitely eight since I have been here. I am number ONE. I am the only ONE.

I am going to Miss Walker's today anyway. Maybe a couple of nights off will make it better for me. I mean, what with Melanie, and her performance. She is affecting my head. For a moment I thought I was the problem, but it was her, and maybe the stress she caused me.

Wait, Melanie?

Nothing on Melanie. Is that what it is? Is that the reason they haven't got it yet? Because they didn't know I had begun. I left the message, but they haven't found her. I grab my laptop and search for any news from home. Nothing. Surely it's been like three days, someone must be looking for her? She can't be that alone, can she?

Although, I have to say, at the end she was a little needy, all that talk about girlfriends and being in my song. Maybe I need them to connect the dots from the beginning to the ONE. They will have my fingerprints on both.

Well, they will have fingerprints on both; they just won't know that they are mine. I need to do everything I can to get them on the right track, and get this thing going.

I can use a burner phone to call them. I grab the bag from under the bed and open one. With the ten-pound top-up from Tesco, it's live.

Perfect.

I dial 999.

"Accident and Emergency, which service?"

"Police, please."

"One moment."

Oh, you do know the word ONE then. I am surprised. One may mean a few for you now. A gang.

"Hello, how may we help you?"

173

"Excuse me, I know I shouldn't be ringing the police but it's my daughter, you see, Melanie Epsom. I can't seem to get hold of her, and I have rung her place of work and they have told me she hasn't been in for a couple of days. I have nobody else to call. I would try to travel to see her, but I live in Spain. I have been so worried. It's not like her. She calls me every day you see, without fail, and I can't get hold of her."

"OK, sir, can you tell me the address and we will send a police car for stopover."

Fuck! I don't know the address

"Oh dear, it's number 6, I know that. It's in Middleton, Essex. It's around the corner from the main bank, Middleton Bank in the high street. She works there, they will know. Oh, I feel so silly now not knowing my own daughter's address, Officer. What must you think of me? If you give me a minute I am sure I can dig it out from somewhere."

"It's not a problem, sir, we all forget things."

Thank fuck for that. Where was I going to dig it out from? Sometimes I need to control the crap coming out of my mouth.

"Thank you, Officer. If you could tell her to ring I would be ever so grateful."

"We will, sir, I am sure there is nothing to worry about."

I hang up the phone and break it in half. That's what they all do on the TV.

Fucking nailed it!

Even had a quiver in my voice. Proper little old man style. There must be something to do with acting that I can't do? But I haven't found it yet. That should start it.

That was it, wasn't it? They didn't know I had started so now they will. And they will tie it all back to Melanie and start

174

thinking more clearly. I can't believe I am having to help them this much. The CSI team don't get help, and they always manage to sort it all out. Even Jessica Fletcher would have tied this together by now. Scooby-Doo, for fuck's sake.

I still need the weekend off. I deserve the weekend off. I switch off the TV. I don't need depressing any more. I grab my luggage and pack enough for the weekend. I also pack my costume. I am coming back from Wimbledon on Sunday night so there are plenty of opportunities for me to bring my number back to the top. I need to keep working. Despite how stupid they are. I leave the hotel and head for the tube station. I expect to see it crawling with police, but it's not. The Metro newspaper is being handed out, and there is a picture of me on the front of it. Well, I know it's me. It's just a person in a black hoodie. I pick up a copy. Think I need to make some kind of scrapbook. Or one of those online ones for when this all takes off. I am sure people will want it for the film. Newspaper clippings, all that sort of thing.

I get on the tube and head to Wimbledon. It's so much busier in the day. Maybe I should work out a way of doing something in the day. Maybe the tube isn't the best idea. The damn press have my head all over the place. How do they not recognise the same killer when he strikes two nights in a row? That Hannibal guy, they recognised his work. Maybe I should be more like him. More shocking. Am I too reserved in my work? I get to the end of the line and get off the tube.

I jump in the nearest cab and give the man the address of the village next to Preton High School for gifted girls. Fifteen minutes later I am in the village. I find the house that backs on to the school. I knock. I knock again. I can hear someone inside, but they don't seem to be answering. I knock again.

I peer through the window and she seems to be dancing to music whilst hoovering the front room. She is so hot. Even as she is cleaning she is hot. I stand and watch her for a while. I tap on the window. She waves and points to the back door.

I walk around the back and slide open the patio doors.

"Oh, Edmund, you came."

She comes running over and hugs me.

"I would have let you in the front door, but I have just mopped the hallway, what do you think of our place? It's lovely, isn't it? I haven't stopped cleaning for two days but it's going to be worth it. I love it here, Edmund, the people are so friendly. Come on, let me give you the guided tour."

I follow Miss Walker around the house. It's tiny. My nan's house is bigger than this one. It has a living room, kitchen downstairs, two bedrooms, and one bathroom upstairs.

"It's lovely."

"It is, Edmund, and I start my new job on Monday which is going to be amazing, I can't wait for a new beginning, Edmund. Now, sit down and I will make us some lunch, and then we can go for a walk in the village. It's so lovely out there."

I sit down at the smallest kitchen table ever. Miss Walker starts to fix us a sandwich and some juice. I watch her as she glances around the kitchen. She looks so happy. It is clear she is not the cook in this relationship. What is she doing to that cheese? Wait, did I say relationship again? I get up and take over. I sit her back down. For a moment it makes me forget the disastrous start to my profession. I don't think she would be so proud of me if she knew how bad the last few days had been. I am amazing in her eyes and that can't change.

"So, how has your week been, Edmund?"

"It's been OK, Mi—" I stop myself. "It's been OK, Emily, I have had better, but it's been OK."

"And your grandmother?"

"She is good, thank you. That has reminded me to text her, to let her know that I have arrived safely though."

I take out my phone and text her. Just to say that I miss and love her.

"You are such a thoughtful man, Edmund."

I place a sandwich down in front of her and she smiles at me. I sit and we eat lunch. She talks about her new job, and how excited she is to be there. I am not really listening. All the time in my head I am thinking about how I can get the ONE more publicity. How can I get them to understand ONE means Number ONE? The only ONE. Not some jumped-up gang from Texas. I am the ONE. I like The ONE. Sounds good.

After lunch we take a walk. The village is really quiet, hardly saw a person, and we must have walked for a good hour. Nothing like Leicester Square.

We arrive back from the walk. She takes my hand and leads me upstairs.

"Now, Edmund, this is the first time in our new home, so let's make in memorable."

No pressure then. I am sure it was Melanie. Not me. I will be amazing.

She slowly starts to undress me, and I do the same to her. The sight of her naked body has turned me on already. Just by standing there she is doing more for me that Melanie ever

177

did. What was up with that girl? She had so much to offer, but just didn't use it. Miss Walker could have taught her a thing or two. Would probably have made her lesbo though. I like the thought of them together. I just don't know if I could do a threesome thing.

We move naked over to the bed.

"Remember, Edmund, slow and hard," she whispers in my ear.

I am on top of her. I am inside of her. Oh, that feels good. I am slow, but I am so hard. With every thrust she makes a sighing sound. My name continues to roll off her lips as I move up and down, up and down. I find myself wanting to scream her name. Miss Walker, Miss Walker, over and over again. I open my eyes and she is looking directly at me. It's not weird. It is exactly where I want to be. I keep going. The smile from the corner of her mouth to the sparkle in her eyes has me captured. I seem to lose myself and time in her. She brings me back when she whispers in my ear.

"Are you close?"

"I am."

"Then together, go a little faster."

I do as she requests. I have flashbacks to our first time. How the harder and faster went. How we lost ourselves so much, we were nearly taking off. My momentum speeds up to the point that she is about to explode and so am I. We do together at the same time. I stay there on top of her. Her eyes are closed and she is exhausted. Seems a while later I eventually roll off her and lay staring at the ceiling.

"I needed this. I needed the break. The last few weeks have been so exhausting. I have worked so hard. It will be worth it, I know it will."

She turns on her side and starts stroking my chest. She is looking longingly into my eyes.

"This is the best place for you, Edmund. This is where it will all start. There is a calmness about the village. It will help you to see clearly what you need to do. You know what the world really wants to see. You just have to give it to them. When do you have to go back?"

"Sunday. I promised my grandmother I would help her with the church fete."

Sometimes I don't know where this stuff comes from. I just need to get back to work. I am in the limelight. Well, the gang are. I need to ensure that I keep it up, and get them to understand who I really am.

"Then let's make the most of the weekend, shall we?"

"Sounds good, Emily."

Wow, didn't mess up that time. She jumps out of bed.

"I forgot to show you the best part, Edmund, come on."

She goes over to the window and I follow.

"There is my school, how cool is that? It is within walking distance of the house."

In the distance is a big stately looking home. Looks like a king or a queen would have once lived there. It is impressive: Preton High School for gifted girls. The place that tried to take Miss Walker away from home. Away from me.

"We have about three hundred students, all girls and all live-in. It's very posh, Edmund. Much nicer than the school we were both at. That was dark and dingy compared to this, and it was full of people neither of us liked."

"Oi! That was my school you're talking about."

I grab her and throw her on the bed. Then I jump back on top of her.

"And it wasn't so bad, in fact, one of the teachers was quite hot."

"Oh yeah? Which one is that, Mr Carson?" She is smiling at me.

"Mr Smith."

She punches me in the arm and then we go again.

Thirty minutes later we are both spent. I turn over and she is already asleep. I cuddle behind her. I needed this. I needed time alone with Miss Walker...

"Edmund, Edmund..."

I can hear someone whispering in my ear. Nan?

"Edmund, there is someone downstairs."

It's Miss Walker, she is whispering in my ear.

"There is what?"

"There is someone downstairs. I can hear them moving around."

I come to my senses. I look over at the clock, it's half ten at night. What type of burglar risks this at half ten? I get out of bed and get my pants on. Then, I walk over to my suitcase and grab my hunting knife out of the bag.

"Edmund, what is that? Why do you carry that?"

Shit!

Didn't mean for her to see that. Should have put it behind my back.

"Just for protection. You never know in London, do you? All these attacks and things going on. It's just to be safe."

Don't think she was buying any of that, but that's not for now. Now there is someone breaking into our house. Never been burgled before. They should have checked who lived here first. This is on them.

"Wait up here, and don't come down until I say that it is clear. OK?"

"OK." She is nodding her head. I know she isn't that silly to follow me.

I creep down the stairs. I can hear the TV on. Did we leave that on? Or has the burglar broken in to watch TV? What kind of place is this village? I reach the bottom of the stairs and I can hear someone moving around. I think they are heading out of the living room and into the kitchen. I stand at the bottom of the stairs waiting for them to come past.

A shape comes around the corner. I strike and plunge my knife directly into his stomach. There is no resistance. He didn't know we were home. He places his hand on my shoulder, I pull the knife up through his stomach and as I do, I can smell it. The blood, it's so strong, there is so much of it.

There is a smash. I look down and he was carrying something, a glass. We are almost face-to-face now and blood starts to pour out of his mouth. The smell is intoxicating. He coughs, and it is in my face. That smell. That scent.

Fuck! I am aroused.

What the fuck, I am aroused? He is a bloke. That can't mean? He collapses on the floor in front of me. I stand on the stairs looking at him. An old man, I would guess? Must be like forty. The smell of the blood has me all in a dizzy spin. I come to my senses as quickly as possible. It has to be the blood, I am not gay. I like women. It has to be the blood. I have a woman upstairs for fuck's sake. Miss Walker, the hottest woman in the world. Definitely the blood. I watch him. He isn't moving any more.

"It's OK. I've sorted it, but don't come down as there is broken glass everywhere."

"OK. Edmund, are you OK?"

"Yes, I am fine. Won't take long. Let me clear it all up first."

I can't leave him here like this, she is going to go mad. She has just finished cleaning this hallway. I pick him up, and start dragging him to the kitchen. I have really sliced him as his insides are falling out everywhere. It looks like an alien has come out of his belly.

I get as far as the kitchen table and stop. I need to try to put it back in him. I lean over the body, and try to pack everything back in.

It fucking doesn't fit!

How is that even possible? It came out of him. It's just making a mess everywhere. I grab the big saucepan on the side and start cutting at him. If I can't put it back in I will take it out. I fill the pot with everything I can get from inside him.

The smell is amazing, there has never been this much blood anywhere. But I am not turned on by it. It's just the smell. Just the fucking smell!

It's in-between my fingers, under my fingernails. Everywhere. I pull the body outside. There is a little garden shed at the back of the garden. I pull the body into it and leave it in there. I then walk back to the kitchen. It's a mess, but I

182

am so glad it's tiled. Not like the Mersons' house, they would have spent weeks getting those stains out of the carpet.

I fetch a mop and bucket and start to clean up. I pick up the glass from the hallway. Who breaks in a house and fixes themselves a drink? What kind of nutter was he? I mean, come in, watch our TV and fix yourself a G&T, why don't you. Making himself at home in our home. Twat.

I mop through the hall, and the kitchen until you can't see the blood any more. Well, maybe a little bit, but you would have to look for it.

"Edmund, is it safe?"

"Yes, it's safe, you can come down now."

She walks into the kitchen and runs over and hugs me.

"Oh, Edmund, I was so scared. You are covered in blood. Are you OK? Are you hurt? What has happened?"

She is checking me all over to ensure I am not cut or hurt. I am not.

Fuck, quick, think!

"I don't think you will believe me if I told you."

Yeah, there is a great big possibility of that…

"It was only a wolf. We must have left a door open or something and it wandered in. I guess that is what life in the countryside is like. We must remember to lock up."

"A wolf? Really?"

"Yes, I know. I came down the stairs, turned the corner, and it attacked me. It's a good job I had my knife. I managed to stop it, but that's where all the blood has come from. When it jumped at me I must have gone backwards into the hallway."

"And you are not hurt? Edmund, you could have been killed."

"No, I am fine, honestly, just a little shocked. I mean a wolf, in our house."

She hugs me again. She likes the words 'our house', I am sure of it.

"What about the glass? I heard the smash."

"It must have been on the side and the wolf knocked it, trying to escape from me."

"Where is the wolf now?"

She starts to look around the room.

"In the shed. I will call animal control tomorrow and we will sort it all out, but it's not for tonight. I think we have had more than enough excitement for tonight."

She smiles and goes over to the sink to get a glass of water.

Who the fuck am I?

Peter the boy who cried wolf. And not to be funny, Miss Walker, how the fuck did you just believe that shit? Oh my god, I must be the most convincing liar in the world. I don't know where this shit comes from, I swear. Is there nothing I can't do? Or be good at? She is so lucky to have me.

I put my hands to my face in disbelief. The smell of fresh blood, and lots of it, nearly knocks me off my feet.

"Are you hungry, Edmund? We haven't had anything since lunch. And we have been exercising a lot."

That playful smile is back. She is like my nan. She knows what I want and when I want it. From food to sex. I suppose that is mainly what I want.

"Yes, a little. But sit down let me fix you something."

I have seen her kitchen skills. It's not why I like her. The smell of blood has my head buzzing.

"Oh, OK. Thank you. That would be lovely."

"Why don't you go in and watch TV as we left it on, and I will call you when it is ready. I will make something special."

"OK. That sounds even better."

She comes over, kisses me, and heads out of the kitchen.

What the fuck!

I am laughing to myself. That was unbelievable. I don't know if it's Miss Walker or the blood that has my head all over the place now. She is amazing, I can't believe we are here together. It's been two weeks. Two weeks and look where I am today.

The blood is so strong though. I pick the saucepan off the side to take it to the garbage out the back. As I do, the smell hits me. It's stronger than I have ever known. My eyes are blinking ten to the dozen. I stop. I don't want to throw this away. I take the saucepan back into the kitchen and put it next to the sink.

All I can think about was those sandwiches I made. The best sandwiches ever. With Caroline and Sophia. I look into the pot. Lots of insides. Lots of what are called entrails or intestines or something. I know you can't use them, they are awful.

"No, they are offal." I burst out laughing.

"Edmund, are you OK?"

She calls me from the living room. She clearly heard me talking and laughing at myself.

"Yes, fine"

I stop myself from laughing. I have no idea where that came from either. When you are happy you are certainly delirious.

185

I sort through the pan, and produce what I think is liver? You can eat liver, right? My nan buys it all the time. I find a carrier bag and throw everything else away. Leaving the liver in the saucepan and all the blood. You can cook in blood, I am sure of it. Black pudding is blood, isn't it? Or is that just a myth? I look around the kitchen and find some onions. Liver and onions is what my nan always makes, and some fresh bread we bought in the village earlier.

It was the bread with the blood that made those sandwiches taste so great. I stick on the cooker and it simmers away. I put it on low as I don't want it overcooked. I clean myself and the table and the rest of the blood up. Light a candle and find a bottle of wine. It's white. I am sure it's supposed to be red with red meat, but beggars can't be choosers. I dish up the food.

"It's ready."

She comes into the kitchen.

"Oh, Edmund, it looks lovely."

"Good. My nan likes it, so I thought we had better give it a try. You will love my nan when you meet her. She is an amazing woman."

"I can't wait, Edmund."

I pull out the chair for Miss Walker. She sits and I pour us some wine.

We clink glasses.

"No, Edmund let's do that again. You have to look the other person in the eye when you clink glasses or it's bad luck."

"Bad luck?"

"Yes, it's seven or ten years bad sex apparently."

We both laugh and clink again looking directly into each other's eyes.

I taste the food. It's the most incredible thing I have ever tasted. The blood is sweet and juicy and hot which adds everything to the flavour. The meat is tender and melts in your mouth.

"Wait, we didn't make a toast? Do you want to make a toast, Edmund?"

"Yes, OK, my toast is to a lovely weekend in the country, and the break we both needed. To your new job at the school. Although it is the school that made you leave town, and nearly took you away from me. I am glad that I am now here."

She is smiling at me. She wants me to be with her. This could well be the real thing for us. The lightning thing they always talk about in the movies. She has had it, I am sure. And I will probably get hit by it soon.

"Oh, and the number sixteen, without a doubt, the number sixteen. Just because I like the number."

Chapter 13

She doesn't look happy as she is waving at me. I think she wants me to live there with her, all the time? What is it with beautiful women and being alone all the time? Men always believe they have a string of men. Maybe that's a secret I have uncovered? Melanie was the same, and now Miss Walker. She could have a hundred men knocking her door down, but I guess not all of them are the same quality as me. Was fun though. Great weekend. I needed that. The pressure I am under lately. I need to ensure that I take time out to enjoy life a little. It can't all be about the work.

The cab driver doesn't speak a word all the way to the station. When we arrive I pay him and get out of the cab. I go into the male toilets in the station and perform a quick change into my costume. Have to go back to work. I know I am on sixteen, but the world doesn't. I want to have the number up to twenty tonight. That will have the press going all over the place.

The ONE alone will then be as big as Jack. I head on to the platform. Sunday evening and there are a lot of people around. Didn't expect this. I get on the tube. There is a space all around me. Why would that be? Nobody is coming to sit close to me. I watch as people get on and off the tube. By the time I get to Earls Court there is still not a single person near me. I smell my hoodie. Does it have something wrong with it? At Earls Court I see four other people get on, all dressed the same as me. All in black with black hoodies. There is also a circle of space around them. Do the people on the train think they are the ONE? Wait, are they cashing in on my fame? I ride the tube up to Edgware Road and then change. Circle line tonight. It's bound to have its opportunity the later it gets. The four pretenders aren't following either.

What the Fuck!

Two stops later and three more people get on dressed in black with black hoodies. Everyone is standing away from them. Do they all think this is a game? They are messing with my fucking career here. Wait, there are police on the tube as well now. They walk up to the three little shits and pat them down. I have my knife in its holdall. If they pat me I am going to be found out. I walk off the tube at Euston Square. I need to change lines. They are obviously looking after the central line. I take the walk over to Euston Station to hop back on to the Northern line.

Are you fucking kidding me!

Two gangs of people on the tube, all in black and more police. What is going on? I ride up to High Barnet. ONE, wannabes and coppers are still on the train. Aren't they getting off? Are they just riding this for fun? I ride back to Tottenham Court Road and jump on the Bakerloo. Epping is about as far east as I can go. There are no black hoodies on the train other than me, but everyone is giving me a wide berth. How am I supposed to do this if everyone is staring at me all the time? The train starts to empty, the further east I go. By South Woodford it's virtually empty. They are all sticking together on the tube. No spacing out of people and certainly nobody close to me. I start to walk down the train to get closer to them. There are half a dozen people left on the train. They all sit together and start a conversation as I get closer. They aren't making eye contact with me. I weigh them up. Three men and three women. Not together. I am good, very good, but I am not sure I could take them all in one go. I sit facing the floor. The tube comes to a stop, the doors open, and I wait till we move again to lift my head. Hopefully leaving me a much neater target.

FUCK!

The train is empty. They all got off. I bet it wasn't even their stop. I ride up to Epping and then go back to Leicester Square. This is a fucking waste of my time. I walk past M&M's World. I don't deserve a treat. I am a failure tonight. I get back to my hotel room, and straight to bed. I just lay awake staring at the ceiling. What am I doing wrong? I am number ONE now, and the world doesn't know who I am? I can't even go to work without someone copying my style. They have brought all the attention on to me in a bad way. If they would let me do my job I will then leave some fame for them. I turn over to go to sleep. Not the end of the weekend I was looking for.

An hour later I am awake again. There is lots of noise in the hotel. I get up and walk outside my room. Drunken people all over the place. Heading into rooms, out of rooms. I walk along the corridor and go down in the lifts. There are more in the foyer. I follow the noise, and find there is a function in the hotel. Some awards ceremony for short films. Must have been something to do with the premiere they were setting up. It's packed.

It's all black tie so I am hardly suited for the place. My hoodie is back in the room and I am just in black trousers and a black T-shirt. I watch as they all stumble about. There are some half-decent women in here. Half of them would get it. Don't know if it's because they are all dolled up though. I would probably feel different in the morning. It is fucking amazing what women can do with make-up nowadays. And with underwear, everything looks lifted and tucked in.

Don't have my knife or my hoodie. I head back upstairs. I lay back on my bed. I can't do anything. If I did I would need to check out and get another hotel somewhere. That's packing and everything. I think better of it and go back to sleep.

An hour later I am awake again. Someone is trying my door. There are giggles from the other side of the door so it's not the police. I get up and listen to the people outside.

"One four two four, we are one four four two, stupid."

The giggling continues, and they move on. I turn and grab my knife. As I open the door I can see the couple walking down the corridor. He is a skinny bloke and she is a blonde. I don't like blondes.

I follow as they turn the corner, and then another. This hotel is like a rabbit warren. They get to their door and giggle at each other as they try to open the door. It opens and they are going in. I run at the both of them. With one big hit I am in. I stab the bloke in the back around the kidney area, tug back on his head, and slit his throat. He isn't going to be screaming.

That fucking bitch is though.

He is on the floor. I jump over him, and grab her. My hand is over her mouth and she is frozen solid. She is silent. Her eyes are wide open and staring straight at me.

"Do you want to live?"

She is nodding yes to me as frantically as she can.

I slit her throat. Don't know why I said that in the first place. Feels like something you would say in a movie. Maybe the awards have inspired me downstairs. Maybe I should make more small movies? No, I am a motion picture kind of actor. The big screen.

When they are making the movie about me, I must remember to have lines like that in there. You have to have catchphrases and things that people will remember. Need to ensure that on the social media stuff as well. One-liners – they go down real well. I suppose that is two more to the number. That puts me clear in front of them now. There is no mistaking it. I sit on the edge of the bed. I sit and think about how I am going to ensure the world knows that all this is me. They need to know I am winning. Five, ten minutes must go past. They start to wake up. I can tell.

"Thank you, both. I thought for a moment that tonight was going to be a total bust."

They are still in shock. I am not surprised. They didn't know they were going to be meeting me tonight. Probably should have worn the hoodie.

"I mean, you wouldn't believe how bad the tube was tonight. I am almost thinking of changing it up a bit. You know, do something different. I do kind of blame myself a little. I think the costume may not have been the right idea.

Kind of stands out, doesn't it? I know you can't appreciate the whole thing as I don't have my hoodie on, but I was thinking when I was downstairs, imagine if Clark Kent walked around in Superman's costume all day. You would know who he was, wouldn't you? I brought it on myself a little, I know."

"Thank you, at last. Yes, black is slimming. I do try to work out whenever I can. I did think that when I was studying for a costume as well. I don't know, it is tempting, and you are a very beautiful woman. I don't want to offend you, but I don't really like blondes."

I hope that didn't come across too harsh? It must be upsetting to her.

"I am sure you were expecting it tonight. No, I am not sure why? Maybe because my mum was a blonde? Maybe it has something to do with that. The thought of sex and a blonde and my mum. Not something that I want to imagine."

I shiver at the thought of that. It's bad enough imagining Mum and Dad together, without me in the mix.

"For sure, yes I will, I will leave you to go at it though. He seems a nice guy?"

I get off the bed. The smell in the air is blood and lots of it. I must admit it is turning me on a little, but blonde, yuk.

I pull the sheets back off the bed and throw them on the floor. I walk over to the blonde and undress her. I give a little lick at her neck as I do. It's sweet, but even that tastes different. Maybe blondes are sourer. She only has a dress on. No underwear? She was obviously out looking for it tonight. I lay her on the bed. I stand back and look at her for a while. Some part of me says experience is good, and change is good.

But, no. The shiver returns. Someone must have walked over my grave.

I grab him from the floor. Very quiet, he hasn't said a word since I got here. Obviously the strong silent type. That's what she was looking for.

"Are you OK?"

As I lift him up his head almost falls off his body.

"Fuck, sorry, I didn't mean to go that deep. It was the excitement of coming in. Sometimes I do get carried away a little."

No wonder he hasn't spoke, I have cut almost through his neck. I must have cut his vocal cords. I drop him, and walk over to the desk. I grab the pen and pull a piece of paper off the pad. I write on it: *Do you want to have sex with the blonde?* I show him the piece of paper. I can tell by his eyes he does.

Twat! He is not deaf.

He just can't speak. No idea why I did that. I get him undressed. As I do, his keys and a lot of change fall out on the floor. Once he is undressed I put him in position, on top of the blonde. He is semi-hard so I help him get in.

"Now, I don't think there is much more that I can do for you guys."

There can't be, for fuck's sake, I stuck it in for him…

"Let's face it, he isn't going to be a screamer, is he?"

I walk back over to the change and keys, pick them up and put them on the side. As I do I notice something else. I can't believe it.

Cheating fuck!

He is married. His wedding ring was in his pocket. I don't think she has seen it. Now I am confused about what to do.

They are at it like a couple of bunnies. Should I tell her he is married? Maybe she already knows? Either way it could be a massive mood killer.

Na, not my place. Each to their own and all that. I head towards the door. I stop before opening it. How are they going to know this is me also? There is no calling card and it's against MO. Do I just leave it and stay in the hotel or do I make an example of it? Tough decisions. I head back into the room and grab the room key from the floor. I go back to my room. Pick up some cards and my black hoodie. I go back to their room. They are still at it on the bed.

"Sorry, don't mind me, carry on."

"No, I am sure. As much fun as it looks, threesomes aren't really my thing. Nearly did once though with a friend of mine's parents actually? He really wanted me to, but, no, it's a little creepy for my tastes."

"I know, who would believe some of the situations I get myself into?"

"I just need to get to the wall behind the bed, carry on without me."

I grab my hoodie and a business card, and with my knife I stick both of them to the wall behind the bed. It's a good job I did shop and bought several outfits and knives if I am going to be leaving them as calling cards.

The bloke falls off the blonde as I try to get off the bed.

"Are you two done already?"

I go over to the desk and compose a note:

Dear Sir/Madam. Just wanted to point out the ONE is not a gang from Texas. I am the ONE and I am the only ONE working alone at my chosen profession. I already am Number

ONE and hopefully look forward to becoming bigger and better in the future. Kind regards, The ONE

I nearly wrote Edmund there. Fuck, that would have been so funny. I read it out to them.

"Yes, I think that covers it. It doesn't say who I am or where I am, it just helps them a little more on their journey. Where do you reckon? The wall? The bed? The desk?"

"I guess the bed is the first place they will look. You have been so helpful."

"Really, again? OK, I can help him get back on."

I set them back up on the bed, and place the note at the foot of the bed. Then turn to leave. It's going to bug me that I didn't tell her. She has been very supportive. I think she needs to know. She probably does, but it's playing on my mind. I walk over and whisper in her ear.

"He is married. Sorry, I thought you should know, as you have been so nice."

"Get out of here. You are too?"

Fuck, didn't expect that. I smile and leave them at it. I am sure both their partners won't be happy when they are famous tomorrow. I head back to my room. I strip down, shower, and lie back on the bed. Not the night I expected, but I didn't waste any of it. Have to check out tomorrow now though, can't be found in the same hotel. I then need to decide what to do about the ONE. I drift off to sleep.

Three minutes past seven on the dot my eyes open. I wonder what it would take for me to sleep till nine. Think my nan has drummed this into me. I get up, dressed and out of the hotel in about twenty minutes. Not picked up my car yet because I want a Maccy D's breakfast. I walk to the corner opposite M&M's World and go in. I order an Egg and Sausage McMuffin meal, and an OJ. The single always tastes better than the double. How odd is that? You would think more would taste better. I pull out my phone and text my nan that I love and miss her. That should keep her happy for a couple of days. I then head back to my car and drive out. I drive south. No reason, it was just the way the road was taking me. I don't know what to do about the ONE. It's captured the imagination of the city, I am sure of it. But it will now be increasingly hard to continue doing it. I think I created a brand image overnight. That's the problem when you are so great at everything you do. You're always going to be amazing and inspirational to others.

I carry on driving. I look up at the road signs and see I am headed back to Miss Walker. Am I doing this on purpose or is that just a coincidence? Is it love or something? I suppose, if I need a place to think this is as good as any. I head to the house knowing full well she would be at work anyway. I pull up outside, go round the back, and through the patio doors.

She said she always leaves them open. I sit in the front room. Need a plan. I go and get my notebook and look through it. Along with the don't dos for getting caught it has a list of the ways to become famous. The best of the best. I read through them. I think I have bettered every one of them in a matter of a few days by creating the ONE. That can't be a good sign. Maybe the ONE can continue, but not the image.

If the hoodie and the tube have gone, maybe the ONE is on vacation. I think I have limited myself too much. Telling the police what I look like and where I am going to work isn't the best idea. They need to be surprised by me. They need to

197

see my creative nature. Miss Walker always said I could do anything I put my mind to. She is, in her own little way, inspirational as well. Being with her, being here, does make me feel more comfortable. This may be the place the magic starts in me.

Holidays, that is when you are most relaxed. Maybe that's it. I grab my phone and google seaside near here. Brighton is the closest. It's fifty miles south. I can be there in an hour and ten. That's the plan. I get up and walk into the kitchen. Grab some paper off the side and write her a note:

Missed you so popped past for a kiss, but was too late. Enjoy your first day. Edmund.

That is going to make her weak at the knees when she gets home from work.

I close the patio behind me and head to Brighton. It's just about lunchtime when I arrive. I drive along the front and there is hotel after hotel. I pass the pier on my right-hand side and then I see it: The Legends Hotel. Must be where I need to stay as I am already a legend. I park in their car park and then go into the hotel. I pay for the week. I tell the girl on reception I might not stay for the week, but I will pay anyway. Forty quid a night B&B can't be bad, can it? And well under my three-year budget.

The big question is, what is next? I walk out of the hotel and end up back on the front looking at the sea. It's not quite the Caribbean and it's dark and dingy, but at least it is the sea. Reminds me of holidays they used to take me on, to Butlins. Loved the place. Always entertainment, and we would eat burgers and hotdogs for a week. But it was always cold and blustery out by the sea.

Also going in late September never helped that cause. I don't understand, with all the money they had that we never went further than Skegness or Bognor? We should have been in Jamaica or Bali.

I walk along the pier and watch as the people feed coins into the machines. It's a grim looking place, but it's quite busy. A lot of kids? Must be some kind of holiday or something. Kids' holidays are all over the place now. They change district to district. Think it's to do with holiday prices, something my nan was saying. I carry on walking down the pier. At the end I watch the fishermen as they cast into the sea from the beach. Who would want to eat fish out of there? Hardly looks somewhere edible to catch your dinner from. I certainly wouldn't want to stand in it.

A simple life though. If that's what makes you happy on a Monday lunchtime – a spot of sea fishing.

I turn and carry on walking down the pier. I am not sure what to do next, but the ONE needs to be known as not just a London terror. It will keep the police second-guessing where I am going to turn up next.

"Bobbleknob."

I look up from the ground. I know that voice. I hate that voice.

Carl fucking Carnegie!

He carries on walking with what must be his parents and his little sister Bethany. What the fuck is he doing here? Shouldn't he be on the school trip to Scotland?

Wait, there is no school trip to Scotland, I made it up. I made it up as we are due to be off school for two weeks. It's all coming back now. Wait, if we are off school why isn't Miss

Walker? Wait, private school or something. Live-ins, Edmund come on. At least keep close to sanity about the whole thing.

Our school is broken up for two weeks and that scum had to come here to ruin my break. Just when I was trying to get things going again.

"Oblong dick Oblong."

The man walking past just looks at me. Sometimes I need to remember to say things in my head, and not out loud. Carl is already well ahead of me. People will think I am mad or something.

Maybe, just maybe, I can turn this to my advantage though.

That's what the ONE needs. Oblong Fitz Oblong, the wannabe dragon slayer.

Chapter 14

I go to the end of the pier and sit in the café. I can see as everyone comes on and off the pier. About an hour later Carl and his family walk off. They head over the road and stop at an all-you-can-eat Chinese restaurant. I go to the bar next door and have a Coke.

Carl Carnegie!

I hate that kid. I can't believe he is here. How has that happened? How have we ended up in the same place? I suppose, practically it's the closest to the seaside from home, but still, here. I think he wants to be like me so much, he has started to think like me. Probably stalking me.

I wait for them to finish lunch, and follow them back to their hotel. They are in the Queens Hotel. I don't follow them in.

I walk back to my hotel, and go back to my room. I switch on the TV. How is there still nothing on the news about the hotel last night? It's like four p.m. I just don't know what I am doing wrong. Am I not big enough now? Does it not shock anyone any more? I blame television and computer games. I swear, we see too much of it, we don't know what is real and what is not. Every other movie is about it, and every video game out there is shooting people and zombies. I bet, if we were ever invaded by aliens with like flying saucers and shit, nobody would run. It would just be another day.

Maybe I just need to think bigger. Stage bigger. Be more dramatic. I have a plan to be more social. I will be using, YouTube, Twitter, Facebook, Instagram, but not until they are looking for me. I can't do their entire job for them. I want them all to be looking for my name. Nobody sends notes to the police saying hey it's me. I need them to announce me. I need the world to know I am a wanted man.

"Arrrghhhhhh!"

Shit, I think I said that out loud. I wait a minute. Nope, nothing, nobody heard me. I switch the TV over. All five channels. Five channels. Who has a TV like that any more? There should be at least Freeview.

Maybe it is out there? Maybe it's on *BBC News* or *Sky News*. I grab my laptop and open it up. No Wi-Fi. Where am I staying? I bet Carl Carnegie has Wi-Fi in his hotel.

I grab my laptop and head back out. It's still light, and I head to the local Harvester. It has free Wi-Fi. I order a mixed platter and a drink, sit down, and trawl the Internet for events on the ONE.

FUCK!

There must be a million postings on here and none of them mention me. Terrorists to Texans are getting all the praise for this. One guy even writes he thinks it is a group of women, by the build. I am fucking quite fit. Nobody has linked it back home. I despair at them all.

Wait, breaking news. The London-based gang known as the ONE have struck in a hotel in Leicester Square. More to follow.

The fucking gang!

Oh my god, I don't know what I have to do to lay this more open wide for them. Short of leaving a signed photo in the room, what else do they need?

At least they think I am London-based. Will have to ensure that they know I can also travel. Going to have to do something special. Bigger and bolder. I close down the laptop, eat my food, and drink my drink. Would have preferred Chinese earlier, but I am not eating it with him.

I go back to my room and change into my costume. I am not going out until it's dark, but I want to be ready. I lay on the bed and watch *Come Dine with Me* and *The Simpsons*. I don't know what people used to do before Sky TV. These channels are full of repeats and game shows.

I nod off for an hour and wake up when the news is finishing on Channel 4. Time to go. I leave my hotel and head along the front, past the pier, and to the Queens Hotel. Don't know why I am standing outside, don't even know if they are in there.

It's too cold to stay out here. The wind from the sea is going straight through me. I head back to the pier. I walk up it and back down. Never noticed it before but the sea only comes to about the last third of the pier. There are still people walking on the beach in the dark.

I can see torches and everything. I walk back down to the café at the end of the pier. Order a coffee as it's cold. Not that I like coffee. I sit watching the world go by. What am I doing here? I wanted to be bigger and better, and here I am in a holiday resort. People dressed up as if it was winter. It's March, for fuck's sake. March or April. Anyway it's not winter.

I have nowhere special to do anything. No trains. Can't really do another hotel so soon, as they will tie the two together. Although, I do want them tying everything together. I need to learn, as I pay in cash, to stop giving them my real name. It's really hard. Someone asks you your name and instantly it's the only name in your head. When I get home tonight I am going to write down ten names, and they can be the next ten people I become.

A bus goes past the window. I suppose I could do something on a bus? Problem is you have to wait until there are only a few people on the bus, and the driver will see you doing it. He will be looking back, pull over the bus and either run, telling them what you look like or, worse, stop and fight. Or lock the bus and you are trapped. No, buses don't make sense.

How about here? There are a half a dozen people in here? I could probably take two or three before they realised what was going on. I turn and look at the counter. I forgot about the bloke who served me. He is a bit big. He also looks like he has done a lot of time in prison. Has tattoos on his arms and neck. Who has tattoos on their neck? It's not like you can cover them up with anything. Other than a scarf.

Fuck, what am I doing here?

I can hardly become famous in Brighton. I take out my phone, go on to Google, and look up the top things to do in Brighton.

One. Hen and stag parties, that's the top attraction? It's Monday night, there are hardly going to be any of those about.

Two. Albourne Vineyard. Are you fucking kidding me? That's the second best thing to do here?

Three. A bird studio. Four. Kayaking. Five. Another vineyard. I carry on scrolling down. Museums, more wine, the football club. Number ten is actually a city walk. The tenth most popular thing to do in Brighton is go out for a walk. Not anywhere, just where you are now.

I keep going through them. More wine and churches. Wait, number thirty, a ghost walk in The Lanes. That could be good. Maybe as everyone is scared I could inject a little fear from the ONE. Leave some calling cards and stuff. That will make the press sit up a bit, and probably give Brighton a little custom off the back of my fame. I click into it. Starts in a pub. Seventy minutes' walk through all the back streets and Lanes. Perfect.

FUCK!

Closed Mondays. I swear, I have come to the only town in the country where I would be wasting my time. If I worked here nobody would be able to tell the difference. I guess this is it. This, the pier, is the only place in town that has anything going on. I counted like three bars just now, although one looks like an old ladies tea dance, and the other is karaoke.

I would be amazing at karaoke, but I can hardly get up there dressed as the ONE. No, the third bar should be the one. Horatio's or something like that. Live entertainment. I should go, sit in there, and see what else is going on.

I walk out of the café and head to the bar. As I do, I suddenly become aware again that I don't have any ID on me?

Well, I do but saying I am seventeen isn't really going to help. I get to the door and the guy on security lets me straight in. I am so chuffed. Clearly I look like a man of nineteen, even twenty. I walk in the door. There are kids running all across the dance floor. It's a kid-friendly bar. That doesn't help me. I walk up to the bar. There are half a dozen people behind the bar. I catch one of their eyes and order a pint of Guinness. I've never had Guinness, but I figured it sounds manlier than, a pint of lager, please. He is still looking at me. I am not sure he heard me or he is weighing up my age. He turns and comes back with a pint.

"Four fifty, please."

I hand over a tenner and he brings back change. I grab my drink, and walk back to the back of the room. I want to watch what is going on everywhere to see if there are any opportunities for the ONE.

I remember these discos. They used to bring me to them at Butlins. All kids, all running around for an hour before the main show used to come on. A couple of helpers showing us all the dances. I was great at them. Always had great co-ordination. I could have been a dancer. Or a children's entertainer. There are lots of them on TV nowadays.

The room is filling up. There must be something good on tonight. I look over at the bar. Something called Horatio's show for an hour, then a band, and a comedian after ten thirty when all under-twelves must leave. I am guessing he has the odd blue joke lined up.

I take a sip of my Guinness. It is close to the worst tasting drink ever. I remember my dad drinking this and he used to tell me that, Guinness is a drink you get used to. So I guess I should try harder. I take a bigger slug. It's better the second time. Not great, but better. I don't think I like alcohol. The G&T at Miss Walker's was bad, and the wine with Sophia. No, I don't think I like alcohol. I am going to just stick to beer from now on. I sit back in my chair. My head turns and about ten tables in the distance…

Carl Carnegie!

Just sitting there with his family. Mum and Dad and his sister Bethany. I often thought about doing her just to spite him. A year younger than me, but YUK! I don't think I could get his annoying face out of my head when I was. Maybe if I did her from behind. I think that is doable. She is not blonde.

They seem to be all laughing and having fun. I hate that. Pretending to have fun with your parents when you are on holiday. I go back to my Guinness. I take a bigger slug. I am not sure I am going to get the hang of this, but now I am thinking that I don't want to drink too much. Carl and his family are here. At a time when I need the ONE to become more famous away from London. That is like fate or something, isn't it? There is a reason my archenemy would turn up as I battle my need for stardom?

I sit back and watch. My hoodie is still up so no one will recognise me.

The show comes on. It's like the ones in Butlins, obvious jokes and some slapstick comedy. The band is someone called Freddie and the Dreamers. Never heard of them. Then Jim Davidson, never heard of him either, but there must be four hundred people in here so someone must know who they are. I watch as the Carnegies enjoy the show. They are even laughing at the silly jokes. So fake. I don't understand why they are not like a normal family, and sit in silence. Who are they showing off for? Nobody but me knows who they are?

Every twenty minutes the mum and the dad take it in turn to go outside. As one comes back, the other disappears. Given the smoking ban is now in full flow, I am guessing they have to walk to the end of the pier in order to smoke. I wait for his dad to stand up again.

Predictably he does. Must be addictive this smoking thing. I follow him. It's only a two-minute walk to the end of the pier. It's cold and miserable. I am not sure why people would want to come here on holiday. Maybe that's why they have so many museums as nobody wants to be outside in this weather.

Carl's dad lights up a cigarette. He is pacing up and down as he smokes. I am staring at my phone as if I am texting someone. I wait until he paces towards the underside of the pier. He does, in fact he remains there as if inviting me to join him. I don't need asking twice.

I walk up behind him, and bury my knife deep into his back. His legs buckle into me and I support him and carry on walking under the pier.

No fight or anything. I stab him a couple more times, and then slit his throat to ensure he doesn't call out. I can't believe how easy that was. I thought he would at least fight back a little. Probably just a loud mouth like his son. When it comes to it, no real substance.

I drag Carl's dad towards the water about halfway down the pier, watching for torches as I do. Nobody is stupid enough to be out walking on a night like this. Wait, I am on the beach on a night like this? I prop him up next to one of the pillars just in case. Maybe they will think he is an old drunk in the dark.

I start to walk back to the bottom of the pier. Wait, the blood? I didn't smell the blood? All I can smell is sea air, and fish and chips from the café. That's why it was a bit lacklustre, I didn't even enjoy it. Is that really the first time I have done this outside? I suppose the tube is also quite enclosed. I am not sure I like that, kind of makes it a non-event and if I am learning one thing lately it's that I need to start making these events. Else nobody is ever going to know that I am here. Let alone become my fans.

I stand at the bottom of the pier and wait. I am convinced at some point they will come looking for him. It took fifteen minutes. I knew they were faking the old happy families. Your husband is missing for fifteen minutes and you don't even notice. Pretending to have fun with your kids. Probably cheating on him anyway.

I stand with my back to the café as Carl's mum walks past. She isn't lighting up, she is just looking around. She is hot for an older woman. I can see why she has strayed elsewhere. I wait until she ends up in the same place as Carl's dad. Just enough around the corner for me to take my chance. This time I ensure that I enjoy it. My knife sinks straight into her throat and I pull it back. The blood's spurting everywhere. Even above the smell of the fish and chips. I lift her with one arm and take her down towards where her husband is waiting for her. She is still moving, so as I lay her down I help her to stop. They are both now resting. There is something about this.

It must take it out of them as much as it does me, as it seems a while before they thank me. They generally do, but it takes like ten, fifteen minutes.

They are a cute couple though. I can see what he saw in Carl's Mum. I bet she was a pretty girl when she was younger. I leave them both up against the pillar. I go back to the end of the pier and wait. It doesn't take long, and I can see Carl's sister walking down looking like a lost sheep.

Fucking Carl!

He is so lazy, I bet he made her come looking for her parents, whilst he sat pretending to enjoy the show. Again I lean against the café as she walks past. Looking directly at the road in front of me. Trying to blend into the background as I do.

"Hi, Edmund."

What the fuck!

How did she know it was me? My hood is up and everything.

"Hi, Bethany."

"I was thinking about you today. I didn't know you were also coming here on holiday?"

What? What is going on here? She was thinking about me?

"Yes."

"Are you with your nan? I saw her the other day in the town. She said she was coming, but not you. I did tell her we were shopping for holiday clothes."

Wait, you know my nan? You spoke with her? Wait, did my nan tell me this story? Is that how I ended up in Brighton?

Is my nan here? I can't stay here if she is here. She will kill me.

"We could have all come down together?"

Wait, is she flirting with me now? Shouldn't she be looking for her parents or something? What is going on here?

"Yes, she is asleep though. That would have been nice."

No, it wouldn't, what the fuck am I saying? I presume she is somewhere asleep. She likes the bingo. She is probably in one of those bingo places. I need to avoid them.

"Although, I don't think there is a lot to do here any more. We used to come as kids, but it's all a bit fuddy-duddy now, wouldn't you agree?"

"Yes. I suppose."

There is an awkward silence. She is just looking at me. I am trying to look anywhere, but at her.

"Are you going back to the show? It's a bit lame, but you can sit with us if you like?"

Who am I going to sit with, your parents are missing, Bethany? Don't you remember? That's why your lazy brother asked you to come down here.

"Don't know yet."

There is silence again. Is she expecting me to talk?

"Haven't seen my parents by the way, have you?"

At last, took your time, didn't you? I almost don't want to tell her.

"Yes, they were here, taking a walk down by the beach, I believe. I saw them wondering off holding hands."

I gesture to the direction in order to persuade her to follow.

"Oh, OK, thanks. I will see you back there then."

She gives me a big smile and turns and walks back towards the pier.

Fuck!

What do I do now? Do I just let her go? That's not thinking grand, Edmund. Everything you do has to be grand. It has to get better. There can't be the one that got away. That makes it sound like you have failed.

"Wait, Bethany?"

She turns and is back in front of me within a minute. I think she was waiting for that. She is almost face-to-face with me now.

"Do you want to walk on the beach? Anything has to be better than that show?"

"Yes, that sounds lovely, Edmund."

No it doesn't, it's cold, wet and miserable out here. Oh, I get it now. She was looking for me to take her on a date. Her smile is obvious, she has a hell of a crush on me. I can't blame her. Probably all the girls a year younger than me do. It's where the following will start from. The younger generation. They always look up to the older man. I grab her by the hand, and we walk under the pier.

"You know…"

This conversation has been confusing enough. I grab her arm and pull her close. She doesn't scream. Wait, I think she is making a kissing face at me. I was reaching for my knife. I pull my hand back, and grab her other arm, and then kiss her. Proper full-on kiss as well. Wait, what is she doing? I think she is trying to fit her whole tongue in my mouth. I have heard of French-kissing before, but this is ridiculous. Either that or she is trying to suffocate me from the inside. Wait, she is. She probably knows what I did to her parents. She is trying to kill me with her tongue.

My god, she is a bad kisser. My hand goes back to grab my knife, and I end the kissing. Three times in the side and then I step back.

"You are a bad kisser. Bad. Awful, I would say."

I cut her throat. It's a little deeper than normal. I guess it's because her tongue was still so far out. I probably shouldn't have said that. No young girl wants to hear that. I feel like I want to say sorry now.

I pull her down to sit with her parents.

"Yes, I am, and yes, he will be hopefully, in the next ten minutes as it is freezing out here."

"Don't blame me, your wife took fifteen minutes to come looking for you, and your daughter was more interested in kissing me than finding you. I am doing this as quickly as I can."

It's all pretence, I know it. Moaning as it's supposed to be a family holiday, and they are not all together. I head back up to the end of the pier.

I am working as fast as I can. Don't they think that I am trying my best here? That's all I have been doing for the last week, and yet, still here I am on a cold blustery Monday night in Brighton.

I stand looking at the pier. It won't be long now.

I still stand looking at the pier, nobody in and nobody out. Wait, it has to be what, at least thirty-five minutes since your dad disappeared, Carl. Then your mum, and now your sister. What kind of brother or son are you?

I would have been a great big brother. I would have taught my brother or sister all about the world and everything. But, no, I bet he is sitting there listening to the blue comedian without a care in the world.

I knew the whole happy family thing was fake from him. He never thinks about anyone else but himself. His parents are freezing out here, and he is just warm and toasty in the bar. Doesn't even care about his little sister. She could be abducted or anything.

I have had enough. I am going to tell him. I start to walk up the pier towards the bar. The door opens in front of me.

It's Carl! Fucking prick finally comes out…

He clocks me walking towards him.

"Bobble…"

Before he gets the last words out of his mouth I stab him in the stomach, and again, and again…

"I knew you were a fake piece of shit. Don't care about your parents or your sister. They are out here waiting for you, whilst you lord it up in your show. I hate you."

He is grabbing hold of my shoulders. I am now fully aware of where I am. On the pier with Carl. Who needs *CSI*? Someone could walk out at any moment? I stick him one more time and back him up to the edge of the pier. With a big push he is over.

I look around. Within a minute the door swings open again, and someone walks out.

"Fuck, that was close."

"Sorry?"

Some bloke heard me. In your head, Edmund, in your fucking head.

"Nothing."

He knew there was a swear word there, but he didn't hear anything else. He disappears again. I walk back to the end of the pier and go under.

Chapter 15

I walk past Mum, Dad, and sister, and go looking for Carl. He is right by the water's edge. That was a big fall for him.

"Fuck!"

I can hear him calling for help. I run over and finish the job. I slit him ear to ear and the shouting stops. I don't think anyone will have heard it. All I can hear are the bars upstairs, and the wind under the pier. I drag him back to his family. How did he survive that fall? It is like thirty foot?

"You're welcome. I did tell your husband I was working on it."

"That is a good question. Now I have you all here, you know, I am not sure."

I sit down in the sand with the family.

"You're a family, right, although I will say that I think Carl is phoning it at times. I told him as much upstairs. Probably a little too harshly which I will apologise for. Those laughs up at the bar, and the fact it took him like forty minutes to start getting concerned. They wound me up a little. I am just saying, Carl, you could be a better son."

He doesn't reply. Still in that adjustment mode, I guess.

"Sorry, I am a little sidetracked. You are like the target audience. Mum, Dad, boy and a girl. The perfect family unit. What would you like to see? How do you think that I can make this bigger, no, better before bigger? I don't think I am going to have any problem being the biggest. I just want to be the best."

"Ha ha ha, I know, not the first time I have heard that, but not something you should say in front of your mum and dad. Oh, and brother, although he is still not saying anything. Adjustment time, I think. I am sure we will make up soon."

No, still nothing. If he had kept this quiet in school we probably wouldn't be here now. We could have been better friends.

"I do know what you are saying, the work is its own reward. But it's not going to make me famous. Not like Jack. Hell, they still write stories and make films about him now. Hundred and twenty years later. I can't be known just for the work. There needs to be more. A flair of some kind?"

There is silence for a moment. Everyone is still thinking.

"Yes, that is what I am talking about. You have a bright daughter there, sir, something that stages the scene... You know, I have these friends called the Mersons. We did something similar. They were nice people too. That was fun."

"Yes, that's the ones. In town. Yes, I was with them that night. Played Scrabble in the end, but when I left there was a certain something about it, a drama, a je ne sais quoi. Think that's how you say it. French for something special."

"No, they haven't, but they won't release all the details yet. I have photos though."

I take out my phone and show them. I think they are all a little impressed, even Carl. Even though he is still not speaking.

"I agree, I think I can become famous for setting the scene. Maybe that is why the press on the ONE isn't very good. It's just the basics. I need to be more... The world needs to know that I am more than anyone else... Any ideas?"

"Good point, good point, it has to be topical to its surroundings. Like with the Mersons, happy family at home... I like it. It means I can work anywhere. In any town. In any office. Really like that. There must be scenes to be created everywhere. Not one specific genre."

There is silence again.

"And, team, we have a winner. Ticks all the boxes, doesn't it?"

I throw a smile at her. If I had the time I could have made her a better kisser, she would have liked that. Sometimes you just need a little guidance in these things. Hell, Miss Walker has taught me no end. And she is still young. You need guidance when you are young.

"Wait right here, I will be back in like five, ten minutes."

I run back to the end of the pier to see if the shop is still open. It is closing up. I persuade the girl to let me buy some stuff nonetheless.

I wonder if ugly people have the same rewards. I mean she must have just served me, because even in this get-up, I am hot. I bet ugly people get closed down on all the time. It's probably fair. There has to be some rewards for keeping these looks up. It's not all natural.

I head back to the family. They are still there. I do love it when all parties are collaborating together. Even if Carl doesn't want to talk. It's the hate you comment, I am sure of it. It is bugging me. Nobody wants to know they are hated.

"I couldn't get any chairs, but I did get a blanket. Some buckets, spades and like these moulding things. I think they are supposed to be shells and seahorses. Oh yeah, and a starfish. That's pretty cool.

"So, this is my thinking. Mum, Dad, laid on the blanket all cuddled up like. And the kids playing down in the sand by the sea?

"Oh, you do speak. I was just thinking to myself, is he going to join in or not? Come on, it will be fun. Your sister is up for it, aren't you? I know you are not kids, but think of the scene. Listen, I am sorry about before and I didn't mean it. I was just cold and tired."

He is looking directly at me now.

"See, I told you she is well up for it."

Could have taken that a little further. But no sense in pissing him off any more.

"Thank you. See, your mum and dad are up for it too. Just join in. It will be fun."

Think I have him back onside. I lay down the blanket and then sit Carl's dad on it, leaning against one of the pillars. Carl's mum, I place with her head in his lap facing the sea. It will be so she can watch the kids as they play. I then take Carl and Bethany down to the water's edge.

"I was thinking of doing a sandcastle or something like that? Maybe with the little sea horses and starfish shells on top?

"Cool."

I start working away at building the castle. I would ask them to help but I always loved doing this as a kid. My mum and dad would leave me to build one for hours. Maybe it was just to get rid of me, but I don't care. It is so much fun.

"Yes. I am. You know, I am quite talented at nearly everything. Not sure why I said nearly there. I guess I didn't want to come across as too cocky. I suppose most things just come naturally to me. Does that sound bad?

"Yes it helps being as hot as fuck as well. Thank you for saying that. I was just thinking about that when I was up at the shop. Ugly people just don't get the rewards we do."

Now that's a line. Any girl would have fallen for that. Not just the ones that are already obsessed with me.

"No I think he is still a little mad at me. He doesn't say a lot, does he? He is normally so talkative in class. In fact, he would probably agree I am the quiet one in class."

I really like Carl's sister she is a lovely girl. Who knew that he could have a sister like that? She is cute as well. She doesn't look anything like him so I am not really sure what I was worried about when I thought of doing her.

I finish the sandcastle. It is awesome. I should do this more. Be like one of those artists who does it on the beach and people give them money and stuff.

"Yes, very happy with it. I was thinking of positioning you building the castle, and maybe we bury Carl up to the head in sand."

She has such a cute laugh.

I start digging. I thought at first about burying him standing up, but fuck, this is hard work. I just dig the length and then drop him in. I cover him over till only his head is showing.

"Ha ha, no, I didn't see that episode. They turned him into a sand mermaid. Should we do that with Carl? That would be funny."

Even I am not that mean. He is a prick, but he doesn't deserve to be dressed like a girl.

"You are so funny. I don't know how we haven't spent more time together before?"

"OK, let's spend more time together now, but let's not do it in front of Carl."

I am willing to give anyone a second chance. Even a bad kisser. She is at least a cute bad kisser. We move over towards the pillars so Carl isn't staring at me. We are up against the pillar. She has quite a fit body for a sixteen-year-old. Her kissing has improved as well. I bet she is thinking about it more after what I said to her. A lot less tongue. Firm and gentle. I hold my hands up to her head and run my fingers through her hair.

FUCK!

"Fuck, I am so sorry, so sorry. I didn't mean to."

Her head has come clean off. I knew I cut that a little too deep. Oh crap, the weight of her body must have completed the job. What am I going to do with her now? Hardly the picture of a perfect family with a beheaded body building a sandcastle. It's not like I have time to find a horse or anything. This isn't *Hammer House of Horror*.

I take her head and the rest of her back to the sandcastle. Maybe I can like lay her down and balance her head on her shoulders a bit.

Fuck!

Really messed this up, didn't I? It's not working. It just won't balance. How do you balance a head on someone's shoulders. I need like a stick or something that I can put in her neck and then stick her head on with it. She is really quiet, I guess like the married man in the hotel; he can't talk as her head has fallen off. That's put an end to any kissing, I can tell you.

"What?

Now he wants to talk to me. Can't he see I am in crisis here?

"Thanks, Carl, that is a great idea. Are you sure you don't mind?"

That is inspiring. I never thought it would have come from him.

"Mate, I am sorry for all the crap we went through. If I had known you would have been this supportive to me as a friend I wouldn't have been so bad to you at school. You have really saved my bacon. And it has the grandiose element as well. Which people are going to love, by the way. I will make sure that everyone knows that it was your idea."

I dig another hole next to Carl and place his sister's body in it. I then walk over to Carl.

"Thanks for this, Carl. I won't forget it."

I take off his head and place it where I have buried his sister's body, and then put his sister's head where his head was. Just enough in the sand that they stand up. I then proceed to write *ONE* in the sand all around them, and place some of my calling cards there. One in Carl's mouth. I want the world to know how much he has supported the ONE. I walk up and place one in each of Mum and Dad's hands, and again write *ONE* all around the blanket in the sand.

I stand back and admire my handiwork. Smart, fun, and stuff a family would do for kicks. Staging the scene done. It is kind of a cool idea. I could definitely become known for this type of work.

Carl isn't that bad after all. His parents are great, and his sister is amazing. This is the kind of thing I need to do more of. I wish I had seen this side of Carl before, but I have left school now so there is no chance.

Now for the selfie evidence. Pictures with Mum and Dad first. Tasteful, not naked like with the Mersons, that was my mid-rampant stage of life. Just some family fun ones. Then with Carl and his sis lying down, and me building the sandcastle. I finish doing the selfies

"You know it's been a great night. Thanks mainly to all of you. I know we missed the end of the comedian, but I am sure these things are on all week. We can catch it later."

"Yes, I am a little tired, to be honest, I am about done in. What with the events of last night at the hotel and today, it's been a long one. But before I go I just wanted to thank you. All of you."

"I know I don't have to, I want to. This works so much better when we are all working together. Tomorrow you will be famous but I will stay in the shadows a little longer. Enjoy the attention, and I will see you soon."

"Oh, and please, if you do bump into my nan don't tell her I am here. It is a surprise."

I wink at Bethany. I can see her blushing back at me. I walk back off the beach to the end of the pier. It's all quiet now. Lights are out, the shows are over and, if it's possible, the place looks a little sadder than it did in the daytime.

I head back to my hotel. I have a key for the front door so go straight in and to my room. Not a soul in sight. I shower as the sand has got absolutely everywhere. I wrap up the costume and place it under the bed. Just in case room service see it. I then lay on the bed. Exhaustion is getting the better of me, I can feel it, but it has been an amazing day. I thought things were going to go wrong down here, but it has worked out really special.

Nine a.m. I wake up. What is going on? Where is my eternal Nan clock today? I must have been totally knackered to sleep through that. I dress and head down to breakfast. I go into the dining room. No wonder they were all in bed when I got home last night. My nan would feel young in this hotel. I feel like I am old enough to be all of their great grandchild's.

At least there was no queue at the buffet, and lots of food to eat. I suppose at their age they only eat porridge and stuff. This stuff must play murder with their teeth.

The TV is on in the corner, but it's not the news. *Come Dine with Me* or something like that. That programme is on ten times a day. There is no talk about the front or the beach from the other guests. I am trying to listen to all of their conversations at once. It's mainly to do with bingo or their children. Old people need to tell you about their children and grandchildren all the time and they keep score. It's like their age; I am seventy-three, you know.

I am eighty-four, you know. What is it about age? As a teenager you want to tell the world you're eighteen, at eighteen you tell them you're twenty-one. From there to thirty-nine you don't care, and over forties till sixty you tell people you're twenty-one.

But old people put a badge on it as if to say that they are still here. Look at me, ninety-three. Still going, you know. Yep, even with this dodgy hip, and the other twenty operations that I need to tell you about.

I don't care much for old people other than my nan. I would work with them more, but I don't think people care enough. I don't think it would be good for my image. I suppose I would be doing most of them a favour.

I finish up and take a walk. I walk past the pier, but on the opposite side of the road. I don't want people recognising me. You never know who may have been watching? I know it was night-time, but I am not sure outside is really for me.

I get so engrossed in my work, and when you are outside you can't cover all angles. Anyone could have been watching me last night, and I wouldn't have known.

There is nothing going on. People are on and off the pier as normal. Has nobody spotted the family having fun on the beach? I carry on walking down past the Chinese and to their hotel. No police outside the hotel. Have the staff not noticed that they are all missing? The more I got to know them, the nicer they were. I am sure you would miss them at breakfast? Bethany is a bright sexy girl, one of the waiters must have been watching her?

The ONE needs to be discovered outside of London.

This must be like that artist feels. Creeps around in the night painting pictures on walls and stuff, and waits for the world's press to release the picture saying another one has appeared.

Although they did take one down and move it. Nobody would have done that, would they? Maybe I have a copycat already? How cool would that be? All the famous ones get them, I am sure I will too. Hell, the train was full of people dressing like me already. I am sure by now someone has graphitised the ONE on a wall somewhere.

I cross the road. I need to know if a copycat has stolen my artwork. It would be just my luck that they have. They are not to know that this is all part of my launch. They have probably figured out what the police couldn't already. If they are my copycat they have to be smart and sexy.

As I walk along it hits me. The fucking water hits me. The sea is that rough that the waves are crashing against the side and up and over. I mean, who would actually go on holiday somewhere where the waves crash over the side? Shouldn't they like build a higher wall or something?

FUCK!

The motherfucking TIDE!

I run back to the end of the pier. The sea is almost at the path. I look down. The Carnegie family are about thirty metres out to sea. No, they are out to sea. I am sure I have read somewhere that the undercurrent will have pulled them out.

They are fucking holidaying in France!

I swear there are actual tears running down my face. What is that all about? I feel like falling on the floor and crying, stamping, and kicking like a fucking kid. What the hell happened? It was perfect, the whole thing. The way it was laid out. The head swapping, even Carl was helpful. Why? Why does this always happen to me? It's like the world is against me. All I ask is to be famous. I am already rich. Why can't I just be famous? I just sit looking at the sea. Am I that bad of a person? I just need to be in the spotlight. I just need people to worship what I have done. I need people to know how creative I am, how smart I am. How utterly unique I am. I stand there hoping that I hear someone scream as Carl's head floats past, but nothing. Nothing.

They are not even going to know it's me? Even if it is discovered in the next day or so the ONE in the sand isn't there, and the cards, I am sure have floated off by now. Nobody will know what I did again. Jack was feared from day one. Why am I not feared? Loved? Cherished? I walk over to the café and sit in. Is falling in love with me so hard? I am trying.

I honestly don't know what to do for the best. I had a perfect holiday story, nice family playing on the beach and everything. What am I going to do now? Stay here and work with the OAPs. Jesus, if they didn't move for a day you wouldn't notice. My head actually hurts from all this.

There are the hen parties and stuff, but that's Friday. It's only Tuesday today. I could do the ghost walk, but again with a bunch of oldies. I am fed up of this. I order a coffee and then pick up a chocolate bar. I put it back. I don't deserve a treat. I have done nothing, but fail since I have started this. It's been nearly a week, and I am no more famous than that band last night. A washed-up has-been at seventeen years old. If I weren't so good-looking I would have nothing going for me whatsoever. Other than the million in the bank and four hundred thousand in the safety deposit box. Absolutely nothing. I sit and drink my coffee. I hate coffee, but it's punishment for poor performance. I don't deserve nice things. I am a failure.

I get up and out of the café and go back to look at the sea again. Nothing. I am not staying here any longer. I go back to my hotel, check out, get back in the car and on the road. I really feel like going home to my nan. At least she appreciates me for who I am. I pull over to the side of the road and send her a text. Good to do that while she is on my mind.

If I was home she would just give me a big hug and things would feel ten times better, but she thinks I am not back for another week. What the fuck am I talking about? She isn't even there. She is here in this crappy place.

It's either London or back to Miss Walker's. I need time to think, and come up with a plan. I start driving. If I go to London I have to park up, get the tube, all that nonsense. If I go to Miss Walker's at least I will have some time to myself. That swings the decision.

I drive back to Miss Walker's house. Enter through the back, and head upstairs for a lie down. I can see straight out of the window and across the fields to where she works. It's an amazing looking school. I would love a house that big one day. Maybe once I have finished my three years we can have one.

I have no idea what time she finishes, just need some time to myself. I lay looking at the ceiling. I seem to be so close yet so far away when it comes to fame. It's not like I am not putting the effort in. The ONE has a name out there, but it's not me. Fame is more important than just a name. I need people to know me. Love me. That's the whole point of this. I have my money taken care of. I know what my next steps are with regards to social media and stuff. I have done my homework, but people just can't put two and two together.

It can't be me. It just can't. I am amazing at everything. There is a knock at the door. It makes me sit up. It can't be Miss Walker, she wouldn't knock on her own front door and I don't have a key to open it. I look out the window. It's an old woman. She must be like forty-five or something.

She shouts through the letterbox.

"Jack!"

Who the fuck is Jack? Don't tell me that Miss Walker has another man here? I almost want to go down and confront the woman, but I don't know who she is. Who is Jack and why would you be knocking here for him? I don't move and she goes away.

I can't believe that she is cheating on me with some bloke called Jack. That bitch. I have been totally faithful to her since we got together. Well, not totally. There was Melanie and I did kiss Carl's sister last night, but other than that totally faithful. And all the time I am away she is shagging some bloke called Jack. Fuck, I am mad at her now. Why do I bother coming back to see her if she is cheating on me? I may as well stay in London. Fuck her and her dodgy Preton High School. I hate the place. Everything that has gone bad has gone bad because of her and that school.

I lie back on the bed, and then get up again. I don't want to lie down. I look out the window, there are girls walking around the school yard. Hand in hand. I walk downstairs and fetch the binoculars on the side in the kitchen. I noticed them at the weekend. I guess it's a village thing; binoculars, wellies and tweed jackets. She has all the gear in the hallway. Bought some for me too by the looks of it. Either me or this Jack bloke. Bitch. I can't believe that.

I look out of the window and watch the activities of the school. It's a busy old place for somewhere that is closed. I can't believe they still have to wear their uniform when it is half-term. Although I must say I do like a school uniform. They feature heavily in some of the magazines I have under my bed.

I watch the window for another hour or so and lie back on the bed. Life is passing me by so fast. I am going to be eighteen before I know it. I need to do something about this non-fame thing. I put on the TV in the corner. It's only a small one, but it has the news and I watch for a while.

Then I take an afternoon nap.

"You fucking cheating bastard."

What? What? I wake up and Miss Walker is running full belt at me. I jump off the bed, and I am backed into the corner.

"What? What are you shouting at me for?"

"You, you know what you did. You came here all sweet and innocent at the weekend, and look at the news today. That is back in our town."

I look over at the TV and there is a picture of Melanie on it.

"They found that bank teller. That was you, wasn't it? Tell the truth. You had sex with her, they say you tried to romance her. How the fuck did you romance her? Why would you romance someone other than me? Why, eh? Why?"

Fuck! Fuck! Fuck! Fuck! Fuck!

What am I supposed to say to her?

"I have no idea what you are talking about? They found her today? Who today? Who did they find? And what? You think that I went home and did this, do you? Went home and what?"

"No, they found her yesterday, but she hasn't been to work since Tuesday. They said Tuesday night it happened to her. Where the fuck were you Tuesday night? Why were you out with this woman?"

"I wasn't out with any woman? I was at home with my nan. We had a quiet night in?"

She is standing on one side of the bed and I am on the other. I don't think I should go to her side of the bedroom. She doesn't look happy with me.

"Wait, wait before you start again. I can prove it." I take my phone out put, it on speaker and on the bed and ring my nan.

"Hi, Nan."

"Hello, darling, it's lovely to hear your voice."

"Yours too, Nan. You were right, I miss not having you there to cook my breakfast in the morning."

She is just staring at me now. That can't be good. Need to get on with proving my innocence.

"And how are you enjoying your little adventure, Edmund?"

"It's good, Nan, but it's not the same as being home with you. I would much prefer to be home with cheese on toast and my nan. Like we did on Tuesday."

I look at Miss Walker as I say that. Scotland now springs to mind. If she mentions it, Miss Walker will think I am ashamed of her and told my nan a lie.

"Yes, darling, that was a perfect evening in, with your CIS programmes"

"*CSI,* Nan. *CSI.* And how is the little holiday."

"It's lovely, Edmund. The weather is not great, but lovely. Are you eating properly?"

"Yes, Nan, even had liver and onions at the weekend like you make it. Me and a friend loved it…"

I am nodding at her to show that I am even willing to introduce her to my nan.

"Oh, that's great as the food's not supposed to be that great up there. I hear they deep-fry everything. Even chocolate."

Quick, get her off the phone. She is starting to discuss Scotland. That will just start her off all over again.

"It's fine, Nan, got to go. Love you. And I will call you soon."

I hang up the phone. She still doesn't look impressed.

"So you haven't told her about us?"

Do you know what, I just can't win? Does anyone ever win with a woman? What did she want me to tell her? I am banging my teacher, Nan. Thought you needed to know.

"What? What are you going on about? I just proved I was home Tuesday. Anyway you are the one shouting at me? Who is Jack? Eh? Some woman came past here calling for Jack. You have only been here a week and already have someone else?"

"There is no Jack, you are just deflecting the fact that you don't want people to know about us. Ashamed, are you? Ashamed of your little secret?"

"What are you going on about, woman? I have come here to see you? How could I be ashamed of you? I wasn't the one moving town to get rid of me. To go to some posh school."

"Fuck you, Edmund."

She is storming out of the room. I hear her go down the stairs, and out the front door as it slams behind her. Am I supposed to follow her? She didn't sound like she wanted company. What is wrong with the woman? She has been here less than a week and this is the fourth, no, fifth day I have been at hers. I just don't know how to please her.

I head downstairs fully expecting to see her sneaking in the back door. She isn't. I look in the fridge. She hasn't even been shopping since I did at the weekend. All we have is four-day-old liver and bread. And some wine. That will have to do. I warm the liver up in the microwave. It doesn't taste like it did at the weekend. My nan's is so much better than this. I wonder if it is like veal. I thought about that when Carl's sister was talking to me. I wonder if the younger the liver, the tastier it is. It would make sense as it's not overworked. Let's face it, by the time you're like forty it must be well overworked.

I switch the TV on in the front room, and look for the news. They have found Melanie. They show her picture. She is really hot. The picture they show is great, better than the blanket photo they always show of me. Shame about the sex though. You would never know looking at her.

They are still not mentioning the Mersons. Surely, by now, they have done some work on this. And absolutely nothing about the ONE. I swear that it's no wonder this country is going to pot if they can't connect these dots.

"Oh, *Criminal Minds*." At last, something worth watching. A double episode also. I sit and watch both of them. I think I am a little of all of them. Morgan's strength and speed. Hotchner's brains. Penelope's IT skills, and even the weirdo doctor, my memory is about as good as his. I think that's why I like this show so much, it reminds me of me. Brilliant and successful.

The programme ends and Miss Walker still isn't home. I reckon she is staying at the school tonight then. I go up to bed. I look out of the window, and I can see the lights on in the school. It is 10.28. I watch for the next two minutes and at exactly ten thirty all the lights go out. You would have thought fifteen to seventeen-year-olds would have been able to stay up later than that. I put down the binoculars and lay back on the bed. Nothing today has helped me with my problem. The Carnegies are probably eating snails and garlic in France and I am stuck home alone when my girlfriend is out who knows where. With this Jack fellow, no doubt.

Wait, did I just call her my girlfriend? What the fuck? There is seriously something wrong with me if I am calling her my girlfriend. She doesn't deserve that title. Not at the moment anyway.

Chapter 16

Seven 0 fucking three.

And the world turns back to Nan time. I walk downstairs. She didn't come home last night. I try the front door and it's still locked. Well, I am not sitting around waiting for her to come home. I am not that type of boyfriend. Wait, I am not her boyfriend. What is up with me? A few dates and she thinks I am hers. I can't be tied down to one woman. That's not how fame works. I look in the fridge. There is still no food. What good is she to me?

I get dressed and head back to my car. The best thing I can do is get back to the day job. I drive to Wimbledon tube station. May as well tube in and leave the car here. Not that she deserves it, but I will be back.

The tube station is rammed; don't know where all these people are going. Wait, I am sure that is the school uniform I saw from the bedroom window. Looks like the same logo. I get on the tube, and so do about twenty girls dressed in school uniform. I am watching out for Miss Walker. Last thing we need is a scene in front of her students, but she is nowhere to be seen. What if she is cheating on me? What if she wasn't at the school last night and she is off with this Jack fellow and here is me leaving my car near her house? What a bitch, why would she do that to me? I am the best she has ever had, she has said so. Why would she sleep with someone else?

Stop, Edmund!

I need to take my mind off my cheating girlfriend. Friend she is just a friend. The girls are all talking and laughing; they are quite well behaved for kids. Although sixteen, seventeen-year-olds in a school uniform are hot. One of their teachers is hotter, but that is playing with fire. Imagine Miss Walker found out about that, and from her new school as well. Maybe that would teach her a lesson? Maybe that's what I should be doing?

The talk is all about boys and music. One Direction are at Madame Tussauds, and that is where they are all going. A school trip to London, Madame Tussauds, what the hell? I remember going to a shoe museum in Northampton once to tell us the history of shoes. These girls are off to London. The more I listen to them, the more I wish I had gone to a private school. It's not like my parents didn't have the money. They just didn't want to spend it on me. I would have been a great lawyer or banker or maybe even prime minister. I could have run the country if I went to a private school.

I follow them to Baker Street. I was going to go back to Leicester Square, but I really want to go on the school trip. Baker Street, Sherlock Holmes. I love Sherlock Holmes, he would have gotten all the clues I left, and I would be famous by now if there were more like him about. Not the idiots we have today.

I head into the queue for Madame Tussauds. This is going to take an hour to get in. The schoolgirls just walk straight in. I stop the guy selling tickets, and for an extra tenner I can go straight in. Result. I get in the lift with some of them to the exhibition.

I get out of the lift and it hits me. The paparazzi. It's like the real red carpet experience. People taking photos as you walk in. This is what my life is going to be like once I make it famous. The red carpet treatment really suits me. I take my time walking in. I need to get used to this lifestyle. I walk into the hall and it is filled with celebrities. Well, plastic celebrities not real ones. I am not mad.

They are all so lifelike though. And all to scale. I take out my phone. This is definitely a selfie heaven, and will look great on my Facebook page when it launches. I walk up and wait my turn to take a picture with Tom Cruise. Thought he would be bigger. Then Brad and Angelina, tiny people, aren't they? They look so much bigger on screen. I am sure these are not to size. Morgan Freeman freaks me out, it could be him standing there. I poke him just to make sure. No, it is plastic. I am two steps behind the girls at all times. I am part of the school trip after all, I don't want to get lost in the ether. Out of that hall. Then Bollywood. Don't really care for that. It's hard enough to watch a film, let alone all the dancing and stuff. I read somewhere it makes billions of pounds. Never watched a single one of them. Although there was that scene in Slumdog. That was quite cool.

The girls are still with One Direction. They all want a picture with them. I don't see the fascination: they are just a bunch of cute looking guys. That's not what it takes to become famous. You need more. You need to be more like me.

I go ahead of them into Film. A selfie with The Terminator and Steven Spielberg. I am still not sure I shouldn't have chosen acting as my profession. I would have made an amazing actor. Hell, if Arnie can make millions at it, anyone can. I know I could hold an audience in the palm of my hand on stage or screen. I wander through sport and the royals and the pop stars. Not really into any of that stuff. A quick selfie with Michael Jackson. Just because he is a real legend, and we legends should stick together.

Now Marvel and Star Wars, now you are talking. Take a dozen selfies with various people. I am a bit Han Solo and Luke Skywalker. Hero and lover. I would have been a great superhero. I wonder if they will put me up here or in the Chamber of Horrors. I am going to be big enough for both. Maybe I will be the first for both. It won't be fair to all my fans to isolate me to one area. What if they are too scared for the Chamber of Horrors? They won't want to miss out on the opportunity of seeing me. Once I have launched I may need to write to them to tell them that. Just to point it out.

I hang around with the superheroes until my school trip turns up. I want to walk the Chamber with them to see their reaction to horror. Real horror.

Thirty fucking minutes later!

Don't know what took them so long. I bet they spent their time drooling over One Direction. They are just boys, you know. And they are not even that good. I wait until they all go in. They are all holding hands as if the world was about to come to an end. I follow them in.

It's all giggles. They wouldn't be giggling if the real Jack was in here. He was like the fourth biggest serial killer of our time. Used to be third till me. I watch as they continue to walk through. Take the opportunity for another selfie with the man. I think he would have been proud to know me. I think they will probably put a whole wing dedicated to me. Imagine if they put all the people I worked with in here as well. Sophia and Caroline, and even my mum and dad. They would need another floor soon. Maybe they will open another Madame Tussauds just for me. That would be so cool.

I wonder if this sort of thing is in the blood. Maybe me and Jack are related? I should look at one of those family tree things.

We get on the ride and then end at the cinema. I am sure this used to be a thing about stars. Now it's superheroes in 4D. I go in and watch. The girls giggle all the way through.

I don't know whether it is the uniform or the fact that they have much cooler school trips than I do, but I feel I am meant to be here. Meant to be with them. It's like a calling. Maybe it is. This is my big break. They say you know it when it happens. I need to do something with the girls that makes us all famous. I am sure they want to be. All the time they spent with their pop stars, it would be the best thing for them to be famous with me.

Schools have been done though. Can't turn on the TV nowadays without some loony running amok in America at a high school. This gun thing in America, it has to stop. The police there must be more stupid than the ones we have. You let them have a gun, and are surprised when they shoot you with it. It's like giving a monkey a banana, and telling him not to eat it.

We come out of the cinema, and head back to the tube. The London Eye is the next stop. I have done those selfies on my first trip to London. I need food. I am starving. She needs to shop more. Can't always be me.

There is a bar on the corner. I go in and order a sandwich and a Coke. Within ten minutes the woman brings my food over.

The girls will still be another thirty minutes. What is it about them that is making me think of them? Miss Walker? Am I trying to protect them as she is not here? Na, that is not me. I think it is, I think it is destiny, but I can't be just another one. I am the ONE. If we are going to do something together, it has to be done Edmund Carson style.

Maybe this is my real debut. My launch, not as the ONE but as me? Maybe I can have double identities. Like that Jekyll and Hyde character, but with more than ONE Hyde. That's a cool plan. Not only is it all me, but me in different styles? This time I leave enough clues that even the police can't mistake it. Like leave my name in clues. Oh yes, that's great. I know how to do it now. That's perfect. The launch of Edmund Carson, also or formally known as the ONE.

I sit and eat my food. I need a plan. That's what, twenty something people in one go. Never been done before. Even the American loonies don't do that many before being taken down. It would need proper working out. Not just in and out. Have to time it and everything. Also, going to have to be silent as not to scare the others whilst I am at it. That's a lot of work to do.

There is a chill running down my back. I think I have finally found the idea in which to launch my fame. I know I can do it. I am amazing.

Fuck!

She isn't going to be happy, is she? This is probably going to get her the sack. It can't be helped. I can't work with another school; it has to be this one. It's my destiny to do it. She will understand in the end, and it's not like we need the money. I have money, and once this is done they will be queuing up for interviews and press reports. We will be set for life.

She still isn't going to be happy though. Maybe I should propose or something. I hear that keeps them quiet for a while. She will be all wrapped up in planning a wedding to notice what else is going on. Or a baby or something. I would be a great dad. And it's something to keep her mind off the fact that she just lost her job.

The girls walk past the window. I finish my drink and follow them. Need to research all of this if I am going to make it happen. And buy a ring, she will like that. Then afterwards I will need to have everything ready: YouTube, Twitter feeds, Facebook, all of it. Ready to go at a push of a button. Because when fame comes you have to grab it with both hands. That bloke always said you each get it for fifteen minutes. Not me. I will be famous for life.

They head into Maccy D's for food. I count them, there are twenty-three of them. Twenty-three and two teachers. That's twenty-five. I need to make up to Miss Walker before I do anything else. She can't be still mad at me and sleeping at the school. Not if I am to work there, and night-time does seem like the perfect opportunity.

I am sure she is not cheating on me. There is no way someone is better for her than me. I am the best. Who would cheat on the best? She was just a little mad at me for cheating on her. She just didn't know how much of a bad experience it was. If she did, she would understand that it has brought us closer. So really, I was doing her a favour.

I watch as they sit down to eat. I take out my phone, and google twenty-five to see if anyone has done anything like this.

Fuck that's creepy!

First thing that comes up is a hand covered in blood, and some body parts. On some sort of website. I am not sure I think you are supposed to move them around to make a face like some sort of ritual. *25,* the *Magazine.* All about senses and stuff. I move on. That's disgusting, who would put that kind of stuff up on the Internet. There are some freaks out there.

Next thing I click on is Matthew 25: The Parable of The Ten Virgins. I look over at the girls. I don't think there are ten virgins there. Maybe six at a push.

Next, Book of Revelations. Twenty-four thrones surround the one throne. Maybe. That has legs. I could get white dresses and crowns for all of them. But it is religion. Do I really want to pick a religion to back? Because if I do that, I may get labelled as some religious nut. And as I don't care for any religion that's not really fair, is it? I don't want to be made famous for any culture. I do not discriminate in my work, other people shouldn't either.

Something about Ezekiel is next, more religion, but nothing to do with my line of work and twenty-five. I think it's another sign. It is what I am supposed to do.

Ten minutes later we are back on the tube and heading towards Wimbledon. I sit on the tube and take some selfies with the girls in the background. A little history on my web pages will go down well with my fans. I think they will like to know how much effort I put into my work. When we get off the tube there is a coach waiting for them. I head back to Miss Walker's house. I use the back door. I want to surprise her. She must be at home as there was nobody at school today.

"Hello?"

Nothing, she is still not home. I don't like the fact that she is not home. I grab my case, change into my costume, and grab my knife. Just in case. I go to the fridge. Still nothing, she still hasn't shopped so probably not even been here at all today. Does she even care that I would have been here all alone? Is this Jack fellow a real problem? Do I need to go and work with him? I can't think about that now. I have work to do. I will discuss it with her later, but I am not happy.

I grab the binoculars and head out the back door. Past the shed. I check. The burglar is still there. Must be asleep as he didn't say a word as I went in. I head out across the field towards the house. The whole thing is in private grounds and the main driveway is tree-lined so I keep close to the trees so they don't see me coming.

I stand just inside the shadows of the trees on the driveway and look through my binoculars. I can see movement in some of the windows, but not all. This isn't going to work from here, I need to be closer than this. The day is getting on, but it's still too light to just walk across the drive. I circle round to the back of the house. This place is huge, takes me nearly ten minutes to get to the back of the house.

Fuck!

I didn't even consider the fact there would be staff as well. I can see two cooks in the kitchen. Looks like they are washing up. I wonder if they live in. If so, I will have to look at twenty-seven on my phone? What if there are serving staff or cleaners also living in? I need to think about this stuff more. I need to ensure I have foolproof plans to do these more. It's all about the prep, Edmund.

So far I have been lucky that everything I have done has been on desire or timing. Nothing planned. Other than Melanie. That was a little planned. Damn, she was crap in bed. Why does that bother me so much? I mean lots of people must be crap at stuff. I guess it's because she was crap at stuff with me. Someone who is amazing at stuff. Upsets me, the thought of her telling people that I wasn't great. She wouldn't do that, would she? That makes her look bad too. That would just be silly.

I watch through the window as they finish cleaning in the kitchen. Must have been an early dinner. After the girls had Maccy D's? I need to check that none of them are too fat. I can't be working with fat chicks. It will knacker me out.

The cook is continually taking rubbish out the back door. I sneak up to the house as he does. I grab a stick from the ground and break it. It fits in the lock of the door. That should keep the door sorted. I go back to the trees and wait for the lights to go out. They do. Five minutes later I hear a car start up. It's both of the cooks, they are leaving. Clearly not live-ins, so back to twenty-five. Don't need to research twenty-seven now. I try the door and it opens. *Criminal Minds* is like the best programme on TV they have taught me so much. I could have been on that programme.

I go into the kitchen, it's huge. They have like five ovens and cookers. I reckon I could have been a chef. They have all the celebrity status as well now. There is at least one programme on a night about them. Girls seem to fall for a man that cooks as well. Most of them have hot wives, and let's face it, they are mainly ugly blokes.

I walk through the kitchen. It leads to a big hallway. It's silent. It can't be close to where the girls are. Twenty-something girls have to be noisy. I stick to the walls and walk around the facility. I can hear laughing down the hall. I follow the noise. There seems to be a common room with at least a dozen girls. I pass the door and carry on walking.

There is a reception area directly at the entrance to the front of the house, and hanging on the wall in reception is a map of the school. Also little leaflets of the school with the same map on. I take one. I can see where they all are now: living quarters, school classes, rec rooms.

There is also a notice above reception. *There are no locked doors in the kingdom of heaven or our school.* They don't lock the doors to the school? There is also something behind reception saying *Locked doors lead to locked minds.* They are serious about this shit. That's almost inviting me in. I knew this was fate. I just knew it.

I walk through reception and into the classrooms. They are empty. They are decked out nice though. Seem to have everything that you need. I sit at one of the desks and study the map. It's a long way between the living quarters and the classrooms. Must be like five minutes walking. I am going to have to time it. I need a time for everything else that I need to do that night. I walk over to the teacher's desk and pull out a piece of paper and a pen.

I write the heading Timings. From lights out to asleep. There is no way these girls just go straight to sleep. They must have like a dozen bunk beds in a room and I am sure that they have pillow fights every night. I have a DVD of that somewhere, I know I have.

Once they are asleep there must also be a timing for breakfast. If we said eight thirty a.m. breakfast, the chefs will be here at like seven thirty... need to watch for that also.

Then there are working timings. Got to be ten minutes per person. I work that out, that's four hours already? Have to be quicker than that. It's all about getting in and out. Moving is another couple of hours. Leaves like what, two hours as a margin. That can't be good and I haven't even thought yet how I am going to get my style? I need to do some things beforehand to save time somewhere. With eight, nine hours tops, this has to be planned.

I am going to have to spend the night tonight to see where I can cut time from. She is going to be mad that I don't come home again, but she will have to live with it. Besides, she didn't come home last night, and I still don't even know where she was? Wait, she should be here. I need to look for her. Not now, but later when they are all in bed. If she is not here then she is with this Jack fellow so I will need to pay him a visit. I am not going to lose her to some random bloke. What is she even thinking? Look at me.

I move to the corner of the room and camp down. It's a few hours before the girls will be thinking about bedtime, with lights out being at ten thirty.

I put my hoodie over my head. Miss Walker is running through my mind. She seriously can't be cheating on me? Can she? Who is that stupid?

I must have been exhausted, I dropped off for a minute then. I check my watch.

Fuck, more than a minute!

It's 10.20. How lucky is that? I wait until eleven and then leave the classroom. I jump back in. One of the teachers. Not the really hot one, but the other one was walking down the hallway. I don't think she saw me. I duck down by the door and she walks straight past. I didn't notice that. I get the map back out. Teachers' living quarters are on the ground floor, about a hundred metres from here. Fuck, I need to pay more attention.

I give it five minutes and leave. I head back along the corridor to where the stairs are to the living quarters. I can't hear anyone from here. The lights are all out. I walk up the stairs. It's just a straight set of stairs, there is nowhere to hide on here. I am looking over my shoulder the whole time. The whole floor looks like a row of hotel rooms. I go to the first door. Alana Simpson. There is a little sliding mechanism on the door that says In or Out. She is Out. I try the door. It is open. They really don't have any locked doors in this school. I walk in. The room is tiny, but it's compact. The bed is by the door and there is a TV, dressing table and a desk area. They even have their own bathrooms. I thought boarding schools were more like orphanages, but not this one. They are mega upmarket. I switch on the TV. There is a sign comes up: *No TV after ten thirty*. Oh, they are efficient. I take out my phone also. No Wi-Fi connections available. They must turn off the TV feed and Wi-Fi along with the lights. I guess that ensures the girls sleep on time. They don't mess about with you at this school, that is proper strict.

I walk back out. The next room is Out too. And the next and the next. I try eleven doors before one is In. I listen at the door and nothing. I open it as quiet as possible, just a bit, and there is a girl in bed. I close it again.

Fuck!

They are all over the place. They all have their own rooms. This place is like a hotel. I go back to Alana's room and take some paper and pens. I am going to have to find all twenty-three girls, and then map them out as I do. I spend the next hour and a half doing this. This is going to make it so much harder. I take the map and sit on the floor.

Not a girl has moved. Nothing. The school is totally silent. At least I know they are good girls. That is going to help. A girl called Debbie Morris is the furthest away from the classroom. I need to time that walk. I go to Debbie's room and march from there to the classroom. A little over seven minutes. That's going to add lots of time on to my plan, and she isn't going to walk it. I know I will end up carrying her somehow.

The Wi-Fi and TV help though. I think they actually go straight to sleep at lights out. I have been walking around for an hour and a half, and nothing. Not a peep from anyone. I walk from the classroom to the teachers' area. They are much closer. They are the same as the students. They have their names on the doors and In and Out slides. Must be something to do with the trust element.

Again first few doors are all out. Then I find the two teachers that are In. They are also silent. I can't seem to find Miss Walker's room. Maybe it's because she isn't a live-in so she doesn't have a room? But where would she have stayed last night?

There are a lot of spare rooms; she probably crashed in one of those. The teachers are going to have to be last. I need to work with the girls first. I go back into the classroom and sit at the desk. I pull out the paper and pen. Twenty-three times seven. That's two hours forty. The work can't take more than five minutes. That's another two hours. Give or take, it's going to be five hours' work to get the girls down. And dressed for school, what's that, like another two minutes?

I get up and undress, my trousers and top, to time myself. I don't care about shoes. Over two minutes. That's another hour. Say half an hour for the teachers in total.

Six and a half fucking hours before I get to being the creative Edmund Carson. I need some prep work as well or else it just isn't going to happen. I can do some work in here before lights out. Stage a classroom scene, I guess.

Maybe a few may go to bed early, but with an open door policy you don't know who will visit them before bedtime. That is too much of a risk. I have to wait for lights out, and then give them a little while to nod off. This is a big job. This is probably why nobody has taken this challenge before. It's a good job I am not just anyone. Takes someone as special as me to do something as special as this. They are so lucky.

I sit looking at the timing on the piece of paper. I need to ensure the press know the amount of work I have put into this. Some people think becoming famous is all about the looks. It's not, I have to work really hard on this.

I can't do any more tonight. I pull my phone out and set the alarm for seven. I need to be back to check on breakfast timings. I set my alarm, and leave through the same door I entered.

Walking along the tree line I head back to Miss Walker's house. She is home. I can hear her snoring upstairs. It's not a loud snore, but enough to know I am not alone. I creep upstairs and climb into bed with her.

"I am sorry."

"Me too."

She doesn't move, she just snuggles back into me. At least we have made up, and she is going to be home tomorrow night. I can't have her distracting me from this. This has to be my focus. I will focus on her afterwards. This is my chance to become all I can be. I lay awake for the next hour planning everything in my head. I finally drift off to the sound of her snores.

Six fifty-five. I wake up before the alarm. I turn over and she has already gone. There is a note on the pillow saying that she loves me. That's a good sign. At least I know she isn't sleeping at the school any more. That is a weight off my mind. I look out the window. Nothing has changed with the school. I can't see anyone moving at the windows. I dress quickly and run downstairs.

I check the fridge. Still nothing. I really miss waking up with my nan, she always had breakfast ready in the morning.

There was always food everywhere in the house. Fruit in the bowl, sweets on the side. I take my phone out and text her: *I miss breakfast with you, love, Edmund x*. That will keep her happy.

Once I have sorted the timings this morning I will do the shopping. I am a modern man, I believe in equality. She works and so do I, so I need to show her I can pull my weight around here. Especially if there is this Jack fellow lurking in the background. She needs to remember I am better.

I am out of the house and back over the fields. I head straight around to the kitchens. It's important I know what time they get in, as that is the end of my stopwatch. And my night. I wait and wait.

Seven forty-five the car pulls up with the same two chefs as before. That gives me a maximum of eight hours and forty-five minutes. From start to finish that is so tight. That's giving them all thirty minutes before I start. I am not sure that is going to be enough. I watch as they prepare breakfast. There is just them and they don't go anywhere else. It's 8.20 before they leave to serve up somewhere. Worst-case scenario is I have till then. And then worst, worst-case scenario is back to researching the number twenty-seven.

Chapter 17

I have the timings for the school and went and did the shopping. I want her to know that I am here for her. I don't expect anything done for me that I won't do myself. The fridge is full, the wine rack is full. Even bought some champagne for us to celebrate with. And I chucked out that leftover liver, it started to smell a bit. Even spent the afternoon tidying up around the house. I have left her dinner in the fridge, and DVD and wine chilling on the side, also a note saying I will be back tomorrow, and we can spend another long weekend together. That has to hold me in good stead. I am like the perfect boyfriend. I do love her.

Fuck, need to stop saying that!

What if I slip up in an interview or something? It will devastate my fans. Celebs are always single. Always.

I managed a two-hour kip this afternoon as well, it is going to be a long night. But hopefully the night of my life. Not just mine. Theirs too.

I leave through the back door, and take the tree-lined walk up to the school. I have my costume on and my kit bag. Need to really think about this costume thing for the ONE. It helps, with the colour and blending in, but I still keep thinking about those people on the train. Everyone is going to copy me and I need my own style. Maybe like a gentleman, like Jack. He always wore the long coat and the top hat. Maybe something like that. I need to blend in, but be classy. Maybe that's Edmund. Classy. And the ONE is one of my egos that is down and dark. Hence the costume. That works. A nice smart suit or something like that?

I make my way round to the back. The kitchen staff are still there. I sit by the tree until the lights go out. I then stand and wait for the car to go past. I head towards the back door.

Thank fuck!

The wood in the lock is still there. I didn't even think about that. That would have been a disaster of a start. I walk through the kitchen. There is just stuff everywhere. Trays and trays of stuff. Must be a hell of a job when the school is in full flow. Maybe a chef isn't as glamorous as I first thought. Unless it's on TV. I would be great on TV.

The hallways are quiet again. I go out into the hallway. I stay next to the walls and pass the girls in the Rec room. They must nearly all be in there, it's packed. There is a movie on and they are all positioned around the TV. I stand by the door to listen in. *Notting Hill* is the movie. I would know Julia Roberts' voice anywhere. Not small or dark-haired, but she would defo get it. She has to be the hottest star out there, other than Sandra Bullock, Lucy Liu and that girl off *Modern Family*. Never remember her name. I listen for a minute more, and then head off to the classroom.

I pull the blind down on the door. Nobody can see me in here now. I need to set a scene. I want them all to be in class when they are discovered. I set to work making sure there are just twenty-three seats in class. I stack the rest in the corner. My plan is to leave one teacher at the desk and one by the easel or blackboard as if they are coaching the class. I can see that picture on the front page now. It will look so good.

I need to leave clues. Clues that any idiot would work out. As this time, this time I launch. I write my name on the blackboard vertically. Can't get any clearer than that. Need to write something which highlights the first letter in each word spelling out my name. Proper Spencer Reid style, he would get it in a second. So these idiots will get it in an hour for sure.

Every
Day
My
Urges
Need
Desires

That's really cool. I think that they will really get that. It tells them that I need to keep doing this. It is part of who I am. I stand looking at the other letters. Nothing is coming to me. Come on, Edmund, think. You are good at this stuff.

I could have been a writer. Mrs Whitaker always said I was talented at this stuff. I should probably write the screenplay to my movie and send it to the studios. That way I would be able to ensure I don't miss anything out. That way it will do me justice.

Could
Almost
Retain

I scrub out Retain.

Replace

Some

Open

Negativity

Could Almost Replace Some Open Negativity. Really needs to read This Could Almost Replace Some Open Negativity. Can't put a T in there. Besides, that is not even the crappy middle name they gave me. I don't want people using the middle name either. Not sure, is that my negativity? As I am not negative. Skilled and awesome, never negative. I write on the bottom two more letters.

From

U

Edmund Carson FU. I like it, it's not awesome, but I like it. Every Day My Urges Need Desires, Could Almost Replace Some Open Negativity. From U.

I feel like there is a sentence or something missing from the middle of the two statements. One tells them I am not going to quit, and the other references I am dealing with the fact that you have ignored me for so long.

But if they don't get my name from that, they are never going too. I am going to leave it there and think about it some more. I can do better. I go and sit at the teacher's desk, and pull out some paper and a pen. I want to write some notes that the girls can pass in class. I start to write:

So cute for an orphan

I think he may be the ONE. That's a cool one.

I hear he is now the best

Best or awesome. Why is awesome in my head? Not a word I use. I am, but not a word I usually use.

Rumour is he killed his parents. A bit obvious but they need to get this.

Miss Walker said he is the best lover in the world. I look at that one, and then I rip it up. I don't want her to take the fame for any of this. She will get fame because she is associated with me, that should be enough. Those celebrity couples never work out when both of them are famous. One needs to be in the shadows, and that's where Miss Walker needs to be.

It begins. That should give them a good link back to Melanie.

Brighton or bust. I saw that on a bus on the way to Brighton. I was going to check whether the Carnegies had turned up or not, but didn't get time. That's enough. If I think of more I will sort it afterwards. It's almost ten p.m. and I need to start getting in place. I look out of the door and nothing. I risk it and go up the stairs. I make it to Alana's room. I sit there in silence watching the clock tick.

This is the longest thirty minutes of my life. I hear the girls all walking up the stairs and past the room. I try counting them, but I lose track with voices on voices.

Ten thirty comes, and I check on my phone. WI-FI goes down. I hear the teacher heading back down the stairs.

How long should I leave it? When I start I need to continue. I wait another thirty minutes. I am not sure. I don't know whether to start or not. Sometimes it takes me longer than thirty minutes to nod off. I give it another twenty. It's

11.20. Surely they are all asleep now. I can't leave it any more or I will run out of time completely. I leave Alana's room, and head to the first room marked on my map. Teresa May. Her sign says she is In. I put my ear against the door. Should have brought a glass or something? It's what they do in the movies to make them listen better.

I can't hear anything. I push the door as quietly as possible. I can see her with her back to me in bed. I walk into the room, and push the door closed behind me. If there is any noise I can't let it wake the rest of them. I stand over her bed. Once this starts I have to go as quickly as possible. It needs to be quick and silent. I could wake up the whole floor if I make one mistake.

I reach my hand over towards her head. If I hold her mouth with my left hand I will have to cut her throat with my right. In two seconds it's done. As soon as the knife is placed in, the smell of the blood hits me. I cut deep to ensure that she can't scream out. She doesn't, she doesn't move. It's as if she didn't even wake up for it. It's a little rude to not wake up, but I can't worry about that, I have a mission to complete, and a deadline. I am out of her room. I switch the sign to Out. I think that is a nice touch. It will show attention to detail. I am in the next room in under two minutes. I am not sure I allowed a timing between rooms. Some of these are quite a hike in-between. This is worrying me. I need to ensure I get these done as quickly as possible. I need everyone taken care of before I start on Phase Two of the plan.

Victoria Raven is girl number two. Again, she is asleep facing away from the door. Maybe it's a girl thing as I always sleep facing the door. I would want to know if someone is

257

coming for me. The same happens again. She didn't really wake up. I am not sure if that is a good thing or a bad thing. I am out and at the next door. I open it slowly. The girl is facing directly at me. Can't be a girl thing. I close the door behind me. I creep up to her.

Fuck!

Her eyes open, she is adjusting to the light. I grab her mouth with one hand and slice with the other. She is convulsing on the bed. Must be a sleep thing. They don't move if they are sleeping. Three down, and the blood is playing havoc with my nostrils. It's not the time to get horny, but it's all I can think about now, especially as she is wriggling about. All I can think about is climbing on top of her. The blood is dripping off my gloves, and my knife. The smell is filling the room. I am hard as hell. I need to stop thinking about it. As soon as she stops kicking out I have to take a minute to compose myself. I can't decide if I should knock one out. Just to get it out of the system. But if I do I am always a little sleepy afterwards. I don't need that right now. I try to forget about it and move on.

I am out and heading to the next door. Time check says it has taken seventeen minutes. That needs to get better or else there will not be enough time. The next three take fourteen minutes. That's better. They were all sleeping. It is so much better when they are. In and out. I wait at the door for number seven. No sound. I think I should just stop the listening, it will bank me another minute or so. I slowly open the door.

There is nobody in the bed. I push the door open to the en suite; there is nobody in this room. I check under the bed. Nothing. There is a glass of water on the side so someone has

258

been here. I go out and check the room again and the fact that it says In when she is not. This is definitely an In. I check the map again. I defo saw someone in this room yesterday.

FUCK! Where is she...?

The last thing I need is to bump into her walking down the corridors. She must be here somewhere. I am out of seven's room and at number eight's door. In and out, simple, that is how it should be, but now I can't just walk to the next room. I am sticking close to the wall in case someone turns a corner. It is dark enough to hide in the shadows if she does. This is freaking me out. She shouldn't be up and about at this time of night. It's against the rules. Why can't people just stick to the rules? Especially girls.

I am going to tell Miss Walker about the fact that her school pupils don't respect her. This is a highly paid school, you'd think people would just do as they are told.

Eight, nine and ten are done. I get to the door to number eleven. No sign of anyone walking the corridors, but each time I come out of a room my heart is in my mouth. The whistle could be blown at any time. I push the door gently and there is another one missing.

What the fuck! Where are these bitches...?

Not tonight. Don't they know how important this is to me? Wait, no, I can hear someone tinkling. She is in the bathroom. I stand behind the door as it slides open. I grab her by the head and mouth, and plunge the knife into her neck. I slide it backwards and forwards to ensure it's done. The blood is so close now. The scent explodes up my nose. I take a lick from her neck. Oh my god, that is good. It's been far too long since I have had that taste in my mouth.

I am now fully aware that she is naked. I go over and place her on the bed. For seventeen years old she is so fully developed. The blood is trickling down her body. I lean over her again and take another lick. That is so sweet. Probably the sweetest I have ever tasted.

Stop. For fuck's sake, stop!

I can only think about what she would be like in bed. Better than Melanie, I am sure of it. I swear she is looking at me. She wants me. Surely that's like entrapment or something. I knew all these girls weren't virgins. You can just tell. I can't though, I really can't, I don't have enough time. I need to crack on.,I whisper in her ear.

"If I get time I will, I promise."

It's been over an hour and I am only eleven, no ten, down. I need to step up. The next six are a blur. I stop listening at the door as I don't have time and if they are still up past one a.m. then they shouldn't be. I get to number seventeen, and open the door.

Number seven, I presume, with number seventeen in bed together. I close the door behind me. They are actually in bed together, together. I get closer and the covers are half off. They are both naked. They must be like lesbians or something. I stand looking at the both of them. I am fixated by it. What do girls do when they are together? I know what I see on the movies I have, but never really quite believed it was true. I look around the room. Can't see any of those big strap-on things or vibrators anywhere. I go back to them both sleeping on the bed.

Now I don't know how to do it. I have to do both at the same time and they are spooning each other. I walk around to the other side. It's easier if I am facing them. I just have to go for it. I grab number seven by the mouth and stab at number seventeen's neck. I drag the blade straight across, she is fitting now. That should have done her. Number seven is biting my hand! I want to scream out loud, but I can't. I cut at her throat. She is mad this one. She is still going.

Fuck, fuck, fuck!

People will have heard that, seventeen is kicked out of bed, and hits the floor. Again at seven and again. At fucking last she has stopped moving. I freeze. There is silence. This place is so spooky at night. It scares even me at times. Some of the other girls must have heard her fall out. I wait a couple of minutes before moving again. I go to the door. I fully expect someone to be walking down the corridor. As I peer round the corner of the door. Nothing.

Fuck, that was lucky.

I go back into the room. They are both in that mad place that they go. I pick seventeen back up off the floor, and place her in the bed. I put them back into the spooning position.

"I am sorry that I disturbed you."

I stand and look at them. On another night, if I had had more time, I would have spent more time with all of you, but not tonight. This is my launch to stardom. I can't deal with this now. I give them a little whisper too.

"I would have considered my first threesome with you two, just not enough time. Not something I have ever really wanted, but looking at you really gets me going. I wish, I wish I had more time."

I still have six more rooms to visit before going downstairs. That was far too close. I exit the room, and complete the next six in under thirty minutes. Amy Parkins. She was the last one fast asleep and didn't move. I watch as she lies on the bed. The blood is flowing on to the sheets like a puddle. The smell is driving me wild.

That's twenty-three in two hours and fifteen minutes. I stand looking over her. It's just gone two a.m. There is a tingling all over my body. All I can think about is Jack. His song is going through my head, *Mack the Knife*. Jenny Diver, Sukey Tawdry, Lotte Lenya and old Lucy Brown, their names are running through my head.

Think that's how they will remember me: Amy Parkins, Debbie Morris and Teresa May? Now that Edmund's back in TOWN. Look out, old Edmund is back!

Yeah, defo need to upload that song on my YouTube account. Maybe even sing it with my name instead of Old Jack's. That will seriously piss him off.

I walk out of the room, and head down the stairs. It's a good walk from there to the classroom and the teachers' area. I wish I had my dad's wheelbarrow now; it would make things so much easier. I get to the first teacher's room: Mrs Cheryl Lee. How is she a Mrs and a live-in teacher? Wouldn't her husband be mad? Shouldn't she be at home cooking dinner and stuff for him? I enter the room. I am surprised they have almost the same room as the children. Maybe another couple of foot, but it's pretty much the same shoebox.

I can see her sleeping, another one that faces away from the door. I lean over her. She is snoring. I grab her mouth and slit her throat. It's deep and the blood has a rich dark smell. I am starting to believe the younger and sweeter you are, the sweeter the smell of the blood. The girls upstairs, they smell amazing. Maybe it's to do with your age or what your diet is like. I think I read somewhere about pigs being fed with acorns taste of acorns. And if you were to feed them fish they would taste of fish. Makes sense really. Imagine what the girls must taste like? The burglar tasted really good, but what about a young girl. She must taste amazing. I give Mrs Lee a lick and try to work out what she had for dinner. I am sure I can taste red wine. I really need to be more adventurous with my diet. Try something new every week. They say kidneys are good for you. Note to self: get liver before I leave. Maybe some kidneys oh, and heart. Heart is supposed to be really good.

I am watching as the blood soaks the sheets. Same as I did with Amy. The colour contrast is amazing even in this light. I think I am slowing down. I need to get some energy back into me otherwise I am never going to be known as an artist. Well, I will, an artist, but not a superstar. I slap my face to get me back up and going. Maybe need some sugar or some chocolate; that normally wakes me up.

The last teacher is three doors down. She was the cute one from the train. I am sure her blood is going to smell good enough to get this show on the road. I leave Mrs Lee and head to the next room.

Why did I just do that? I listened at the room. It's a good job that I did as I can hear a TV going. How is that happening? I listen again it is definitely some kind of movie playing. It must be like two thirty in the morning? Shit, I am unsure now what to do. Is she awake? Is she alone? The door says Miss Lisa Stanners. She is not married then? I don't have a choice, I don't have enough time. I push the door. The lights are off.

She isn't moving on the bed and facing the side window away from the door.

That's lucky. I notice the dresser. There is a laptop playing what looks like a movie. I walk up slowly behind her. She isn't moving. I can see her breathing deeply. I am sure she is asleep. I walk around to where she is facing. Yes, she is asleep. Thank Christ for that. Wait, what am I worried about? Nobody can hear us. We are all alone here. I walk towards her and slowly close the laptop.

Fuck! Dropped it on the floor.

Shit, she is awake...

Her eyes are adjusting. I wasn't ready. I grab for my knife behind me and I drop it.

Fuck, fuck, fuck!

"What the fuck is going on?"

I am on the floor and just about grab the knife, I am up, and she is the other side of the bed. That's not really good language for a teacher, is it?

"Who are you and what the hell are you doing in my room?"

I don't have an answer for her. I wasn't prepared to speak. No. No words are springing to mind. I just dive across the bed at her.

Fuck, missed.

"Help! Help!"

I am sure there is no one else here, but I need to shut her up just in case. I am off the floor and up again. She is up, and out of the room. Fuck, where is she going? I run after her. She is knocking on Mrs Lee's room. I see her burst in. That screaming isn't going to help you, love. I run in after her and into the room. She is standing over Mrs Lee's bed having a right fit. She is facing me head-on now. She does not look impressed.

We are at a Mexican standoff: one of us has to attack. She hasn't stopped screaming, but she is stooped to attack at me. I dive again and she punches out. She connects right at the side of my head. I am on the floor in front of her. She moves backwards. She hits fucking hard for a little woman.

"Fuck that hurt."

I don't think she cares that it did. I can see it in her eyes. I am up again and facing straight at her.

"Don't, just don't." She is mad.

I dive forward again. I have her. I plunge my knife into her side. Somewhere between the ribs, I think, as I felt a bump as it went in. She is still hitting. I think she thinks that puts me off, but it doesn't. In fact it is just what I need to get the blood going again. I hold on to her.

I was thinking about bringing my knife up and slitting her throat, but I want the fight more. So I just wiggle it backwards and forwards where it is. There must be some sort of vital organ there somewhere. She is still punching and kicking at me. I am horny again now. The blood is sweeter and stronger. I can feel it trickling down my hand. I so much want to lick it. I need her to slow down first, else I will end up with another right-hander from her. It's almost five minutes before she gives up the fight. I lay her backwards, and pull my hand up to my face.

My eyes pop out of my head, I am sure of it. That's amazing. This must be what drug addicts feel like when they get a hit. This has cost me time, but I need this. I need this moment with the blood. I need to remember why I chose this profession. Not only because of how skilled I am at it, but the fact that I enjoy doing it. They say if you choose the right profession, you never have to work a day in your life. That sounds like me. This isn't work, it's life. This is my life. I need this to keep me going for the next five hours. In fact, I need more than just the smell of blood. I wipe the glove all over my face. I need my blood to be pumping in all areas of my body.

I strip Miss Stanners naked, and within minutes so am I. I throw the clothes in the corner where I was standing. I need this, I need my heart to be racing. I need my blood at full pelt.

I cut her at the throat. She is leaking. Not spurting, but leaking. I think all the pump has gone. But the smell hasn't. It has me harder than ever. I lay down on top of her. I am going to fuck her like she has never been fucked before. I deserve this. I have worked hard for this.

"Fuck!"

I am up and grabbing at my clothes. I am covering myself with my shirt.

"I am so sorry, Mrs Lee. I forgot all about the fact that you were here?"

I am so embarrassed. I almost gave her the show of a lifetime. Imagine that getting back to her husband. They just came into my room and got down to it.

"I know, I know, I would, but then I have to come back and move the clothes and stuff."

"OK, that's a great idea. Thank you, Mrs Lee. You are so generous."

I put my T-shirt on. At least it covers the main parts of me.

266

"Sure, I will help you."

I take Mrs Lee back to Miss Stanners' room. I place her in the bed and tuck her in. I do hope she doesn't tell her husband what happened. The last thing I need is an angry husband after me. I close her in. I don't think she wants to listen to us.

"I am so sorry it took that long. I wanted to make sure that she was comfortable."

She isn't talking to me. What is it about the mood time? Ten minutes or so and they are happy as Larry. Whoever Larry is?

I am back on top. I enter her. Oh my god, I have missed that. The first push, the first feeling and I nuzzle my face into the blood on her neck. She feels amazing. I am slow and hard, slow and hard.

I keep thinking of my girlfriend. Shit, my girlfriend will know her. What am I doing here? She will never speak to me again. Hold on, she doesn't know me. I just have to use a false name, and that will be OK. She looks like her though. Maybe that's why I started slow and hard. The mood time is over.

"I could hardly come straight in and say that, could I? Is it hurting? Do you want me to stop?"

"OK, a little faster."

"Thanks I try to work out when I have the time."

"OK, I promise next time I will just get straight down to business."

Does she want to talk or fuck? She is better than Melanie, that is a plus point. The look in her eyes is more mischievous as well, which always makes me hornier.

The blood has my heart pumping at a hundred miles an hour. I am so eager for this. This is my reward for the work so far. I deserve a reward. Fuck, it's going too fast. Too fast, too fast.

Shit!

That was over way too fast. She is disappointed. I can tell by the look on her face. She did tell me to go faster, she has to take some of the blame. That can't have helped my performance. And the Mrs Lee thing, I also think she affected me.

"Sorry, I am so sorry. I guess, what with the excitement of the night and everything else. It has never happened to me before, I can swear that to you. Honstly, I am a great lover. I can get people to verify, you know."

"You're too kind. I am not normally, I can assure you. Normally forty-five minutes to an hour at least, at least, and that is after foreplay"

I don't think she believes me. What is it lately about the women I choose? They seem to have some kind of voodoo on sex. Either not exciting enough or too exciting.

"We can, we definitely can."

We can't, not now. Now I have stuff to do.

"What if we leave it like an hour and a half? I will fetch your laptop, you can watch your film and then we will have another go at this?"

"Perfect."

I help her to Mrs Lee's bed, tuck her in and then get dressed. I go next door and fetch her laptop. Mrs Lee is snoring so she is sound asleep. Maybe I should have stayed here with her. Maybe it's because Miss Stanners and Melanie have both looked a lot like my girlfriend that the gel isn't working. Maybe I should be looking elsewhere? Should I try blondes? I go back to the room, and set everything up for her. Blondes? No, I just can't see it.

"I know, I love that film. I was just saying the other day I love that film."

"I know, right, in the shop. I'm also just a girl, standing in front of a boy, asking him to love her. How could he say no? I would have melted on the ground, I am sure of it. The girls were watching it earlier as well, I believe. It is a proper chick flick, isn't it?"

I press play and leave the room. I think it's safe to say there is no one else here or they would have heard all that going on. I go to the classroom and prop the door open.

Fucking Result!

Didn't notice that before. In the corner is one of those trolleys that they move boxes of paper around with. That will help no end. Even has a strap. Better than my dad's wheelbarrow. Things are really looking up. I grab hold of the barrow and head towards the stairs.

This is the hard part. Helping all the girls down the stairs. Given what we are doing, you'd think they would be more excited to help. They are going to benefit from this no end.

Miss Stanners will be all right. I will be back and better than ever. I can't leave another one without making their bell ring. At least once. Maybe she just isn't into long sex. She may have some kind of knack that makes men come quicker. Maybe does exercises down there to keep it tight and stuff. I heard women do that. Yeah, she has a knack. Like Miss Walker does with delaying them.

Yeah, it's her. I can never believe it's me. I am a god.

Chapter 18

I bump the barrow up the stairs and to the first room. That was more tiring than I expected. Teresa May, she was nice and quick and easy. The sleeping thing took the fun out of it, but I am glad that some of them were asleep. If not, I would be completely knackered by now.

I look in her wardrobe and find her school uniform. Then the drawers, and find some underwear. I lay her out on the bed and start to dress her. Pants and skirt go on easy.

Not sure how a bra really works. I place it over her breasts and then try to reach underneath to fasten it. Never done one up before, it's not easy.

Fuck!

I flip her over on the bed, do it up, and then flick her back and wedge her boobs back in there. How do they do that every day?

I then button her blouse and put her kerchief around her neck. I think the blazer is a bit much for in class. I pick her up and get her next to the barrow. I can't hold her with one hand and then strap her with the other, it's impossible. I just can't. I put her next to the bed again.

Think, Edmund, think.

There must be an easier way of doing this. I lay the barrow down and then lay her on it. That's it. That's the one. I can strap her in. I stand the barrow up. She is still in there, perfect.

I have just noticed she hasn't said a word the whole time I have been doing this. That's not like a teenage girl.

"Are you OK?"

No, nothing? They aren't normally mad at me. Something must be wrong? I sit on the bed facing her. I want to make sure the girls enjoy it as much as I have. I am a great person to work with.

"Are you sure everything is OK? You have been really quiet. I want you to know that all of you girls are special to me. And let's face it, you were the first? When the story is told they will say Teresa May, and then the other twenty-two?"

That has a reaction out of her. I can see it in her eyes. But still nothing.

"As first, I tell you what, I think you should be at the front of the class, by the door. So you are the first person they see when they walk into the classroom."

Her eyes are dancing around the room at that, but still not a word.

Fuck!

I get up and check her neck. I knew it: I knew it when I came in I was over forceful. Nearly took the poor girl's head off.

"I am so sorry, Teresa. I thought you were mad at me and not speaking. Do you know what, I thought I had been a little hard when I started. I should have known that's why you weren't talking to me?"

The look in her eyes says she forgives me. I hold her head in my hands. Gently this time. I don't want a Bethany. I kiss her. A real kiss though, not a school playground one. That will make up for it. I stand up, and wheel her out of the room.

Fucking hell!

Sounds like they are having a fucking party up here. The girls are shouting and laughing. They weren't this noisy when they were in London. I suppose they have never been up after ten thirty. This must be like a sleepover party for them all.

"Yes, yes, I have started, and yes, you will all be in the classroom soon."

"No, I wish. I wish I did have the time."

"No, I don't know what one is. If three people are a threesome, it's not a twenty-foursome, is it…? Besides, there are teachers too?"

"Yes, Miss Stanners is hot, seventeen. Trust you to notice."

For the life of me I can't remember that girl's name.

"Soon, soon."

I bump Teresa down the stairs and along to the classroom. I untie her and put her in the first seat.

"Pride of place, Teresa."

She is happy. I check the watch.

Twenty-one fucking minutes!

It's gone three a.m. At this rate it will be what, twenty-four times twenty-one… Half fucking eleven just to get them in the room. I can't do that. It was that damn bra. Takes so long to put on.

I run up the stairs with the barrow to Victoria's room. I need to get better at this.

"No, no time. I wish I did, really I do."

I grab her uniform. No time for underwear, just the basics. I put her skirt on and start on her blouse.

"I wish I was as well, but today I will be mostly putting clothes on."

I find her kerchief and then lay down the barrow. I lay her on it.

"I do, I do find you attractive, in fact you are just my type. But we don't have the time."

I stand the barrow up. Good, she is strapped in.

"I did kiss her. News travels fast around here, doesn't it?"

I suppose it's only fair. They are all going to be playing their part in my launch. I kiss Victoria. Good kisser. Firm. Not a lot of tongue.

"Now we have to go. I am sorry if this gets bumpy."

We are out of the room. I think they wait for me to come out, and then all start screaming my name. This is what it must be like to be a pop star. It's deafening. I feel sorry for those One Direction guys now. We are down the stairs and in the classroom. I sit Victoria next to Teresa.

"Because she was first. Don't worry, you will be known as the person I went to next."

They are fussy about these things, aren't they? Popularity in girls is nonsense.

Fourteen fucking minutes!

Not good enough. I mean, it's better, but that is still nearly nine o'clock. Needs to be better still. I can't wait with the barrow. Maybe I carry them? I run up the stairs and in the third girl's room. I want to say Elle? It's on my map, I am sure. I put her skirt on and her blouse, but don't do it up. I throw her over my shoulder and run down the stairs. stick her in the seat, do up the blouse, and BAM. Ten minutes.

Fuck, I am knackered.

I don't think I can do that twenty times. I turn to leave the room.

"I am sorry, slipped my mind."

I go back and kiss Elle. The other two are not happy. Shouldn't have really done that in front of them, even though everyone is talking about what a good kisser I am. I can hear them.

"I forgot when I was in the room, that is all."

"No, I mean, yes, Teresa, you are special and, oh, I don't know."

I run out of the classroom as fast as I can. I don't need that shit. Jealous girls, don't they know I have a job to do?

I am back upstairs and in the fourth girl's room she is in PJs

Fuck it!

She is going to class like that. I don't have time for all this dressing nonsense. As long as they are not naked then that will have to do. She is down, and in class in just under eight minutes. Better. Not great, but better.

I run back up the stairs again. I need another plan. I can't be doing that another nineteen times. I am fit, but I need to reserve some energy to take care of Miss Stanners. They are going to have to be in class in their PJs. It's not ideal, but I don't have the time to dress them all.

There are only three of them naked. Seven, eleven and seventeen. So they need to be last. I go into Maria's room. Number five. I think she has gone back to sleep. I suppose it

274

has been a while since I visited her. I lean over her and give her, her kiss. She is awake.

"I know, I am sorry. This is taking longer than I thought it would."

"Thank you, you're right, I suppose, you can't rush an artist. I just need a better delivery service."

"I know, I am fit enough to take more than one, but I have other stuff to do tonight."

"Believe me, if I had time I would. You are beautiful. I wish you were the other stuff I needed to do."

The vanity on these girls is amazing. Although I so wish I had a weekend to do this. Would be a lot of fun. A lot of fun.

I look around the room. There isn't anything. Nothing that can help me get them down the stairs quicker and I am going to run out of time. I am just going to have to run it. I go over to Maria and throw the blanket off the bed.

Fuck the blanket!

Maybe that's it. Maybe I can drag them down the stairs.

"Carefully, yes, carefully. It will help with the timings so much, if you don't mind."

"Thank you."

I place Maria on the blanket, and pull her out to the hallway.

I then go and fetch two more of the girls. I kiss them in the rooms. I am not going through all that nonsense again. Girls can be so petty. I grab the blanket and start to pull. It's easier.

"Sorry, yes, of course."

They are right, I should pull from the head. Not fair to be going feet first. And let's face it, I don't want to lose a head tonight, not tonight. I take them down the stairs and into the classroom. As we come in, the girls give me a round of applause.

"I know, I took my time but I figured it out finally."

I set the girls up in the classroom and repeat. By four fifteen I only have three left to bring down. And dress. I run upstairs and head into Kate's room. Number eleven. I kiss and dress her. And pull her out into the hallway on the blanket. She is a little mad I didn't come back after surprising her out of the bathroom. I do understand that they all want more time with me. I need to think about that for the next time. The people I work with also have rights. And they shouldn't be rushed into anything. This is as much for them as it is for me.

I enter the room they are both laughing.

"What is so funny?"

"Oh, this whole time, eh? It must have been what a couple of hours?"

"But you are finished now? When I say finished, I mean finished."

"Good, as we need to get you dressed."

"I would love to, believe me. The night I have had so far. There would be nothing I would rather do."

"Yes, even a threesome would have been on the table."

I am warming to the idea of one, but I am not convinced I am a two-women man. I take number seven off the bed and dress her. I take her out to the hallway and towards the blanket.

"What?"

"That doesn't matter, does it?"

I place seven down by the wall and walk over to Kate.

"I can't believe that you judge people because of their sexuality. It doesn't matter. Boys, girls, hell, I don't care if you sleep with a goat. Love is just love."

That's so short-sighted. In this day and age as well. I drag Kate down the stairs on her own. Feet first. I place her in the classroom. The girls are so loud now. I guess it's all the excitement about the press coming and the fame thing.

I go back upstairs to seven.

"I am so sorry about that, some people, eh? I think it is great that you have found someone."

"Yes, I will get her dressed and the two of you can come together."

"Ha ha ha, yes, not for the first time."

I go back into the room. Seventeen is still lying on the bed.

"Now don't start, you know we are up against it on time."

"I can't do quickly, I wish I could."

I clearly can do quickly, but the less people know about that, the better.

"School uniform?"

"I kind of like it. Haven't been able to stop thinking about it since the school trip. It's defo a turn-on."

"Yes, I was there, I was with you. It was a good day."

"You did? They did? Thanks, I don't know about hotter than Brad Pitt, but it's nice to know you noticed me."

I grab her clothes and start to dress her.

"Slower?"

I do as she asks. This is very hot. She is very hot. If I didn't think that Miss Stanners was a one-off I would try and fit it in, but I don't really have the time. I wish I had the time.

"Stop that, I can't concentrate."

With every touch she is making little sighing noises. It's so horny. I finally get her dressed and take her out to seven.

"Yes, we were a long time."

"No we didn't. Your girlfriend here though is a right tease."

They are both chuckling. I must admit, that is a tempting sound. I suppose I am going to have to get used to women throwing themselves at me.

I lay them both on the blanket.

"How did you hear that from here?"

"I am a good kisser, that part is true."

"OK, but quickly as I have to get on."

I lay down on the blanket with both of them. I kiss seven. As I do I am conscious that seventeen's hands are all over me. It's a bit freaky. I then kiss seventeen. She is a good kisser, but now seven's hands are all over me. Both of their hands are all over me. There are too many hands here. I can't concentrate. It's making me all confused. I jump up.

"OK, that's enough, we don't have the time."

I am not sure I could do this threesome thing. I am not in control, it's like they are smothering me. Some people see that as normal. They are weirdoes.

I take the girls gently downstairs. The move from upstairs to downstairs hasn't stopped them. All the way down to the classroom they are all over each other. It's hotter in real life than it is on the DVDs. I take the girls into class and sit them at their desks next to each other. My god, these girls are noisy.

"I said, we need to keep it down. Your teachers are only next door."

"I know, I know, but I promise you all, you will all be famous. This is just the start of it. I wouldn't be surprised if they don't name the school after one of you. Or at least there will definitely be plaques with your names on them."

"No, not reality TV famous. Those people last for about a year or so. You girls are going to be legendary famous. I am sure that you will all have your names in songs as I will."

Seven and seventeen are still giggling to each other.

I need to stop calling them that. I have their names all written down on the map, but they just feel like seven and seventeen to me. I am sure they are doing it to see if I will change my mind about a threesome, but Miss Stanners comes first. I can't have her telling the police about what happened. I am hardly going to be a superstar if people find out I lasted about thirty seconds. All superstars are five times a night, that's what all the papers say.

I am not sure it is true, but the press is king when it comes to turning normal people into legends.

I didn't plan enough time. I stand looking at them all. I wanted to dress them all in school uniform, but it's too hard. I think it's because they don't want to get dressed around me. I have never been good at getting girls to dress. Undress, yes, but to put clothes on around me. Must be a hard thing for them. I do understand that.

"Yes, I know. I need like thirty to forty-five minutes, and then, I swear. Name badges, notes handing out, and I will get the teachers as well. And, yes, I know I am not sure it works on the blackboard either. In fact that is your challenge. Think of something better for me. By the time I come back."

I leave the room. My god, they don't shut up, do they? I am so glad I didn't go to a same-sex school as well.

I go back to Mrs Lee's room. The film is finished. I can see the park and they are lying on the bench. Wait...

"Do you know I never noticed that before? She is pregnant, isn't she? I think I have watched this film a million times and I thought the ending was all about the old couple sitting beside each other. I thought that is what they were going for. I am glad though. That looks perfect."

I walk over and close the laptop.

"Yes, we do."

I climb into bed. Time to go to work. I strip and cuddle up next to her. I start stroking her body.

"Thanks for waiting."

Something is missing: I don't seem to be rising to the occasion. Work, for fuck's sake, don't you let me down. Come on, work.

"I am sorry, I don't know what is up with me, I am all over the place tonight. This is never a problem, really never. Half the time I have to hold the thing down. Or just knock one out to get rid of it."

"I am tired. People don't realise this job isn't easy. Moving the girls has really taken it out of me. And I know I am on the clock, but that is no excuse. I am going to be famous and work some long hours. I can't be in relapse before I have even started."

"Cuddle? OK, but that's not my normal style."

I cuddle up to her. The blood on her neck does the job. Within seconds I am back. And everything is rock hard. That was it, I just needed a pick-me-up. I lick her neck as if it were the only ice-lolly left on a hot day.

"No, there is nothing in my pocket. I am naked."

I knew what she meant. We are at it like a couple of bunnies. Now this is what I am talking about. No slow and hard, hard and fast and faster. This has my heart racing again. Stop, Edmund, stop. I pull out. I am not doing that again. What the fuck is wrong with me? I was seconds away again.

"I just need some water."

I go and fetch some. I take my time. I need to calm down a little. What is going on tonight? Think I am on overdrive. I hope it's not the girlfriend thing.

I am picking them to all look alike. Maybe Miss Walker is playing on my mind when I am cheating with someone else. Maybe I should sleep with a blonde so I don't think about her. Maybe I have some guilt somewhere down deep inside when they look like her. That can't be good for my performance, Somehow something is off, whichever way I look at it... It's either Miss Stanners' or Miss Walker's fault, that is for sure. It's not me.

I go back, a quick sniff and we off again.

Fuck!

What was that like, ten pumps and bang?

"I swear, I honestly swear, this never happens."

She doesn't believe me. I can tell. I get out of bed and head back to the bathroom. I stand looking in the mirror. It's Miss Walker, I know it is. She is in my head. What is she doing to me?

I can't let this stop me being a superstar. I have a reputation to uphold. People will be talking about me in generations to come.

I leave the bathroom.

"Look, I swear, before I go we will do this. Not like the last two times. I will be back and I will leave you feeling as if you have been fucked by Edmund Carson."

Fuck! I told her my name.

What is up with me? Now she is going to put two and two together? She will tell my girlfriend… Friend, fucking friend now! I dress and I am out of there. Before I even get to the classroom I can hear them all laughing. They can't be laughing at me, can they? They wouldn't know what just happened? Well, not unless they have just been texted. She wouldn't do that. Or would she?

I don't want to go in there. I go and fetch Mrs Lee. They won't laugh when there is another teacher in the room.

I take Mrs Lee into the classroom, and sit her at the desk. The class are a little bit quieter, but not a lot. It would seem they don't really care for authority at this time of the morning.

"I know I promised. I always keep my promises."

I start to hand out some notes to the girls. Some are mid passing them. That's good. The police will be looking for the piece of paper in their hands.

I take some of the books off the desk, and hand them out.

"I am sorry, I didn't know."

Really need to sort name badges.

"Look, let's swap them around once we get the badges. But all I wanted to do for a start is for some of you to be writing at your desks. It's all about the staging. People will want to know that we are artists. We have created something here that will be as famous as that bloke's sunflowers."

"Yes, you will still be famous even if you have the wrong books. You girls and I are all going down in history after tonight."

For a clever school I am still concerned about the IQ level of some of these girls. I help some of the girls draw some pictures. A love heart with my initials in seems to be their favourite. I guess that is something I am going to have to get used to.

"My god, you two never shut up."

I give them a look as if I mean it, but playful at the same time. Seven and seventeen, it's like they are obsessed with me. I do understand it, but it's so time-consuming. I go over and whisper in both of their ears.

"You know you are both my favourites."

They are not the only ones I let down tonight. Don't they know that if I had my way and another day or so, I would have probably spent time with all of them? These girls are special, and I would have loved to make them feel even more so. If I had time. Maybe I will come back in a couple of weeks.

"Do I have a girlfriend, is that what you are saying?"

Miss Stanners never texted them. Or they wouldn't be asking. I don't think I am supposed to answer that. All these famous people, they never own up to girlfriends, do they? Not until they are due to get married. It hurts their fanbase. You have to give them the hope that they have a chance with you.

"No, I am single. What with my job and everything I just haven't met someone who is willing to stand by my side. I am not looking for a girlfriend. More a soul mate. I really want that someone to share everything with."

There is a giggle from the classroom and a dozen offers. Think that is the answer that they wanted. They are all going to be dreaming about me now. My caring sensitive side also.

"You are too kind, all of you."

I wink over at seven and seventeen. That should keep them happy.

They are not all sitting upright in class. The room doesn't look right. They need to be paying more attention to the teachers. I try sitting them up. It's OK for a few to be bent over writing, but not all of them.

I leave the classroom. I need some rope and utensils. I left my bag in the kitchen on the way in so I go and fetch it. Tools in hand, I go back to the classroom, and start work on making sure everyone is in position.

This night, wait, nearly morning, isn't getting much better. I am knackered. I spend the next forty-five minutes making sure all the girls are in position. It is amazing what some rope, hammer, nails, and school rulers will do. They don't shut up all the way through it though. Edmund this, Edmund that. Can I be your girlfriend? I love you, Edmund. I guess that's what fame is going to be like. I am going to need some time to get used to it. It's almost as if I have been an overnight success, when I have been working for weeks, but nobody noticed. The classroom is a lot better. Looks more like the scene I imagined.

I go back to Mrs Lee's room. I have a job to do before I leave here. People need to know I stay until the job is done right.

"I am sorry, it took longer than I expected."

She is not mentioning Miss Walker. Maybe they aren't that close. That would be so good if they weren't.

"I know, it's like six thirty. The whole night has gotten away from me, and it will be nearly breakfast so the chefs will be here."

"Really?"

I leave the room, and go back to the kitchen. She is right, there are pack-up bags everywhere. I knew there was a lot going on in this room when I came in. Right next to where my kit bag is as well. How didn't I notice the pack-up? I open one: fruit, breakfast bars and orange juice. I open one from the next tray: sandwiches, crisps, and more fruit. I don't think they were planning on making breakfast this morning.

I can't believe I have just spent the last six hours running around like a mad man when I had hours to do this. The cooks aren't coming in, are they? Why didn't someone just tell me? It's not like they haven't been talking. They haven't shut up since two a.m. Their breakfast and lunch is already laid out for them.

I go back to Mrs Lee's room.

"You are right. Don't know how I missed that. Pack-up everywhere. I have been in and out of that kitchen as well."

"I guess we do. Time to do this properly."

I undress for the third time tonight. I have time. I don't need to rush this. It's all about the mood setting, getting relaxed. I lay on the bed stroking the hair. The smell of blood isn't as strong. In fact it is hardly there now.

"If you don't mind?"

I take my knife off the side, cut behind her ears, a little tear on her stomach.

"I know it's been a hell of a night. I think it is enough though, don't you? I think this is the point which will excel me into stardom?"

She is a chatty one, this one. I am not sure I could put up with that full-time. The only thing Miss Walker says through sex is my name. That's exactly what I want to hear. She knows exactly what I want to hear. Like she can read my mind.

"You? You are going to be where you belong. Centre stage of the class."

That should loosen her up a bit. I lean over and kiss her. The blood is stronger now. My knife has done the work. On that, and me. As her blood leaks down her neck mine returns to its rightful place. I climb on top of her and we go again. Slow and hard. Slow and hard.

I can hear Miss Walker's voice in my head. I close my eyes, and it is her I am imagining. Does that make me weird? I have heard about men fantasising about other women when they are with their wives, but fantasising about your girlfriend when you are with another woman. I am still going. This is great. There is no burst this time. I can feel myself falling into the rhythm. I open my eyes, I can tell she is on it this time. I whisper in her ear.

"Told you I knew what I was doing."

"Thanks, I know."

I am bigger than the average man. And I bet a lot of men can't go three, four times a night. I am getting faster. I can feel it. I am looking at her. She is ready to explode. I keep going harder and faster, harder and faster, and I wait for her to go first. I need to ensure she has multiple ones to make up for the last two times. She does, and I come almost straight afterwards.

"Now that's what I am talking about. You are welcome."

I lie on the bed next to her. She is not going to tell anyone how bad I am now. Three times a night. And not just any night, the night when I had this much work to do. People are going to know I am a legend that doesn't quit.

"I agree. Time is getting on. There may be no cooks, but I don't know if anyone else is due today."

I need to get her ready. She is right, she deserves to be dressed and in front of the class. I get dressed, and go to her room. Go through her closet, and find a skirt and a blouse. I head over to her drawers and open them. They are full of all kinds of underwear, stockings, suspender belts, teddies. I bet she looked hot in all of these. I pull out a teddy. I would have gone full-on stockings and suspenders as it's my favourite, but she is teaching class. Besides this looks easier than a bra.

I go back to the room, and show her the outfit I picked out. She likes it, so I help her get dressed. She is fit. As I get her dressed I can't help but notice that she almost has a six-pack. No wonder she wanted it three times in the same night.

I take her into the classroom. There is a cheer from the girls as I get into the room. Other than seven and seventeen. They don't look impressed at all. I think they think that I have deserted them for Miss Stanners. I whisper in her ear again.

"Whereabouts would you prefer?"

I try and lean her up against the blackboard. It's not working, she is going to fall down. I need to get my bag and do a job with her also. A slide rule and twelve nails later and she is in position. There is a round of applause from the class. I take a bow. She looks great there. She really commands her students. Wish I had a teacher like her.

"Do you know what, I think I agree? I haven't referenced enough the ONE. So class, how do you think I should?"

They all shout their opinions. Seventeen the loudest. I think I need to give her something. Just as a way of saying sorry for not joining their party.

"And we have a winner."

I take off my hoodie and dress her in it. I then place her chair behind seven's and put my knife in her hand, and seven's on her shoulder.

I write on seven's pad: *He is the ONE.* Think that might just do it. I go back to the front of the class. There is another round of applause. Maybe I should have gone to an all-girls school. It would have been so much fun. Or become a teacher in one of them. I could teach, and people would listen.

"So girls, any ideas on the board?"

I stand looking at it again.

"Dissolving instead of Desires, I like that, it's punchy, and means I need to work every day."

I walk up and change the board. I still don't like Carson FU.

"I am sorry, I forgot all about the name badges."

I pull out my map again, and stand by the window writing on the windowsill.

The badges are more important than the board. It's only fair that they all become famous too. Not as famous as me, but they will get their fifteen minutes in the spotlight.

I start to stick some of the names on the girls. I am sure they are lifting their chests just so I place the sticker on them. They want me to touch them.

Fuck! A car.

I can see the lights coming up the driveway. It can't be the cooks. There is pack-up everywhere. I start pulling down the blinds in the classroom so they can't see in here. It's getting closer. It's a good job that it is a stately home with a long driveway.

Just as they are about to pass the last blind is down. I stand in the corner, and look out of the window through the cracks in the blinds. It's a van. It's not the cooks. I can just about make out the words on the side: Gardeners.

They are here to cut the grass? Two men get out. Surely they won't come in here, will they? Maybe they need to plug stuff in or get water or something. What am I going to do? I look back at the girls. I can see them looking at me.

"I don't know, there are two of them."

"I know I am, but is it right that they should share in your fame. Now that is the question? This is about us."

I look back through the window. I am fast and I am skilled, but one of them must be six foot six. Looks like he could be a wrestler. What if he is stronger than me? I mean, I am strong and fast. But what if? Then the whole plan goes out the window. What would Miss Walker say? I can't risk it. I come away from the window.

"Thanks, yes, I agree."

She is so bright that number seven. If I were to just take care of them, it would ruin the whole staging thing. The whole point is for the girls to be made famous for this.

No, they will have to just do what they are doing. I look back out the window and they are both getting back into their van. But it doesn't pull away.

Time for some selfies with all the girls. I spend the next fifteen minutes making sure all the girls get their picture with me. They are lucky, it won't be long before I have to start charging for these and for photographs. I promise to send on the good ones. I am going to need a new phone. What with the tube, and now this.

I think I have done enough. I can't do any more.

"Look, before I go, I just wanted to say thank you. Thank you for all the help and encouragement that you have given me tonight. Thank you for letting me come into your school and help it make a part of history. What we have done here tonight is going to be remembered for decades to come. Your names along with mine will be linked in history and yes, I will wager, in song for an eternity. I couldn't have done it without you."

There is cheering from the girls. I am almost welling up. There is a smile from Miss Stanners. There is a real connection there, if it wasn't for Miss Walker, I think we could make it a real thing. If she had been a little less chatty maybe. Chatty women do my head in. Remind me of my mum.

"OK, OK. Good luck and I guess by this time tomorrow we are all going to be world-famous."

I grab my kit and leave them in the classroom. I stop just outside of the door and have a moment to myself. I can hear them all clapping and cheering inside. That was great. A real piece of art. This is what I was destined to do. I head out the back of the kitchen where I came in. It's colder than it looks out here. I could have done with keeping my hoodie. The last thing I want is to catch a cold before becoming a legend.

I don't really have time to be on my sick bed for the next couple of weeks.

I head over to the trees and walk just on the inside of them down the lane. The gardeners are still in their van drinking tea by the looks of it. Within ten minutes I am at the back of Miss Walker's house.

I don't know what to do. If I go in and she is awake she is going to be able to tell I have been up to something. Plus she will probably want sex due to me being so sweet yesterday. And then what? I fall asleep and wake up to the tune of police sirens? They are defo going to knock door to door in this village as soon as they find them. Especially this house. It's practically in the grounds.

No, I need to get out of here. Sleep and then sort the plan. I stand at the window. The wine and DVD are still on the side. Is she even home? Did she go to bed exhausted? Is she with this Jack fellow? I can't deal with all that today. Not today.

She is probably in bed fast asleep. I go back round and take the car back to Wimbledon tube station. There is a greasy spoon café to the side, and I wash up in their bathroom. I need to find a hotel. I may as well stay here.

I pull out my phone and google hotels. There is one around the corner about four hundred metres, the Justin James. I manage to bag myself a room. Had to pay for last night as well as the next two, but I think they needed the custom. It's a bit olde-worlde, but it will do.

I get to my room, and take a shower. I stand under the water as it beats down on me hard. I think this is shock that is waving over me. This must be what stars are like when they finally finish a movie. I think it's relief and excitement all wrapped into one moment. I don't know whether to laugh or cry with happiness.

I get out of the shower and lay on the bed. I have so much work to do, but I am not going to be doing it justice unless I get some rest. I need to look my best tomorrow for the camera.

I lay looking at the ceiling. I have done this a lot. Seem to always be looking up at a ceiling somewhere. I grab my phone and set my alarm. Four p.m. I need a good six hours' sleep. Then I need to get on, and sort it all out. The world can't ignore me any more.

Chapter 19

The alarm wakes me up. I slept straight through to it. I must have been exhausted. I switch on the TV. Nothing. No news. Not sure if I am surprised or not. Something this big is not just going to get out in the press in a matter of hours. They will want to investigate first. I order room service. I need to keep remembering to eat. It feels like ages.

As soon as it arrives I sit on the bed and eat. The TV is on in the background, and I am waiting for the breaking news moment. Nothing.

This is what I had planned though. I thought I would get some time to set up the social media sites. When things this big happen they like to get their ducks in a row before coming out to the press. I have seen it on *CSI* and *Criminal Minds*. They need to work through to find the right description of the unsub.

Facebook first, it's the safest. Nobody can see anything until I friend them. I start through the process. I need a good selfie picture as my profile. One that ensures the world knows what I look like. I use the one from the night outside Sophia's house. It's a little dark, but you can see it is me. Plus it was the night I first met Miss Walker for real. She will be happy I chose that one. I start uploading lots of selfies. All with little straplines like, *me at the Mersons, me with the girls, seven and seventeen, my favourites.* They will love all this stuff; it will make them so happy.

I do everything in the right order. That way it will look like I have been doing it all along. Well, unless they look at the dates. As I fill in all my personal information it keeps recommending people I know.

Carl Carnegie has a Facebook page. I think he should be my first friend when I kick-start this. I think we are friends now. He did help me with the old head thing. And I think it shows how much I have grown as a person since I started this job. I have come a long way to get to here.

Relationship status. I can't win there, can I? If I put in a relationship I am going to upset millions of girls. Maybe boys too. I am not fussed who worships me. If I don't, she is going to go mad. Best leave it blank and say I missed it, if she asks.

OK, Facebook is ready. Now for Twitter. I check it out. I am going to have to leave it, until I am famous. People can follow me straight away. Then they will see everything and be ahead of the game. I want to launch my social media all at the same time.

Now for the big one. The YouTube channel. I need a video introducing me to the world. I've watched how these YouTubers or vloggers do it by adding in photos and little captions. I can do that. I can make stuff pop up over the video. That's the plan anyway.

But I need to look my best. I pull out a shirt and trousers and iron them in the room. I also need to shave. I want to look my best. I shave and dress and look in the mirror. I look good. I think they will probably clip and edit the video once it's worldwide to make posters and picture frames like they sell at the markets of pop stars and stuff. So I have to look my best. I pull out my last hoodie, it's all clean. I have been saving one for the video.

I sit down in front of my laptop with the webcam on.

"My name is Edmund."

No, that's not going to work. It needs to be punchy, it needs to be fast paced. Like the others do. It needs to be scripted. I am a great writer and director, that's what I need to do. I need to script it to ensure I cover everything and then I will know when and where to link in the pictures. I grab a pad out of my bag, and start to write. Placing little boxes into every point that I need to add the photo.

I read it over and over again until it is right.

Fuck, is it really eight p.m.?

I sit back in front of the camera. Switch it on.

"That's right, it's me, The One. The only One. The number One. Edmund Carson."

Takes me about an hour to record it. Went over it a dozen times to make sure I can edit everything together. I turn on the TV again. Still nothing. Surely the gardeners would have gone into the school? If not, the cooks would have been there for what like four hours by now. What are they playing at? I mean it's hard to miss, isn't it? Twenty-five people are hard to miss? I need to stop thinking about it.

Fame is coming, it is just a matter of time. I have to edit this now and insert all of the photos. It's going to take me ages.

I start and it does. Four hours to get it right. I play it over and over again. It's perfect.

I am so fucking talented, sometimes I even amaze myself. This is my launch on to the big stage. I deserve this. I have worked hard and I really deserve this. It's nearly two a.m. I switch the TV back on again. Nothing.

What the fuck is going on?

It's almost been a day since I left there. All I can think of again is copycat. What if someone else is taking credit for my work? This is my work.

I forgot to eat again. I head out of the room. Down the stairs and out on to the street. I am still dressed as the ONE as I was on the video. I have my knife with me too. I shouldn't be going to work, but this is pissing me off now. I am pissed off and hungry at the same time.

It's a couple of minutes' walk to the high street, but about a minute after leaving the hotel I see someone standing down the alley. This is pretty close to my hotel. Maybe they haven't announced anything yet as they knew where I was all along? What if this is it? They are coming for me? They are coming at me from all angles? The guy is facing the other way and looking down the alleyway. Probably waiting for all the backup. They know they need an army to catch me. Probably he is formulating the plan from down here. What if they are already in my hotel and this is the secondary squad? I am not going without a fight. They need to know I mean business. I stick to the walls, but walk down the alleyway towards the man. He is still facing the other way. I come up behind him and slit his throat from behind.

"Fuck!"

Something burnt my hand as I did. The man drops a cigarette on the floor and then falls to his knees. It's not a cop.

It's a cook from the hotel or one of the restaurants. He was just outside having a cigarette.

"*Fuck!*"

Edmund, you are so stupid. You have just spent the last forty-eight hours planning and executing the perfect event to show the world you are a class act. Not a normal everyday run-of-the-mill person. I am better than this. What am I supposed to do with this guy now? He is on the floor. He isn't speaking. I am not surprised. I would be mad at me also. I can't take this one as an Edmund Carson. Even the ONE would be embarrassed to say he did this.

I walk over to the wheelie bin and lift the lid. I go, pick him up, and place him in the bin and close the lid. I am just going to forget that it ever happened. Certainly not claiming it as one of mine. It's the police's fault. They have me all wound up because they haven't told anyone yet. I come out of the alleyway, and head back to the high street. I find a kebab shop open called Yummies and order a kebab and chips. They have a few tables and chairs and I sit down with my food and a can of pop. It's not great food. I don't even know what meat is in a kebab? Beef? Lamb maybe, it's just brown stuff.

People are walking in and out. Most of them look like they have been drinking. Every one of them orders extra chilli. That's normally a sign of too much alcohol. No taste buds.

I look up at the small portable TV that is in the corner of the shop.

FUCK!

That's a picture of the school. They are talking about the school. I jump out of my chair and head towards the TV.

"Excuse me, mate, can you turn that up?"

Foreign-looking guy behind the counter reaches over to the remote control, and turns it up to seven. He then goes back to serving the people at the counter.

"Breaking News, police have confirmed the massacre at Preton High School for girls. It is believed up to twenty-five bodies have been recovered from the school in what is being called the single biggest attack in UK history. More to follow."

I can't move. I can't breathe. I am just staring at the TV. I think my mouth is wide open. I am frozen solid. Am I dribbling? I am sure I can feel it running down my face. I am conscious I haven't moved in like five minutes.

"Are you all right, mate?"

I can hear someone talking to me, but I still can't move.

"Mate? Are you OK?"

I turn around and there is a man standing in front of me with his kebab in hand. I notice mine has dropped to the floor.

"Did you know someone at the school? Been on the news for the last couple of hours."

My mind is a blank. It takes a second to sink in.

"Yes, yes I did."

"Then I am really sorry, mate. It doesn't look good. There are some right nutters out there, pal."

I am looking directly at him. I heard the words, but they didn't register in my head. Shock has waved over me. I walk out of the shop leaving my kebab on the floor and run. I run straight to the hotel and up the stairs and switch on the TV. It's there again. Mass murder, Horror, Attack. Killer, Killers, the words are all floating under the screen. It's like a movie. Something just hitting you. I knew it was coming, but it's here. It's really happened.

I lay backwards on the bed. I can't believe I feel like this. I can't believe that it is out there. My head is spinning with the words: Killer, Murderer, Mass murderer, Single biggest attack in history. What have I done? What have I done? What have I created? What is everyone going to think of me? My nan, my friends, my… Okay I don't have any other family, but what about Mrs Green, people like that. What are they going to think? I sit straight up in bed.

"They are going to think I am a fucking LEGEND!"

I am actually jumping up and down. I am a fucking legend. I don't care if they call it dad dancing, I am doing some of it. I swish my arms backwards and forwards. This is it, this is my moment. I am about to be promoted as the best in history.

I sit glued to the screen, but nothing more is happening. Surely they have the clues? Surely they know what is what by now? Maybe they are trying to put two and two together. Sherlock would have been here at my door by now. I can't contain my excitement. It's like winning the lottery, and the, well, the other lottery all rolled into one.

I sit glued to the TV. Two hours pass, and it's still basically the same report. Nothing is happening tonight and I need to get my sleep pattern closer to normal. I turn off the TV and lay back on the bed. Time for some sleep. I set my alarm for noon and go back to sleep.

I am awake at eleven a.m. I am buzzing from the time I wake up. I switch on the TV. It's headline news. I am headline news. I turn the volume up.

"Last night's discovery is still shocking the nation. The police are yet to make a formal statement on the event, but eyewitnesses have confirmed to the BBC the sight of the black hoodie at the scene. Is this the work of the gang known as the ONE who have been terrorising London?"

The gang, the fucking gang!

You stupid morons. There is just me, I am the ONE. I can't give you any more clues than I already have. It's like they don't listen. What is up with today's press and police? I swear if I lived in another country I would be locked up or worse by now.

Breathe, Edmund, fucking breathe.

I take a minute. I suppose it is a point that they are so useless I will be doing this until my retirement. It's a matter of time, they are only speculating. The girls will help them to ensure they know it's just one person. Seven and seventeen won't let me down. I took more selfies with them than anyone else. I know they have my back in this.

I order room service. It's lunch as I keep missing breakfast, but a sandwich is a sandwich. I sit glued to the TV, but nothing. They aren't saying anything. They can't have got this wrong, can they? Maybe they are out looking for me already? Maybe that's it. Maybe they knew all along it was me, and they are waiting to catch me before telling the press. Maybe I already knew that was what would happen and it spooked me last night into doing something I shouldn't. I should only be doing stuff that keeps me at the top of my game.

But what do I do in the meantime?

I am ready to go with the social media stuff. I can't just sit in a hotel and wait to be famous. I sit and watch some more news. Various people commenting on the events at the school. Even from Miss Walker's village. Maybe that's it, maybe that's where I ought to go back to… Miss Walker's.

It's a little close though. I mean, all those police, and me being walking distance away from them. Maybe tonight when it's dark. Maybe I should stock up on supplies: clothes, tools. It is going to be a lot harder to shop once I am famous. They close down shops for superstars, don't they? I guess they will probably do that for me, but best to get ahead of the game.

I get dressed and head to the high street. Every window in Currys or PC World has a picture of the school on it. It won't be long before that picture is of me.

Fuck!

They are going to use the blanket picture, aren't they? I hate that picture. I look nothing like that boy now.

I need the social media thing to kick off as soon as. They can use some of those selfies as the wanted posters. Maybe I should do like a calendar of twelve shots. I could update my Facebook page with them every month. I can wear like a Santa's hat and hold like a piece of holly or something. That would be cool for my fans. They would like that.

I stop and buy another suitcase and then head to Next. Shirts, T-shirts, jeans, shoes. I fill the trolley up pretty quickly. Generally dark colours. Not just for the ONE. They look a lot better on me in the photos. And there will be lots of photos.

Then I head to B&Q for some more tools, rope, tape. I drop the bag back in the car and head back to the hotel to watch the news. Still nothing on me. They must be getting close. I lay and watch for the next hour. At last some movement. The police have said they will be issuing a statement at twenty hundred hours this evening. That has to be it. That has to be me. I need to be ready for that. I need to have social media ready and the world will see me.

I probably need to share that moment with Miss Walker.

Girls get funny about those things, don't they? Life moments and all that. She will want to know how much our life is about to change. I check the video on my laptop. It's a great job of directing. I think the world will be watching this more than that stupid gang dance song.

I stay and watch the news until six. It's dark enough to travel now. I check out of the hotel and head towards the village. It's so quiet, I almost expected roadblocks and stuff. But given it's been almost two days since the project started, I guess they think I am long gone by now. They would never believe I would be coming back to the house at the bottom of the drive.

I park in the centre of the village and walk back to the house. I only take my laptop. As soon as it is announced, Miss Walker and I can load up the video together. In fact I might let her do it herself.

A little treat as she is going to be with me at all the red carpet stuff. Maybe they will get Sandra Bullock to play her in the movie. That would be so cool. I clearly want to play myself. That is only fair. I am a good enough actor. I am an amazing actor, to be fair.

I arrive at the house. There is police tape across the front door. What the hell is going on? I run around to the back, go into the house and shout for Miss Walker. Nothing.

I search the house. Nothing. I don't know where she is. She must be here, it's not like she would have gone to school today. I search the house for a note or anything and there is nothing. I am worried now. What if something has happened to her? What if that copycat guy has been here and worked with her? What if this Jack fellow was the copycat guy? Getting close to my girlfriend on purpose. The wine and the DVD haven't moved. I check the fridge. She hasn't touched a single piece of food. Or the dinner I made for her. Has she gone with him? Has this been her plan all along? Wait, am I the fucking copycat? Is someone taking credit for my work and I am going to be the patsy that gets nothing.

Bitch!

It's that Jack guy, I am sure of it. She has run away with him. And they are going to be famous and it's going to be all about him.

Calm down, Edmund. You are letting your mind wander!

She is probably just missing from the school. That's probably what the police have been doing here. She is a missing person.

Because she has fucked off with him! Bitch!

How could she do this to me? After all the work I have put in to make us famous. Not today, today of all days.

I wanted to share this with her. I sit down in the front room.

Breathe, Edmund.

I need to watch my temper and mind talking.

Maybe she has done this on purpose. She never wanted the limelight, she just wanted to teach. She is a good teacher, in more ways than one. Maybe that is all she wants. She will have left for me. Not because of me. Because I am amazing and she knows that. She knew that my life was about to change and that no doubt hundreds of women are about to start throwing themselves at me.

I am only human, after all. I am not going to be able to resist them all. Maybe that's what it is. She is the amazing one. It's the kind of thing she would do. There probably isn't even a Jack fellow. Silly old bat probably got the wrong letterbox. I am just playing games in my head, aren't I?

Fuck, the school!

I can see it from the window upstairs. I run upstairs, and look out the window. Blue lights and white tents are camped out across the lawn. It looks like some kind of festival. I use the binoculars and watch as they all run about.

It must be amazing up there. I can't see any of the girls or Miss Stanners, just a lot of people in white coats and blue uniforms. All running around as if their lives depended on it.

Miss Walker was right. This is the place. This is the place it all starts. She said that. She knew from the beginning. She is amazing.

The press are all there too. Must be nearly thirty vans parked up. Way more than the fire at my house. I check my wallet. I still have a couple of BBC business cards from the time I called about the flowers on the first anniversary. I need also to email them the video.

That way, the police won't be able to keep anything back. I open my laptop and set it up. All social media open and then I switch on the iPlayer for BBC News. There is still fifteen minutes to go till the press release. They are still talking about the ONE. I am sure this is going to get cleared up in fifteen minutes. There will only be me then. They will know this has nothing to do with a gang.

I run downstairs and fetch the bottle of champagne I bought. I thought we would be celebrating this moment together, but this is probably for the best.

I also set up the email to go to the BBC. They don't mess about. I fully intend it to be out there within hours if they are on the case. Through the binoculars I can see them all fussing around a podium outside the school. I turn up the volume on the laptop but watch through the binoculars. I want to see the faces of the audience more than the police.

I think Tom Cruise does that. Doesn't go to his own premiere and would rather sit and talk to the audience and fans. That is what we do all this work for. The fans. They are the most important part of this fame thing. He is a good guy, that Cruise. Maybe he could play me in the series version on TV of my life.

It's time.

The chief constable is walking to the podium.

"At precisely four forty-five yesterday afternoon we received a call from the chef of Preton High School informing us of an incident in one of the classrooms. Officers were dispatched and by six p.m. we had secured off the school. I do not want to repeat what we found in the classroom live on air for the sake of the families of the victims, but what I will say is that walking into that room is the worst moment of my career. Twenty-three teenagers and two teachers sadly lost their lives in this school. All the families have now been contacted, and I ask that you all give them time to grieve at this tragic time.

"We believe this horrific crime to be caused by one man. This man is Edmund Carson, aged seventeen."

Fuck, that's my picture!

And not the one in the blanket, that's a school one. They must have been to my school. That's so cool.

"We believe Edmund Carson to be responsible for at least another nineteen murders including the death of the local groundsman of the school, Mr Jack Devers. We strongly believe that Edmund Carson is also known as the ONE. The ONE that has been terrorising the London Underground. If you see this man, do not approach. I will repeat that, do not approach. He is, and will be, armed and dangerous. At this time Edmund Carson is the most dangerous person in Britain. There will be a further briefing tomorrow morning at nine a.m."

Nineteen? Where the fuck did he get nineteen from? One, three, seven... Oh, who the fuck cares? The most dangerous man in Britain, and they think I am what on forty-four... Forty fucking four! They must have said my name like a dozen times. There is no mistaking it was me. No fucking way this time.

I watch through the binoculars. The press are almost chasing him down the road for questions. They are going to be hungry for me now. And less than a month ago they wouldn't come and see me grieve on my parents' grave. Bet they wish they did now. Bet they all wish they had got in on the ground floor.

Fucking hell!

I can't help it. I get up and jump about the room. I did it! I did it! I am bigger than Jack, bigger than the doctor, and the odd couple put together. I am number ONE. I feel like I am about to explode. I grab the champagne, my hands are trembling, but I open it. It sprays all over the bedroom. I drink some. It's horrible. But I have to get used to it. It's all they serve at these big parties and things. I shake it up and spray it around the room like the racing car drivers do. I have always wanted to do that. I am a fucking legend...!

Fuck, right, need to stop.

Focus, Edmund. I sit at the laptop. First, send the email to BBC. Let's get them started on the case. They are going to love me. Wonder if I can get on their morning news? Then Twitter. I upload lots of selfies and comments. Sophia and I on our first date, that sort of thing. The last one hashtag forty-four hashtag Edmundiscoming hashtag beafraid. That should get the ball rolling.

Then I befriend everyone from school on Facebook. Carl first. He deserves it. That is going to shock them. They never thought I would amount to anything and here I am, the most dangerous person in Britain. I wonder if it scares the crap out of them. I hope so. Most of them anyway. I think Mrs Whitaker will be proud. She always had a soft spot for me. I say soft, probably damp is a better word for it.

Now the YouTube account. Upload. Done.

I play the video. The opening screen is the countdown. All the numbers go off like bombs as they hit the screen.

"Five... Four... Three... Two... ONE. Yes, One. The ONE the Only ONE."

And boom there I am.

"That's right, it's me, The One. The only One. The number One. Edmund Carson."

I pause for effect, they will all be wanting to look at me at that point. This is the first close-up the world will get. Fuck, I am hot. Girls will be wetting themselves.

"I was going to open with I have been waiting for you, but it's been you who has been waiting for me."

Another pause. I can hear them screaming now, we have, and we have.

"Where to start, no, actually before I start I just want to thank my family, my friends and my… friend Without all the support of these people I wouldn't have gotten to where I am today. The people I have been working with over the last year or so as well. Let's not forget your parts in this. You have helped shape me into the best in the business. OK, with that done, I begin with my parents."

Up pop pictures of old Mum and Dad. They are good pictures. Nan will like those ones.

"If you had asked me two years ago, I figured they hated me. We didn't talk, they didn't listen and when I wanted things, well, I just didn't get them. They led me to believe that I wasn't important enough in their lives. Yes, there was a gas leak. Did I cut the pipe to cause the gas leak? Most certainly, but as I said, I felt as if they didn't care about me. Move the clock forward to my seventeenth birthday after the fire. Imagine my surprise to know exactly how much they cared. I must say, we would have had a totally different relationship had I known."

Banknotes flutter down the screen. I love that. It's amazing what you can do on a laptop.

"When I turned seventeen, it made me a man."

I am looking directly at the camera for that. So funny. She will love that. Number seventeen. She wanted me to turn her. A little play on words for the fans never hurt anyone. Secret messages are what keep you on top of your game.

"I needed to celebrate. My nan who I love more than anyone. Hi, Nan."

I chuck her a little wave and blow her a kiss. They will be talking about her in the WI this week, I am sure. What with a famous grandson and everything.

"And I met a lovely girl called Sophia, at a flower shop, actually buying flowers for my nan. Her favourite are orchids if anyone wants to send her any."

Fans do that sort of thing to get close to the stars, I am sure of it.

"Sophia and I, we had a wonderful night. We went to the movies and shared a bottle of wine. Then back to her house to meet with her and her family."

Up pop selfies with the Mersons. I edited some to be tasteful. Just blacked out the naked parts. Last one is the one by the door. That will be the photo that launches across the Internet. I look hot as fuck in that photo.

"We laughed, we cried, we even played Scrabble together. Thank you for all your support and kind words. If truth were known, Mersons, it was you that highlighted my skill set, and showed me the direction that was meant for me. I will never forget that. It means the world to me."

Up pops the Scrabble photo.

"This is my favourite picture of us, I do like to play games, but sadly the time for games was over."

I darkened the picture a little there. Just to show things aren't as rosy as they once were. They will get that. I am a great editor.

"I am a man now, and I needed a job. Nothing against normal jobs, but they were not for me. So I decided to become the best at what I do well. And to be the best I needed to outsmart the rest."

Good catch line. Leave them with something they can requote in the press. I can see that in tomorrow's headline. Edmund Carson, the best, outsmarting the rest.

"Melanie, here."

Up pops her selfie.

"Helped me sort the funding. I couldn't have done this without you. Thank you, Melanie."

Was going to have a hidden message in there. Something about me, not her, to make her feel better. But let's face it, it was her, not me.

"I have been researching this role for a good two years, and I know what I need to do to become successful. I have worked hard on this, and I just wanted to point out I will continue to work hard at my job. Push boundaries and strive until I reach the ultimate goal of number one. But not just of Britain, which I already am by the way. Thank you, but I will be number One worldwide."

A ONE business card flashes up on screen, and holds for about ten seconds. They will all be wondering what is coming next. And then, back to me in my hoodie.

The hoodie comes back down.

"I knew you were waiting for me to tell you, but yes, I am the ONE. The Only ONE. There is no gang. This has nothing to do with America or anywhere else. It's just me. That is the amount of effort and sacrifice I have put into this job so far. I must admit, at first, the copycat lookalikes did annoy me when I got on the tube. I needed to do my job, and they were making it difficult. But I guess fame is something that takes time to deal with. Fans need to feel close to you so I have no problem with the ONE having a following. In fact, I love that. I hope to work with all my fans one day."

I make the heart gesture with my hands. That's a screen shot for a front page if I ever saw one. I wonder if they will pick up on the message about working with them. I really would work with them. The screen lightens up again, showing my playful side.

"To give the ONE a break I took a trip to the seaside. I am so glad I did as I met a classmate, and we settled our differences. I am so proud of us for that, Carl."

Up pop the selfies with the Carnegie family. Bethany looks so sweet in them. There's a real holiday feeling about it.

"We had so much fun on the beach together. That sandcastle, I made that. I know, amazing, isn't it? Again, thank you to the Carnegie family. The support you showed that night was amazing. Even though the weather was horrible. I hope you are enjoying France, and send me a postcard."

Screen a little darker again. Mood lighting is so important in these things.

"The holiday, it gave me time to reflect on myself, and my performance so far. Whilst I think I was doing well, I didn't quite manage to capture your hearts. I think I needed to work with more, give you more, and give you something you would remember. It was when I was actually returning from holiday that gave me the idea"

Up pop the selfies on the tube with the girls.

"Look who I bumped into on the tube. We had a great day, Madame Tussauds, seeing Jack in the Chamber of Horrors."

Up pops a picture of Jack the Ripper.

"Makes you what? Number four now, Jack. You must be a little disappointed in that. Now there is a new kid on the block."

Another good line. That will link me to the songs. Edmund Carson, new kid on the block.

"So inspired, excited and ready to wow the world, I set about the events at school. I will say, they are an amazing bunch of girls. Every one of them. We laughed so much. They are a credit to their families, and the teachers. The teachers couldn't be more proud of them. I know I spoke at length with Miss Stanners and Mrs Lee. Remarkable women."

Selfies with Stanners and Lee pop up.

"And I know you are not supposed to have favourites, but these two."

Selfie with seven and seventeen dressed in my hoodie pops up.

"These two, they are my favourites. We laughed so hard, and they gave me the run-around on the night too."

I nearly pointed out where I found them at that point, but I figure it's up to them to come out to their parents. Not me. Those are hard things to do. They shouldn't be judged on who they love though. And besides, they must be a little bit bi as they both wanted me.

"All the girls were special. Amazing, special girls. This is a small video of the pictures I have taken."

Picture in picture boom. It flicks through all the pictures from the school in the top right-hand corner.

"It was an amazing night, you know, I was going to say debut, but it doesn't feel right. So let's call it what it was, a launch party."

The screen goes darker still, and my hoodie goes back up.

"And from a launch party to the main event."

The boxing ring bell rings to show I mean business. This bit is full of dramatic pauses. I love it. The camera zooms in with every line.

"Edmund Carson is real."

"Edmund Carson is the ONE."

"Edmund Carson is the UK number One."

The screen goes black and bang I am back in my hoodie staring directly at the camera. You can just about make out my piercing eyes.

"Edmund Carson is... COMING."

And finish! That is fucking awesome. I can't believe my video is going to be a worldwide hit. I bet it has a million hits within a week, and it tells my story from now to here so well. It's important they know where my humble beginnings came from.

I need to like do one every other week to keep the world up to date with my events. They will want to see regular updates on my work and my achievements. Nothing worse than a celebrity off the radar for a while, and trying to make a pathetic comeback. Has to be fast paced and regular. Maybe I should do it on location, and then send it when I am hundreds of miles away. That would be a great idea.

I look back out the window at the hustle and bustle of the tents and the police. The laptop is pinging everywhere. People sending friend requests. Re-tweeting.

Fuck, fuck, fuck!

I stand up and smash the laptop. IP addresses, they will find me. That was so close. I go back to look at the window. It's fascinating me. It looks so much fun up there. How much closer could I get to the school? Now that's a selfie I would want. That is a selfie that my fans would want also. I have to think of them now with everything that I do.

Caroline!

For fuck's sake, I didn't mention Caroline. I just mentioned my parents as that would have been the first time they remember me. Fuck! I can't leave her out.

I am going to have to do something special for her as she is going to be pissed at me.

My phone rings downstairs in my jacket. I bet that is her, she is going to be so mad with me. I have launched in to the public, and I forgot to mention my first. I walk down to get it. I will just say to her that I thought she was too special for a general broadcast. Besides, she probably still thinks that she is my girlfriend. And I did mention a girlfriend. Didn't I? I will say that was her. Yeah, that will do it. As my first she deserved a broadcast of her own. As my girlfriend she was special. That should keep her back on track.

I pick up my phone. It's not her. It's my nan.

FUCK!

That's either her ringing to tell me how good I look on TV or to... No, you twat! I break the phone in half. My nan never rings me. Do they think I am that stupid? *Criminal Minds* one 0 one. They are obviously at the house and trying to track me. Besides, my nan is at bingo tonight. She wouldn't ring me at bingo. She will probably ring about ten p.m. If not, I will ring her in the morning.

I fetch a burner phone from my bag. Have to keep on top of this now that I am on the social media stuff. Pay as you go sorted, I am back online.

I go back upstairs, and look out the window again. It's good to know they are stepping up the game. At least we can start the real work that I have been planning. All of this is just the introduction to me. Like the trilogies. Set the scene in the beginning, lots of action in the middle, and by the end the audience know how amazing you are. The world will know how amazing I am. I use amazing a lot. I need more words for how great I am.

I want a selfie at the school. My fans want a selfie at the school. That's never been done before. Even Jack wouldn't have done that.

I am out the back door and in the garden. I check the shed. The burglar has gone. I guess it is a bit cold to be out here for a week. I am over the fence, and in the middle of the trees. I was going to walk the tree line, but that is way too dangerous. In the middle nobody will see me. As I get louder, the people get noisier.

I start jumping from tree to tree like The Coyote in *Road Runner*. That's a funny cartoon. Nobody is looking at the trees, they are all looking at the house and the lights in the house. All the cameras are faced that way also. I am almost at the front of the house. I stand at the tree, and take some selfies with the press behind me. A big BBC logo is in one of them. That will go down well on TV. They will use that on their channel.

Need the others too. Find ITV, Sky, and Channel 4 and take selfies with their logo in the background too. Channel 5 are there but I don't bother, I am not sure anyone watches that channel. This is cool. I am going to need to tweet these to the press.

There is a lot of noise at the front of the house. I decide to work my way round to the back to see if they found my wood in the door. Takes me almost ten minutes to get back round there.

And there it is. They have taken the door off. I can see it inside a white tent with someone still looking at it. They can't be doing that for fingerprints, can they? They know who I am. Maybe they are taking memorabilia already. Probably going to sell it on eBay or something. I should really think about merchandising: own clothing line of hoodies, knives. Maybe even launch my own perfume? Carson or something like that.

It's not as busy out here. There are only the people in the tent, but that whole house is lit up. It is quite impressive. I should have really taken the full tour.

Fuck!

I dive on the floor. It's only the fucking chief superintendent, walking out the back door. Fuck, that scared me. I am sure he can't see me from here. There are a lot of cars around anyway so he won't be looking for me. I sneak a peek over the car. He is lighting a cigarette. I thought policemen wouldn't smoke. They are supposed to be role models and all that.

Maybe that's why he is out the back. He doesn't want people to know that he smokes. He is now on the phone.

Fuck!

What if he is calling for backup, and only pretended not to see me? He isn't looking in my direction. He looks like he is in a heated debate on the phone. What if that is acting? I look over to where I came from. Some of the press and police are leaving. They wouldn't be doing that if he was calling for backup.

Fuck!

He is walking this way. I need to get out of here, but I have nowhere to go. If I run, one of the press might see me. He is almost at the end of the car. Being here probably wasn't one of my brightest ideas. I forgot how open it was. And didn't realise that the police would be everywhere.

Don't be a twat, Edmund!

All I can think about is a selfie for my fans. They would love that. They really would. I turn my phone around and see if I can get him in the background. I love the fact you can actually see the photo now before you press.

Only fucking got it! Selfie with the main man. He is arguing with someone on the phone. That is going to go down in history. History.

"I don't know, Julie, I don't know. I will be home as soon as I can... I know we were supposed to be having dinner, but this is a little bit more important... For fuck's sake, Julie, this nut job has massacred a school. A fucking school. Give me a break..."

He doesn't sound happy. I guess that is married life for you.

"I am sorry, I shouldn't have raised my voice. I will wrap this up as quickly as I can and then get home. Yes, I could do with a drink. Ten drinks, to be fair. We have to catch this boy, Julie."

Boy? Doesn't he know I am a man?

"He is escalating."

Yes! I knew I would. They said it on *Criminal Minds,* and here I am living the dream itself.

"We think forty-four, forty-four that we know of, but who knows what the real number is or is going to be. Forty-four, Julie."

"Forty-five, Julie."

My knife is across his throat, I slice deep, and drag him down by the car. Nobody was watching as I was watching them in the tent. He is not even moving. The blood is strong and rich. I take a real selfie now as he is still bleeding out.

I log straight on to Twitter.

Fuck me!

I have two thousand followers in what, an hour? I am going to be huge. They will probably give me my own social media. I upload the photo and tweet:

Good to be back at the school#45#Justthestart #helpingwithenquiries#edmundiscoming#the ONE'

That will go down a bomb. Maybe one more:

Edmund is coming...#beafraid#Veryafraid.